Ralph looked dow

In some odd ... e's beauty. Strain ... hes of her face—bc ... hat she would remain ... er first youth had gone.

He was surprised a ... w soft and silken she felt against him, and at the temptation that she presented to him, a man who could usually coldly control his desires and appetites. All the same, he could not prevent himself from kissing the top of her head.

Paula Marshall, married with three children, has had a varied life. She began her career in a large library and ended it as a senior academic in charge of history in a polytechnic. She has travelled widely, has been a swimming coach, and has appeared on *University Challenge* and *Mastermind*. She has always wanted to write, and likes her novels to be full of adventure and humour.

Recent titles by the same author:

EMMA AND THE EARL
A BIDDABLE GIRL?
THE LOST PRINCESS
NOT QUITE A GENTLEMAN
DEAR LADY DISDAIN

AN AFFAIR OF HONOUR

Paula Marshall

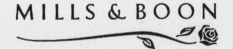

© Paula Marshall 1996

MILLS & BOON

*All the characters in this book have no existence outside the
imagination of the author, and have no relation whatsoever to anyone
bearing the same name or names. They are not even distantly inspired
by any individual known or unknown to the author, and all the
incidents are pure invention.*

*MILLS & BOON, the Rose Device and
LEGACY OF LOVE are trademarks of the publisher.
Harlequin Mills & Boon Limited,
Eton House, 18–24 Paradise Road, Richmond, Surrey TW9 1SR*

© Paula Marshall 1996

ISBN 0 263 80007 5

*Set in 10 on 12 pt Linotron Times
04-9612-84066*

*Typeset in Great Britain by CentraCet, Cambridge
Printed and bound in Great Britain
by BPC Paperbacks Limited, Aylesbury*

CHAPTER ONE

RALPH SCHUYLER first saw Clare Windham at Bitsy Bentley's cocktail party given to celebrate her engagement to Charles 'Woofer' Clifton Jones: Woofer because his hobby was breeding dogs. Since Bitsy hated all forms of animal life—apart from men—and dogs were high on her list of detestation, the future of the marriage looked a bit rocky. Bets were already being taken on how long it would last.

Clare was standing in a corner, alone, examining a rather dull Landseer painting which had been hung away from the light; deliberately so, pictures of gory dead animals not being in fashion at the moment. The Bentleys were always in fashion, if nothing else.

It was her face which interested Ralph. It was not conventionally beautiful, but was striking: fine dark eyes, straight nose, determined mouth, all crowned with a great fall of cream-caramel coloured hair, straight, and worn longer than the current fashion. Her dress was dated, too. A Fortuny, all golds, ochres, and burnt siennas, but it was at least five years out of fashion. Ralph, being a Schuyler male, knew all about female fashion, what was chic, and what wasn't.

Ralph was immensely chic, and knew it. Not over-tall, broad and dark, like most of the Schuyler men, his face was formidable, all strength and bone. His eyes, golden like those of a predatory beast, were intimidating. His mouth was the only redeeming thing about him, being a little softer than might have been expected, considering the rest of him.

He put his flute down—he had been drinking champagne, he detested cocktails—and walked over to where Bitsy was holding court amongst a crowd of men, none of them her future husband. At the sight of him she abandoned them all: Ralph Schuyler was a somebody.

Exactly what sort of somebody no one was quite sure. In any case, being a Schuyler and some sort of relative of Gerard Schuyler, Lord Longthorne—that man of destiny who controlled Cabinets without being in them—he was most definitely worth knowing. A bachelor, very rich, with some sort of decorative position at the Foreign Office, Ralph carried with him an aura of cool sophistication. He had won an MC in the Great War, but like many other survivors rarely talked of it.

Like all the Schuyler men he was reputed to be a devil with women, but discretion had long been his middle name. Bitsy had thrown herself at him once—those looks, that money—but he had held her at arm's length in the most charmingly vague manner.

'Ralph, so glad you could make it. What are you doing these days?'

It was typical of him that he ignored every word she had said and went straight to the point.

'Bitsy, my pet, who is the woman in the corner, on her own?'

'Where?' Bitsy swung around, a little piqued that Ralph's interest was not in her. She had chased him hard and fast, and had only accepted Woofer in lieu of him—and now he was interested in another woman. Well, he wouldn't be when she told him who his mysterious beauty was.

'Oh, her? That's Clare Windham—you know, the notorious Clare Windham, the one Boy Mallory shot himself for when she jilted him five years ago.'

'*That* Clare Windham. Hmm. . .' Ralph's reply was carelessly non-judgemental. Anthony Mallory, always known as Boy, had been part of the crowd Ralph ran with, although he had been out of England at the time of his suicide and had consequently missed all the excitement.

'What is she doing here, then? I thought everyone had dropped her.'

'Oh, we were great friends before the scandal. Went to Cheltenham Ladies College and finishing school together. I met her by chance last week in Piccadilly. Thought I'd do her a good turn by inviting her; someone said that she was having a struggle making ends meet. After all, she's been cut dead by everyone since Boy. . . Bit of a mistake, though. No one will talk to her.'

'In that case,' said Ralph, renowned for doing the unexpected, 'I will. I've always wanted to find out what a man thought it was worth shooting himself for.'

Deserting an annoyed Bitsy, he picked up two flutes of champagne from a passing tray, and walked over to where Clare Windham was now inspecting a small group of portrait miniatures as though her life depended on it.

'Hallo,' he said, totally without preamble, and handing her a flute at the same time, 'I'm Ralph Schuyler, and Bitsy tells me that you are Clare Windham. How do you do. I'll bring her over to make a proper introduction of me, if you think it's worth the trouble. Otherwise. . .here I am.'

She turned those great grave eyes on him.

'So I see. One of *the* Schuylers, I suppose.'

He raised his glass to her. 'Sort of. But I'm still expected to work for my living.'

Clare responded by raising her glass to him. 'I thought all Schuylers worked—rich and poor. Tell me, are there any poor Schuylers?'

'If there are, I haven't met them,' acknowledged Ralph. He was privately conceding that whatever Miss Clare Windham was, she was no fool. 'Working, though, is a family tradition—even in the lesser branches.'

'So, a twig off the family tree—and you are working here? By talking to me?'

Her reputation might be shot to hell, but she was not allowing it to prevent her from speaking frankly. No, Miss Clare Windham definitely had her wits about her. He remembered Boy Mallory talking about her on the telephone a few weeks before he killed himself.

'Clever girl, Clare. Never thought I'd marry a clever girl. She's great fun, though, and that makes up for the brains.'

His careless comment had jarred a little on Ralph at the time. Bitsy had said that she had dropped out of society after Boy's suicide. He had also heard that her parents had turned her out after she had jilted Boy— which explained the dated Fortuny.

The Windhams were an old gentry family, dirt poor, in danger of losing the family seat. Boy Mallory had been immensely rich, and the marriage must have seemed like a godsend, Clare being their only child.

'Not exactly,' he told her, snatching another pair of flutes from yet another passing waiter, and handing one of them to her, without so much as a 'by your leave'. 'I'm at the Foreign Office. Poodlefaking at do's like this one tonight is part of my job, but that's not why I am here. I was at Oxford with Woofer.'

He didn't say that he had been there with Boy Mallory, too; it might not be tactful.

Clare Windham, for whatever reason, was not going to allow him to be tactful. She had put down the flute he had just given her without drinking from it. Ralph noted that she hadn't finished the first one which he had given to her, so her frankness was not simply due to drink talking.

'You must have known Boy there, then.'

Ralph nodded, before gesturing in the direction of her discarded flute. 'You don't fancy champagne?'

'One glass at a time, yes.' Her smile was almost mocking. 'Moderation in all things, Mr Schuyler, has always been my motto.'

'Ralph,' he said. 'Ralph. And was it always your motto? In the past?'

His dark eyes were challenging her. His whole stance challenged her. Neither of them quite knew why.

'You heard what I said.' Clare's voice was as frank and forthright as her expression. She was refusing to be moved by his scepticism. 'I never say what I do not mean.'

'Most rare in a woman.' Now he was mocking her a little, trying to disturb her lovely calm. 'But it's a good claim to make—even if difficult to believe.'

'You may believe what you please,' she told him coolly. 'Most people do, I find.'

'Ah, you have me there. A useful point for philosophic debate—but not at a party hosted by Bitsy Bentley, I think.'

She did not answer him, but merely inclined her head a little, so to provoke her—and again, why should he want to do so?—he continued, 'No, indeed. Poor Woofer would be out of his depth a little if challenged

on the matter. And he was never a good swimmer. Are
you a good swimmer, Clare?'

He was baiting her by playing with double meanings
and innuendo, she was sure of it. His eyes, dark amber
with little points of light in them, betrayed him—and
the slight twist of his mouth. Like most people whom
she met who knew her story, he could not forget Boy
Mallory and his dreadful end.

Nor could she, for that matter, although lately it had
disturbed her less and less. She had been a fool to take
up Bitsy's invitation, but curiosity had overcome her
and, in a weak moment, she had ignored the advice she
had always given herself: never to go back.

She answered him in the two-edged manner he was
using to her. 'I was a good swimmer once, but no more.'

'A pity. You should take it up again. Or are you
afraid to?'

'Not at all, I have other interests now. More pressing
ones.'

Now why did she not simply move on? Was it that,
for the first time in five years, she was back in the
society which she had once expected to live in for the
rest of her days as Boy Mallory's wife, and she was
looking at it from the outside and finding it wanting?

Ralph Schuyler represented all that she had come to
detest: idle, rich, self-indulgent. Any intelligence which
he possessed was devoted to amusing himself, regardless of the fact that outside this room was a world of
individuals who found life a struggle, the more so
because the end of the War had seemed to herald a
more promising future. But 'the land fit for heroes to
live in' had never materialised—although anyone visiting parties like Bitsy Bentley's would never guess that.

'Such as?' Ralph's gaze grew more searching.

He wondered how she was earning a living, and also wondered if he could provoke her into telling him. He wanted to see her animated, agitated even. Her calm reproached him, annoyed him. A woman with a reputation such as hers had no business to be calm.

'Oh, this and that.'

It was giving Clare great pleasure to thwart him. By his manner from the first moment he had met her, thrusting a champagne flute into her hand, it was obvious that he expected any woman whom he favoured with his attentions to fall at his feet—which Clare had no intention of doing.

'This and that, eh? Tell me, Clare, do you prefer this to that? Or are both equally fascinating?'

His smile was intended to take the edge off the slight hostility in his voice and in his question. He had not intended to subject her to such an inquisition, but she had got under his skin. And Boy Mallory had been his friend.

Clare's straight stare at him at last grew hostile.

'I'm not quite sure what point you are trying to make, *Mr Schuyler*, but you are beginning to bore me. You will excuse me if I leave you, and the party. I have been made quite well aware that I am not wanted here. I have to believe that Bitsy meant it as a kindness to invite me, but I am tired of being a raree-show for inquisitive fools.'

She turned her shapely back on him. Ralph admired it for a moment, from the nape of her neck to the elegant lines of her graceful bottom, before putting out a large hand, a strong Schuyler hand, backed with fine black hair, to detain her.

'Oh, no. You are not to run away from me just as the conversation becomes interesting.'

His grasp of her elbow had been strong enough to swing her round, strong enough to turn several curious and knowing eyes on them. Clare ignored them all, her cold gaze freezing even him.

'Mr Schuyler, *I* am not interested in having a conversation with you, interesting or otherwise. I have work to do in the morning, and I value my rest. I have no reputation to lose so, if you do not let go of my elbow, I shall have no hesitation in kicking you in the shins. Hard.'

What in God's name had Boy Mallory done to provoke her to jilt him? She was as lovely a creature as he had ever seen, and possessed a rare spirit.

And why was he so determined to provoke her in his turn? Was it the knowledge of her reputation or some odd chemistry which had sprung up between them from the moment he had first handed her the champagne flute?

Well, he was not a man to be played with. He held on to her elbow just long enough for it to be in defiance of her wishes, only dropping it when he saw her eyes change, and the determination to kick him grow in them.

Now, what *was* interesting was that as he did so she gave an involuntary and unwilling smile which transformed her face. For a fleeting moment there was a touch of mischief there, a hint of humour, long suppressed.

'Schuyler common sense asserting itself,' she asked sweetly, 'or is it simply that you value your shins?'

'Neither,' he murmured softly, so softly that those near them could not hear what he said. 'I think that I am more careful of your reputation than you are, perhaps.'

He had touched her! He had pierced the carapace of indifference which she carried around with her. Her mouth softened, and her eyes shone. For a moment he could have sworn that tears stood in them. And then she was as cold as ice again.

'Oh, no, don't try to fool me with pretended concern. And don't try to follow me when I leave.'

He didn't. He would grant her that favour. But as soon as she had gone, after saying her farewells to Bitsy, he was across the room to ask Bitsy for her address.

Bitsy's laugh was a little shrill. 'What, Ralph, do you want her to insult you again? You must be a glutton for punishment! I would never have suspected it of you,' and she became the second woman that night to give him her shoulder, after refusing to tell him Clare's address.

Ralph was not to be denied. He did not, as he had done with Clare, try to detain her physically, he simply said, as softly as he could, 'I don't think Woofer would like to discover what went on between you and the Prince of Wales last year, do you, Bitsy? He's not the sort to be pleased to learn that his future monarch had been there before him.'

This had Bitsy turning round to face him even more swiftly then Clare had done. Her hand flew to her suddenly ashen lips.

'How?' she exclaimed, and then, 'You wouldn't. . .?'

'No,' agreed Ralph. 'Not if you give me Clare Windham's address. Otherwise. . .'

'Oh, very well.' Bitsy flung at him the details of the Chelsea back street where Clare rented a flat on the first floor of an old Victorian building, before, with a toss of her bobbed head, she left him to go to Woofer.

Presumably, thought Ralph wryly, to reassure herself

that he was still her faithful cavalier. Never mind, he
had gained what he wanted and had found one thing
out. At that humble address it was unlikely that Clare
Windham had a lover, or protector, and her claim that
she needed to be up early to work was probably a true
one.

He wasn't very proud about having to blackmail poor
silly Bitsy, but Clare Windham had presented him with
an intriguing puzzle which he wanted to solve. After all,
he earned his living solving puzzles. It hadn't been a
discreet thing to do, either. Even flighty Bitsy might
start asking herself how in the world Ralph Schuyler
could know of her secret rendezvous with HRH, and
what exactly was his role at the Foreign Office which
allowed him to be aware of such royal secrets?

What might have intrigued him was that as Clare
made her way out of the party—curious and unpleasant
glances following her—and reached the flagged
entrance hall, she was stopped by one of Boy Mallory's
oldest friends, Jeremy Peele.

'Clare! Clare! Bitsy told me that she was inviting you
tonight. I'd no idea where you have been hiding or I
would have got in touch with you before. You're not
leaving already, surely?'

'I must, Jeremy.' Clare was biting back tears as she
spoke. It had been a mistake to come. She should have
known that, even after five years, no one would have
forgotten the old scandal which had ruined her. 'I
shouldn't have come.'

'Oh, no,' he said, sincerely, his honest face troubled.
'Surely not. Bygones ought to be bygones, you know.
But if you aren't staying, do leave your address with me.
I need to get in touch with you. It's perhaps not

important, but it's about Boy. Something I think that you ought to know.'

Clare looked at his simple, honest face. Of all Boy's many friends he had been the least sophisticated, the most ordinary, perhaps, and that had been his strength. She doubted that there was anything about Boy which she did not already know, but to make Jeremy happy she took a card from her small evening bag with her name, *Clare Windham*, *Secretarial Services*, printed on it, and her address, *5b*, *Camden Place*, *Chelsea*, beneath it.

'No telephone?' queried Jeremy, his frank face looking puzzled at the notion that anyone whom he knew might not have one. 'Never mind, I can telegraph you, I suppose, or send a letter.'

He would have said more but a petulant-looking beauty, her hair cropped as short as Clare's was unfashionably long, put her head round the door, and sighed at him. 'Oh, come on, Jere, do. I didn't come with you to wait about while you talked to other girls.'

Her disapproving stare took in Clare, standing in the shadows of the front door. 'Oh, it's Clare Windham, isn't it? Surprised to see you here, I must say. Oh, *come on*, Jere, do!' And she disappeared again.

'You see how it is,' he told Clare awkwardly, 'must go. Daphne will never forgive me if I delay. But I will be in touch.'

And how many people had said *that* to her, since the dreadful day when Boy had been found shot, only for them never to be heard from again? Although to give him his due Jeremy had sounded rather urgent, and he was a well-meaning soul, if a trifle wanting in the brains department.

At least she could go home now, and regret in peace

ever having seen Bitsy again, let alone come to her party. But Clare's evening was not yet over. Whilst she and Jeremy had been talking another man had entered the hall and stood in its shadows until Jeremy had gone to join Daphne.

He moved forward, and said smoothly, 'I thought that it was you, Clare. Wherever have you been hiding all these years?'

'I haven't been hiding anywhere.' Clare's reply was frosty. 'I have been busy earning my living.'

She tried to recall who he was, and it was only when he stood tall under the light and she could see him properly that she recognised him as Gordon Stewart, another of Boy Mallory's old crowd. He had been strapped for cash then, but he was evidently not short of the ready these days. He was wearing impeccable evening dress, shoes by Lobb, a Patek Philippe watch and his ash-blond hair had evidently been cut by a master. Clare assumed that he had come into money.

'I'm sorry,' he said, looking suitably contrite. 'I didn't mean to hurt you.'

Clare's response was heartfelt. 'Well, that's a relief. Gordon. No one else seemed to think that was a consideration.'

'The more fool they,' he returned robustly. 'You've had a hard time of it lately?'

'No more so than most people since the War.'

'Properly rebuked.'

Gordon's smile was conciliatory. She had not remembered him as such a handsome man. Five years had changed most of her old friends, some for better, some for worse. With Gordon it was for better. There was a sleekness about him. She remembered suddenly that Boy had always patronised him, even though he had spoken of him as 'my best friend'. Perhaps the poor best friends of the very rich were always patronised.

Clare pushed the thought away, and said, 'I must be going. It's getting late.'

'May I call you a taxi? Or could I give you a lift?' He was obviously trying to make amends for his tactlessness. He had always been very willing to please.

'Thank you, no. I have made my own arrangements.' She did not say that the arrangements were a walk, a journey on the Tube, and a further long walk at the other end. It was no business of Gordon's—or of Ralph Schuyler's—how she arranged her life.

'You're sure?'

'Quite sure. Good night, Gordon. Nice to meet you again.'

'Good night, Clare. I'll be in touch.'

Well, he was the second man that night to say that to her, Clare thought, as she walked briskly through the balmy summer night towards the Underground station whose distinctive lamp beckoned her.

Perhaps one of them actually meant what he said! She had not given her address to Gordon, so perhaps he had merely said what he did out of politeness, and the memory that he had been Boy's best friend. From a discreet distance, unnoticed, she had watched Boy's funeral cortège enter the church and he had been so broken that Jeremy had had to support him.

On the whole she rather hoped that she would never have to meet any of her old set again. Or Ralph Schuyler, either, with his mocking eyes and sardonic humour which had made her feel uncomfortable all the way down to her toes.

Clare did not ask herself why that should be so—which was perhaps just as well.

CHAPTER TWO

RALPH SCHUYLER was dissecting a Manx kipper at breakfast when the telephone rang. Armstrong, his valet, who had been his sergeant in the war, put his head round the dining room door, and said, 'It's Mr Gis Havilland, sir. He wishes to know if you are willing to speak to him at this early hour.'

Ralph looked at the clock which said eight-thirty. 'Not so early as all that, Armstrong. Yes, I'll come.'

He threw down his table napkin and strolled into the hall where the telephone stood. 'Well, Gis. What's early about the hour? And what is it this time? What problem do you need solving?'

A light laugh at the other end preceded a mellow baritone voice saying, 'How well you know me, Ralph. Yes, it's early hour for me to arrive in London, and yes, I do have a problem. Can you meet me at the Travellers' for lunch? Twelve o'clock, sharp. I need your know-how, cousin.'

Ralph thought a moment, then said, 'Certainly. Nice to know you do visit town occasionally.'

'As little as I can, Ralph. As little as I can. See you later,' and he rang off.

Ralph thought that Ghysbrecht Havilland, always known as Gis, was either very silent or very talkative, with little in between. He was also one of the few men whom Ralph respected, both for his brains and for his physical prowess. If Gis had a problem with which he

18

needed help, then the problem must be a large and difficult one.

Meantime, he had a few problems of his own to solve. He made a beginning on one of them by putting his head round a colleague's door as soon as he reached the Foreign Office.

'Pryde, you can help me if you would.'

'Really, Schuyler, old chap. I thought that you never needed help. Still I'll do my best.'

Ralph, who wasn't sure whether he was being complimented or insulted, ignored Pryde's facetiousness, and simply said, 'I was out of the country on that Balkan job, when Boy Mallory shot himself after Clare Windham jilted him. Fill me in, if you would.'

Pryde swung round, and began by saying, 'Why?', then, on seeing Ralph's expression, muttered, 'OK, OK, no names, no pack drill. It was all quite simple, really. Clare and Boy had been what you might call soul mates since childhood. Took one look at each other...you know...when they were about eleven.

'And then...two days before the wedding, two days, mark you, all the guests notified, two Cabinet Ministers and three Bishops among them, church booked, wedding presents all laid out, honeymoon at the Cap d'Antibes arranged, all the trimmings...and then... with two days to go she jilts him, no explanation given.

'Gets up one morning, tells her parents the wedding's off, she's given him his ring back, no reason offered other than that she's changed her mind. Two days before *that* they'd been lovey-dovey at Ascot. Season's biggest sensation, as you can imagine.

'A week later, Boy shoots himself. No note. Only explanation possible is the jilting. Parents throw her out. She disappears. Someone said she was at Boy's funeral, but if she was, she was disguised. And that's it. Why do you want to know?'

'And that really was it?' Ralph said at last. 'And no one questioned that he shot himself for any other reason than Clare Windham jilting him?'

Pryde shrugged. 'Cold-bloodedly, I suppose, I would never have thought of Boy doing it for *that*. But what other explanation could there be? He had no money worries, nothing gone wrong in his life. And look at it this way. It must have been a God-almighty shock when his beloved jilted him so near to the altar.'

'Yes, I suppose it was. I met her last night. She didn't seem the type to have jilted him without reason—any more than I would have thought Boy was suicidal.'

He saw Pryde's face change, and added sharply, 'Yes, what is it, Pryde?'

'Funny, that was what Milford claimed. Said Boy wasn't suicidal and the whole thing a bit odd. Said he was going to do some snooping around.'

'And did he find anything?'

'Think not, old chap. And he's not here now to ask,' Pryde volunteered as he saw Ralph beginning to open his mouth.

'It was another tragedy which happened when you were in the Balkans. He was killed in a car accident shortly afterwards. Drove one of those sporty Bentley's—like yours. Used to race at Brooklands. Must have taken a bend too fast. Hit a tree. If you want my opinion, nothing in it. The Boy Mallory thing, I mean. Some chaps driven mad if their girl rejects them. Boy one of them.'

'So I suppose.' Ralph's tone was dry. 'Thanks, anyway. I'm lunching with my cousin at the Travellers' today. Fill in for me, will you?' And he strode out of the room without further explanation, leaving Pryde to shake his head at him.

Another bee in Schuyler's bonnet! Well, they usually buzzed to some effect, but he thought that Ralph was on to what the Yanks called a 'bum steer' this time.

Clare Windham found work difficult that morning. She bitterly regretted having gone to Bitsy's party. It had brought back too many memories. Even the concentration needed to translate a French novel which had been shortlisted for the *Prix Goncourt* could not drive what had happened out of her mind.

She had just decided to make a cup of coffee, one of her few indulgences, when the door bell of her flat shrilled.

Eleven-thirty! Who could it be? Not the post. That had come and gone, bringing nothing of any value. And surely not Jeremy Peele, so soon after last night's meeting? He probably wasn't even up yet.

Like Ralph Schuyler, he had a nothing job at the Foreign Office. The sort that rich men who liked to think that they were working were handed to give the place a social cachet.

She was right. She opened the door to find not Jeremy, but Gordon Stewart standing there. He was holding a great bunch of white roses and, as on the night before, was impeccably dressed. This time he was wearing the uniform of a perfect gentleman—pinstriped trousers, black jacket and a soft Homburg hat. He was as fair as Ralph Schuyler was dark, with a pair of cold silver eyes.

Just before she went to sleep last night, Clare had remembered that he had had some sort of junior position with a merchant bank, and it was likely that he had been promoted several times since she had last seen him. So what was he doing on her small landing in the middle of the morning?

Clare didn't ask him that, but simply accepted the roses and the charming compliment which went with them.

'Beauty for the beauty,' he said, and stood there, apparently waiting for her to invite him in.

'Oh, they're lovely, Gordon,' she exclaimed. 'I'm working, and everywhere's a mess, but if you care to come in, I can offer you a cup of coffee.'

'Delighted,' he said. 'I had a couple of hours off, so I thought that I'd look you up.'

It was the work of a moment to put the kettle on, find a suitable vase for the flowers, and carry it into the living-room, to stand in the empty hearth.

'I really am very grateful,' Clare said, her voice shaking a little with emotion, it was so long since anyone had done her such a kindness. 'I can't afford to buy flowers, and these are so beautiful. I can't thank you enough. And how did you know where I live?'

Gordon, who had draped his elegant self in her one armchair, said lazily, 'Think nothing of the flowers, Clare. My pleasure is in giving them to you. As for your address, I winkled it out of Jeremy.'

He stared about him. 'You have a nice little *pied à terre* here.'

Now that was going the pace a bit, thought Clare sardonically, looking round the small and shabby room which did duty as living-room, dining room and study. But if Gordon thought to please her by saying so, then so be it.

He read her expression correctly and leaned forward to say earnestly, 'I think that you had a rotten deal after

Boy's death, Clare. If I'd known where you were, I would have come to tell you so.'

'You were right to say last night that I had hidden myself away,' Clare told him frankly, moved by his apparent sympathy. 'I shouldn't have been cross with you. Things were. . .difficult for me after Boy's death, but I'm settled now. I lived not far from here with my mother's sister until she died.'

'And how do you manage, Clare? I know that your parents. . .' and he hesitated.

'Threw me out.' Clare was frank again. 'Oh, I do some translations for a publisher, and type theses for professors and students at several of the London colleges. Aunt knew a bigwig at King's College, and things took off from there. I do a lot of casual work as well.'

'All very different from being Boy's wife,' said Gordon gently.

She would not discuss Boy Mallory with him—or with anyone else, for that matter, so Clare simply smiled and quoted Shakespeare. '"We know what we are, but we know not what we may be." I never thought, when we read *Hamlet* at school, how much those words would apply to me.'

'Oh, what we did at school. . .' shrugged Gordon. 'Now that I have found you again, you will let me keep in touch with you, Clare? A last link with the old days. You really don't see any of Boy's old friends these days?'

'I don't see anybody's friends these days, old or otherwise,' riposted Clare drily.

'Ah.' Gordon cocked an enquiring eyebrow at her. 'It was just that I thought that I saw you with Ralph Schuyler at Bitsy's party, having quite a. . .tête à tête.'

'I never met Ralph Schuyler before he introduced

himself to me last night, and we weren't having a tête à tête. Quite the reverse. It wouldn't worry me if I never saw him again.'

Clare was not quite sure why she found it so necessary to disclaim any interest in Ralph Schuyler. If she denied him so vigorously to Gordon, perhaps he would do her the favour of walking out of her head. Furthermore, why was Gordon so interested in whom *she* might have a tête à tête with?

She didn't flatter herself that Gordon might have an interest in her, or had suddenly been smitten with her charms. From her memories of him in the past, it was only rich girls with promising financial futures whom he had taken the trouble to chase. She could only wonder what had brought him to her flat with flowers.

As though he had read her mind, he said apologetically, 'It's only that Ralph Schuyler has the reputation of being a woman chaser, Clare. And on top of that he has a long-standing involvement with Eva Chance-Smythe. I wouldn't want you to get hurt. A word to the wise and all that. Besides, seeing you again brought back the happy times I shared with you and Boy.'

'Well, that's very kind of you, Gordon,' Clare's reply was a dry one, 'but I can't see myself having anything to do with Ralph Schuyler in the future. More coffee?'

He rose. 'No, thanks, I have to be on my way.'

Clare rose, too. 'Duty calls at the Bank, I suppose.'

He smiled, a little awkwardly. 'Not the Bank, Clare. I'm with Hoffman Goldsmith, the investment people now. I struck lucky a few years ago.'

Well, that explained his new-found sleek affluence. Clare saw him to the door, where, his Homburg in his hand, he said earnestly, 'Why don't we meet for dinner at Quaggers some time soon? I'm a little busy at the moment, but I'll be in touch. It's a promise, Clare.'

Clare's answer was a vague one. She had never cared greatly for Gordon in the old days. He had been too much of a toady to Boy for her liking, but the years seemed to have dealt kindly with him. Now he had come into money he appeared to have changed for the better.

She wasn't sure that she wanted to dine with him at Quaglino's, but despite herself she found, as she closed the door on him, that the prospect had a certain attraction after years of penny-pinching over food.

One good thing his visit had done for her was to drive Ralph Schuyler from her mind. Such an odious woman-iser was sure to have some notorious society beauty in his pocket. Eva Chance-Smythe, indeed!

Even Clare, cut off from that world in which she had once lived, had seen her notoriously beautiful face and body plastered about the picture papers. It had even been rumoured that a prominent Hollywood producer had offered her a contract to star in his new spectacular.

Well, she was welcome to Ralph Schuyler, and he to her, thought Clare, as she struck the keys of her typewriter more viciously than usual. They were a prize pair. . .

Ralph wasn't thinking of Eva Chance-Smythe that lunch time. He was too busy enjoying himself being his cousin's guest at the Travellers' Club in Pall Mall.

Several years of marriage and a young son hadn't changed Gis Havilland. He was still impossibly hand-some, even if his face had hardened and matured now that he was approaching thirty. What had changed was that he was no longer the dandy he had been in his youth—Ralph had taken over that role. But, even in his informal clothes, Gis remained as elegant as ever.

They talked of nothings as they ate—the politics of the day, who might win the Derby, as well as the somewhat troubling news coming from Germany, still in economic difficulties after the war.

'You know my opinion,' Gis ended, as the waiter brought them coffee. 'There will be another European war shortly when the Germans try to reverse their defeat in the last one. I know I'm in a minority when I predict that, but there it is. . .'

He stirred his coffee reflectively, and looked a little sideways at Ralph, whose dark face was a perfect foil for Gis's fair one. 'Which brings me to why I have come to the Great Sewer to seek, among other things, your advice.'

'Flattered, I'm sure,' murmured Ralph, wondering what was coming next.

'It's this. I set up Schuyler H to design and build aircraft. The point is, I'm not satisfied just to reproduce a slightly better version of what is currently flying. I want, instead, to do something really revolutionary and produce a monoplane as safe and effective as the biplanes of today are. I'm pretty sure that I've made a design breakthrough and we should be going into production shortly.

'So far so good, but here's the tricky bit. I've had two break-ins recently, rather ruthless attempts at burglary, and I'm convinced that what the thieves were really after were the plans for my new plane. They didn't succeed, and some money *was* taken. I've no evidence to support my belief that the plans were the target.'

He looked sideways again at Ralph. 'I've a built-in something or other, which if I were a woman would be called intuition. Now I know that Uncle Gerard possesses it, and I believe that you do. The problem is, I didn't notify the police—I don't want to jeopardise the hush-hush nature of what I'm doing—but I do want someone I can trust to go after the villains—whom I assume are agents of a foreign power, Bolsheviks or whatever—so I've chosen you.

'How they know about the plane is a mystery, except that these things can't be kept completely quiet, as you are well aware.'

Gis leaned back, and favoured Ralph with his sweetest smile, before going on, 'And I've come to you to track them down for me before we start production, when they are likely to have another try. Kudos for you with your masters if you do, and a period of safety for me. How about it?'

Ralph said slowly, 'Why me? I'm only a poodlefaker at the Foreign Office. Decorative attaché when I'm abroad...'

'Oh, come off it, Ralph. Don't try to fox me. I'm a Schuyler, too, remember. I know you, and I know your masters, and I know what you were doing just after the war, in Hungary. You weren't an attaché then, and it was the most risky poodlefaking I've ever heard of. Unless it's a new name for being a member of the Secret Service...'

'Dammit, Gis. How...?'

'Don't ask, little cousin. I have my secrets too. Name my name to your masters, and you'll find that they'll have you on the trail, instanter.'

Ralph's laugh was unwilling and admiring. 'Hell, Gis, you're the most consummate—'

'Bastard?' Gis's smile was pure fun. 'Oh, little cousin,

remember Edmund in *King Lear*. "Now, gods, stand up for bastards!"'

His look at Ralph was wicked. 'We're a good pair of wrong-side-of-the-blanket Schuylers, and consequently should help one another at all times! Never mind what God might, or might not, do for us.'

'So you know that, too.' Ralph was half-disgusted, half-admiring. 'But you know everything don't you, Gis?'

'Not quite everything.' Gis was abominably cheerful. 'But I do know that, contrary to popular belief, Uncle Gerard, the revered Lord Longthorne, isn't your father. My betting is that you're Uncle Gerard's half-brother, Grandfather Joris's unacknowledged son of his old age. Mother unknown—to me, at least.'

'So, because of that I should listen to your half-baked intuition?' Ralph knew, though, that he was going to do as Gis asked, but he was going to have to pay for it a little.

'I know you will, and there's more. I have information—from a source I can't divulge but which has the ring of truth to it—that there's a high-powered ring of spies at work in London. My informant was too frightened to give me all the details, or even the country they're working for, but he seemed pretty sure that they were near to the crowd you run with. And that about five years ago they brought off a real coup.'

'And that's it? Your intuition and an unknown informant.'

'And the fact that when we were boys we swore a musketeer's oath to help one another to the death. And even cut our arms and mingled our blood to seal it. I'm calling in that oath, Ralph.

'I won't give *your* secrets away. Poodlefake on, old

fellow. I'll look the other way! If I had the time, I'd be after the villains like a shot, but I've a plane to build—for the war that's coming, and in which I may even fly again.'

He should have remembered what a devil Gis Havilland was, behind the pretty face.

'Very well.' Ralph stood up. 'I have to go now, but I'll do as you ask. I warn you, I may call on you for help—or whatever else I might need. Give my love to your wife. I wonder if she realises what a conniving bastard you are.'

Gis's face was alight with mirth.

'Even more than you do, old fellow. Even more.'

But Ralph had the last word. He was halfway to the dining-room door before he retraced his steps to offer Gis his parting shot.

'Oh, by the way, Gis, the important thing about me is not who my father was—but my mother!'

CHAPTER THREE

'I REALLY do need to speak to you, Clare!' exclaimed Jeremy Peele breathlessly. They had met by accident in Piccadilly Circus, not far from Joe Lyons' big Corner House where Clare was, for once, hoping to enjoy a cheap meal not prepared by herself.

She had just delivered the translation of the French novel when she had heard Jeremy calling her name. She had heard nothing from him in the three weeks which had passed since Bitsy's party, and she had assumed that his promise to get in touch with her had been an empty one.

He was now staring anxiously at her. 'I can't talk to you here,' he said. 'Could you come to my place this evening, at seven? I'm still at Half Moon Street.'

Clare shook her head. Gordon Stewart had sent a special messenger to her yesterday with a note asking her to dine with him at Quaglino's, either that night or the next. The messenger had had orders to wait for her reply, and she had written a letter accepting for the next day, even though she wasn't sure that she wanted to dine with him at all. It was difficult for her to rebuff him altogether, though. He was, at least, being kind to her—for whatever reason.

'I'm sorry,' she told Jeremy sincerely, 'but I've an engagement this evening.'

'Then tomorrow,' he said urgently. He seemed to Clare to be labouring under some strong emotion. 'You will come, won't you, Clare? It's about Boy.'

Clare nodded, and watched with puzzled eyes as he hared off down Regent Street in a manner quite unlike that of his usual easy self.

She remembered this encounter when sitting opposite Gordon at Quaglino's that evening. She and Gordon had arrived early and had just finished eating their asparagus soup when a sardonic voice greeted them.

'Evening, Stewart. Nice to see you again.'

Ralph Schuyler, impeccable in evening dress, a woman on his arm of such glamour that Clare was almost blinded by it, was staring down at them.

Gordon rose. 'Oh, hallo, Schuyler. Long time no see. And Eva. You know Clare Windham, I believe.'

Was it Clare's imagination that Ralph's dark harsh face grew even harsher at this? 'Oh, yes, I know Clare Windham,' he agreed, 'but I don't think Eva does, do you, Eva?'

Eva's stare was inimical. She didn't speak, but shook her head in the most bored manner she could summon up. She was making it quite obvious that she neither knew Clare nor wanted to. Ralph's manner grew colder still as he introduced Clare and Eva to one another. Clare had never felt more uncomfortable, and she regretted all over again that she had accepted Gordon's invitation.

Gordon appeared to notice nothing. He was as warmly polite to Ralph as Ralph was cool to him, and after some further meaningless formalities Ralph and his partner moved on, leaving Clare with the impression that Ralph disapproved not only of Gordon, but even more of herself. She wondered desperately what she had ever done to annoy him.

'Conceited ass, Schuyler,' Gordon told her nastily, in

complete contrast to the almost servile manner he had just been using to Ralph. 'Never could see why everyone takes such a shine to him. Rumour is, he isn't even a Schuyler at all. Not a legitimate one, anyway.'

Her throat closed, Clare couldn't answer him. This whole evening was a mistake. She wondered if Ralph and his partner, now sitting in her line of sight, could possibly be feeling as wretched as she did.

Certainly Eva was not showing much enthusiasm for either Ralph or the meal—tossing her head indifferently when the waiter proffered her the menu, and looking over Ralph's shoulder at the other diners in the room, waving once to a man and woman who had come in after them.

The beautiful food was like straw in Clare's mouth. She suddenly realised that Gordon had asked her a question, was waiting for an answer and she hadn't the slightest idea what he had said.

He had just noticed that she was *distraite* and said gently, 'Are you well, Clare? You look very pale.'

She gave him a grateful smile. 'I had a hard day today, Gordon,' which was true. She had promised Professor Clarke at Imperial College that she would do a rush job in typing a clean copy of his much written-over manuscript by five o'clock.

'Then have some more wine.' He refilled her glass with the excellent Sauterne which he had ordered. 'You'll feel better. You should go out more. I saw Jeremy talking to you at Bitsy's. He had quite a pash for you when you were were engaged to Boy.'

So that was what had been on Jeremy's mind, and explained why he was so anxious to entertain her. This news, instead of exciting Claire, only served to depress her further. She had liked Jeremy, but only as a friend, and had no wish for him to be her suitor.

For some reason, perhaps it was Gordon's earnest face, she felt compelled to say, 'If I had known that, I wouldn't have agreed to meet him at his place tomorrow evening. I suppose I shouldn't have. . .' Her voice trailed off.

Gordon shook his head. 'Oh, Jeremy's a perfect gentleman, Clare. You'll be safe with him, I'm sure.'

Clare nodded again. 'I suppose you're right. It wouldn't be fair to cry off when I said I'd go. He seemed very insistent, though. Kept talking about Boy.'

'Natural of him,' said Gordon kindly. 'We all liked Boy. Now do eat your fish, Clare. It's delicious.'

The rest of the meal passed agreeably enough and Clare even began to enjoy her food. Particularly when she saw Eva Chance-Smythe suddenly start to her feet in the middle of the meal, strike Ralph Schuyler hard on the face, and stride out of the restaurant, an excited buzz of voices following her.

The only unmoved person was Ralph Schuyler, who, after a shrug of the shoulders, continued to eat his meal as though nothing had happened, drinking the whole bottle of claret which he had ordered and of which Eva had only accepted a half glass, with the most apparent enjoyment.

Yes, he *was* quite shameless, Clare thought, and she became especially pleasant to Gordon, laughing and talking so that if Ralph looked her way he would see what a good time she was having. But not such a good time that she was prepared to invite Gordon in for a coffee when he drove her home.

She had to concede that he had behaved like a perfect gentleman, quite unlike Ralph Schuyler. . . She wondered gleefully how happy *he* was feeling after Eva had made her dramatic exit.

What Ralph Schuyler was feeling was relief. He had been trying to shake Eva off for months, not quite having the guts to tell her that their affair was over. She had picked a quarrel with him in the taxi on the way to Quaglino's, and had continued it once they were alone at the table. He had been neglecting her, which was not true; he disapproved of her decision to accept the Hollywood producer's offer to make her a star, which was true.

After a quarter of an hour of Eva's shrewish vituperation, Ralph's patience had finally snapped.

'My dear Eva,' he had drawled, 'if you are determined to set yourself up as a cockshy for every cheap columnist in Los Angeles, don't expect me to approve of what you're doing.'

At that point she had slapped him hard in the face and stormed out. So far as Ralph was concerned she had saved him from having been the one to give the *coup de grâce* to their dying affair. It was plain that she was as bored with it as he was. He was honest enough to acknowledge that love had never entered the equation for either him or Eva. He was also honest enough to admit that he was growing tired of the life of a successful Don Juan. He had reached thirty-five and it was time that he grew up.

In the meantime, he had to watch Clare Windham enjoying herself with Gordon Stewart, and was surprised at how much he was resenting her pleasure. It was surely not possible that he was feeling jealousy, but all the same he was relieved when they left. Except that he then had to worry about whether she was inviting Gordon into her home or bed!

What he ought to have been worrying about was his latest assignment.

Three weeks ago, when he had told his master at the Foreign Office, Colonel B, of Gis Havilland's request for help, Ralph had not been in the least surprised when the Colonel had nodded at him and had said briefly, 'Good man, Havilland. If he thinks something odd *is* going on, then something odd is going on. His HQ is near Bedford, I understand. Be off there, and find out what you can, report back to me as soon as possible.'

He had already been opening a file before Ralph had time to leave the room. He was a man of few words, all of them meaningful. His full name was Hugh Beauchamp, and he was a member of a family that had secretly served the State in some capacity or other for over a hundred years.

If he thought that Ralph was a sound, clever and discreet operative—which he did—he never told him so. Ralph was simply there to do his duty, as Colonel B was, and that should be enough for him.

Ralph had returned earlier in the same day that he would seen Gordon and Clare at Quaglino's and had reported at once to the Colonel.

'Well, Schuyler?'

'Not too well, sir.' And he had begun the recital of his visit to Gis Havilland's HQ as tersely as he could. He had gone there as a vacuous Schuyler cousin being given a guided tour of Schuyler H's plant.

'Why Schuyler H?' he had asked.

He had adopted a monocle and a silly-ass drawl to

allay any suspicions of what he might be up to, and had jammed the monocle into his eye as he questioned Gis.

'Oh, that's so no one confuses us with the other Havilland building planes. The H stands for Havilland, and the Schuyler acknowledges who I really am.'

'Um. . .' Ralph had drawled, and then began to ask silly questions of Gis and the foreman who had accompanied them.

Later he had sat in Gis's small office and discussed the one interesting fact that had come up. Not long before the break-ins the foreman had hired a mechanic, Geoff Watson by name, without telling Gis, and the man had remained at Schuyler H for only a fortnight and then had disappeared. Ralph was later to discover that the home address he had given was a false one. It was likely that he had been paid to ferret out Schuyler H's secrets.

Gis had heaved a sigh at the news. 'I'm always telling Humphreys that it's not necessary to come back to me to vet temporary staff. I don't like to breathe down my men's necks too much—it destroys their initiative. But I have to admit that his judgement—and mine—weren't sound in this case.'

'Hmm,' the Colonel had grated as Ralph had ended his narrative. 'I see Havilland's point, but he should have been more careful—given the circumstances.'

He had fallen silent and stayed so for some moments, before saying suddenly, 'Nothing further to be found there, you say, everyone long gone. You remember that you told me that Havilland's informant talked of a coup happening five years ago. . .? Well, five years ago we suffered a massive leak of information, by whom and to whom we're not sure. What we *do* know is that several of our agents in the field were captured and executed as a result.'

'The Soviets?' Ralph had ventured.

'Perhaps. . .' The pause this time had been a long one. 'Boy Mallory shot himself five years ago, Schuyler. He was in the FO. Not in the secret division, I admit. I'm going to tell you something no one knows. Milford was sure that there was more to Boy's death than disappointment over Clare Windham. He started making inquiries. . .'

He had paused again, giving Ralph the opportunity to say, 'I gather that Milford was killed in a car accident, or so Pryde told me.'

'Indeed, but what Pryde didn't tell you, because he doesn't know, was that it wasn't an accident. His brakes had been tampered with. Oh, I know that he drove his Bentley like a maniac, but it wasn't that which killed him. I think that the so-called accident was arranged to put an end to the inquiry. He was due to report to me in person. Like the careful fellow he was he left nothing behind in writing. I let the matter go, it was all so tenuous, and what Milford might have found out had died with him.

'Now I'm beginning to worry that *my* judgement might have been faulty in not carrying on with it.'

No answer had been required, so Ralph hadn't made one. Another lengthy pause had followed before the Colonel offered, almost reflectively, 'Know Clare Windham, do you, Schuyler?'

Ralph had wondered what was coming next, so had said cautiously, 'I've met her.'

'Good. Among your other duties I want you to keep an eye on her. Watch her, in fact. Something odd about Boy's death. Odd about Boy altogether—and about her. Why did she jilt him? Milford interested in her, too.'

Good God, was the old man getting softening of the brain? What on earth had Clare Windham to do with Schuyler H?

The Colonel did some mind reading, and had said, 'If there was a spy ring operating five years ago—a high-powered one—I have to believe that it's still in existence. A successful one wouldn't have been disbanded. The membership might have changed, though.'

It had been apparent that the old man hadn't told him everything he knew. So Ralph had said in his most silly-ass voice, 'It might be helpful if I knew exactly which country is running it.'

'As I hinted earlier, I'm not quite sure. I'm pretty certain that the Bolsheviks are behind it, but it's for you to find out. And, I don't want anyone in on this but the pair of us. We may have a traitor near to home. Oh, and by the way, Clare Windham lives at 5b, Camden Place, Chelsea.'

He had picked up a file and begun to read it. His usual mode of dismissal. Useless for Ralph to continue to argue. All he would have got would have been a polite stare...

'Oh, blow,' was Clare's dismal response to a snag in her silk stocking which rapidly ran into a long ladder. She was changing into something a little more glamorous— the new word from Hollywood—than the working clothes which she usually wore these days. She didn't want Jeremy Peele, or anyone else for that matter, to know what a hard time she was having keeping her head above water. She slipped off the damaged stocking and replaced it with another.

Fortunately, her hair was cut in a simple style which cost her very little to keep in trim at the small hairdresser's around the corner, and she still had a few items of good clothing left over from happier times. She didn't want to wear her Fortuny again, so she made do instead with an austere navy blue and white striped dress which had come from another local shop. Cheap though it was, she knew that she looked chic in it: it had the obligatory low waist and ended mid-calf. Boy Mallory had always boasted that she knew how to wear clothes to show them off to their best advantage.

Finally, she slipped on a long white knitted cardigan, and a small navy blue cloche hat. All that remained was to pick up her clutch purse and take one last look in the mirror to check that everything was in order. The seams of her deep blue silk stockings were straight, which was fortunate since they, and the elaborate clock motif on each ankle, were very visible. Satisfied by her appearance, she set off for her appointment with Jeremy.

The evening was a balmy one and Clare strolled slowly to the Tube station, unaware that she had a follower.

Ralph Schuyler was following the Colonel's orders. He had spent the afternoon watching the house where Clare lived, and had been rewarded by seeing her go shopping—and then come back. He was seated in his car—not his sporty Bentley which reeked of money, but in a battered grey two-seater Austin which he used on occasions such as these. He was parked diagonally across from her door, in the shade of a large plane tree.

He was half dozing when Clare at last came out, and he almost missed seeing her. Fortunately for him, he caught a glimpse of her just before she turned the corner of the street, and he set off after her at a slow pace, his hands in the pockets of a cheap suit worn to make him look as little as possible like the elegant Ralph Schuyler who graced Mayfair drawing-rooms.

His cap, pulled low over his face to disguise him further, was another disgracefully shabby object, so that when he boarded the same coach of the train as Clare, sitting as far away from her as possible, he was unlikely to be recognised.

'A single to Green Park, please,' she had said in her clear pleasant voice at the ticket office, and Ralph shadowed her all the way there, wondering who it was she could be visiting. Quite a number of her old set had houses and flats just off Piccadilly.

A rather attractive tart solicited him as he left the station, but he waved her away, walking some way behind Clare as she set off in the opposite direction from Piccadilly Circus, passing Clarges Street before turning into Half Moon Street.

Peele! She must be visiting Jeremy Peele, one of Boy's oldest friends. They had been at prep school together, Ralph remembered. He stood at the corner, watching her push open the door before walking up the stairs to Peele's flat. He had the two top floors. Ralph knew this because his man, Armstrong, was a friend of Jeremy Peele's Sutton who, like Armstrong, had his rooms on the top floor.

Ralph debated whether to keep up his vigil—it might be useful to find out whether Clare intended to spend the night with Jeremy—so he retreated across the road to a small alley, put a shoulder against the wall, and kept watch. . .

Unaware that she had been followed, Clare mounted the stairs. Five years ago she and Boy had often made this trip together. She pushed the unwelcome memory away as she reached the landing—to discover that the door to Jeremy's apartment was slightly open.

She hesitated a moment, wondering whether he had left it open for her, and decided to ring the bell anyway. Jeremy might get all the wrong ideas if she just walked in.

The bell rang—but no one answered. Probably Jeremy's man had the night off—in which case she might expect Jeremy to let her in—or was that why he had left the door open? She put her head round it and called softly, 'Jeremy?'

No one answered. Was it possible that he had forgotten that she was coming? Surely not—he had made such a point of her visit. Whether it was the open door which had disturbed her, or the silence, Clare didn't know. She debated whether to leave at once, and decided against it. It might be an idea to reconnoitre. After all, she knew her way around from her previous visits with Boy.

She pushed the door open and walked in. The pleasant living-room was empty. Two glasses, two small plates and a pair of damask napkins were laid out on a low copper-topped Indian table. It was evident that she was expected. The *Daily Telegraph*, open at the crossword, was thrown down in a large armchair. Jeremy's, presumably.

Clare took off her cardigan and hat and sat down on the sofa before the empty hearth to wait for Jeremy to return—if he had slipped out for a short time, that was. She picked up a copy of the *Tatler* from the sofa table laid out with society magazines, put it down again in favour of *The Illustrated Sporting and Dramatic News*. Only to put that down and look in *Vogue* instead.

It opened at a picture of Ralph Schuyler playing polo, Eva Chance-Smythe gazing adoringly at him in the middle distance. Could she never escape the man?

A quarter of an hour passed, and still no Jeremy. Hesitantly, Clare opened the door to the small kitchen where Sutton presided when he was on duty. That was empty, too. But someone—Sutton?—had laid out a coffee set, and milk and sugar and a plate of sweet biscuits. A kettle stood ready for use on the gas stove. Yes, she was expected. Quite definitely expected.

Back in the living-room, Clare hesitated again. She knew that Jeremy's bedroom was along the small corridor off which the kitchen and bathroom opened, and that he used it as an extra cloakroom when he gave parties. Could he possibly be there?

Perhaps he had been suddenly taken ill. Not that that was likely, but there must be *some* explanation for his non-appearance. She called his name again, more strongly this time; when he still did not answer, she walked down the corridor to tap on his bedroom door.

Still no answer. Curiouser and curiouser, as Alice had once said in Wonderland. It would be stupid to go away without looking in the bedroom—to find out if there was any explanation for his absence there.

Clare threw open the door, to see immediately an explanation which was so shattering that she retreated backwards, her handkerchief to her mouth, trying to stifle her screams. Jeremy *was* in the flat, after all, but he was quite unable to welcome her. Covered with blood and very dead, he was lying across his blood-drenched bed, his blind eyes staring at the ceiling. . .

Outside, a bored Ralph Schuyler glanced at his watch, saw that twenty minutes had passed, slipped off his disreputable cap and decided that enough was enough. He would visit Jeremy Peele, try to find out what was going on. He could think up some excuse for his presence—after all, Jeremy was an old friend. He started briskly across the road, rehearsing what he was going to say.

Upstairs, Clare was being sick in the bathroom which opened off Jeremy's bedroom. Recovered a little, she walked back into it, engaging in a wild hope that she might have been dreaming, and that Jeremy was playing some sort of mad trick on her, would be standing there, laughing at her. . .

But it was all the bitter truth. And now she had the problem of deciding what to do. Duty said that she ought to ring the police immediately—she had no idea how gong ago Jeremy had been shot. A revolver lay on the carpet before a large wardrobe, some way from the bed, so suicide could be ruled out.

Might not the police think that she had killed Jeremy?

Clare began to shiver violently, although the night was warm. She remembered the cruel questioning which had followed Boy's death, and the unspoken suggestion that she knew more about it than she was confessing to.

What on earth would they say when they discovered that not only was she involved with another violent death, but that the victim had been a friend of Boy's? She could almost see them raising their eyebrows at this odd coincidence.

Nevertheless, she had her duty to perform. She rose stiffly to her feet and decided to use the telephone in the living-room to ring Scotland Yard. She had hardly reached the bedroom door before it opened. . .

Clare prepared to scream if it proved to be Jeremy's murderer who had been hiding, disturbed by her arrival and ready to kill her as well... Instead, it was Ralph Schuyler who stood there, staring from her to Jeremy's body on the bed and back to her again.

It was all too much.

Clare had never fainted in her life before, but she did so then.

Perhaps it was the expression on Ralph Schuyler's face, or her fear that it was *he* who had shot Jeremy and had been hiding in the flat all the time—although why he should do such a thing she couldn't imagine. Whatever the cause there was a violent buzzing in her ears, everything swam before her and she fell into a black pit of unconsciousness.

To be caught by Ralph Schuyler, his face more disbelieving than ever. Whatever he had thought to find when he had mounted the stairs to Jeremy's rooms, it was not this...

CHAPTER FOUR

'WHAT are *you* doing here?' were Clare's first blunt words when she recovered consciousness again.

Well, they were at at least more original than the usual 'Where am I?' was Ralph's ironic internal comment. What he actually said was, 'I came to visit Jeremy—and found you, and that—' and he waved towards the closed bedroom door. He had carried Clare into the drawing-room and laid her on Jeremy's sofa from where she was gazing at him with puzzled eyes.

'Oh, I see.' Not that she really did, but her mind didn't seem to be functioning properly. She was so shocked that she didn't even register that Ralph was wearing cheap, rough clothing. She sat up, tried to stand and decided not to. Ralph, meanwhile, was busying round the room wiping all the flat surfaces in it, as well as the magazines which she had left on the sofa, and the room's various doorknobs, with a handkerchief which had once been spotless.

'Did you touch anything else?' he enquired abruptly. 'In the bedroom, for instance? Did you pick up and move the revolver?'

'Move the. . .' A wave of nausea swept over Clare. 'No, of course not, why should I?'

He made no answer to that, simply continued with his self-appointed task until Clare asked, 'What are you doing?'

'You obviously don't read thrillers,' was Ralph's dry comment. 'I'm erasing any fingerprints which either of us might have made since we came in. Try not to touch anything more. There must be no evidence that we have been here.'

Of course, she should have thought of that, remembering what had gone on at the time of Boy's death. On the other hand, when they rang for the police it was going to be apparent that they had been in the flat. . .so why remove their fingerprints. . .? In her shocked state Clare found it difficult to think logically and, for the time being, gave up the attempt.

Later, she was to think it strange that Ralph had never once asked her whether she had shot Jeremy. She tried to remember what she had done before she had found his body.

'I touched the door knob when I went in the bedroom, of course,' she said at last. 'Otherwise, nothing. I was too shocked at the sight of Jeremy. . .'

'Um.' Ralph was giving her a hard basilisk stare. 'And in here? I supposed that you had been reading the magazines. Anything else?'

'No. I don't think so.'

He paused, and Clare now noticed that his hands were gloved, although he was indoors.

'You're sure?' When she nodded, he said, still short with her, 'Have you recovered enough to walk, d'you think?'

Well, he might have offered her a glass of water, thought Clare a little aggrievedly, the kitchen being so near, but she answered him as coolly as she could. 'I think so, why?'

'Because we ought to leave as soon as possible when I've removed all trace of our presence here.'

'Aren't we going to phone the police?' she asked him,

her eyes wide at such a breach of proper conduct in the face of the criminal act which was Jeremy's death.

'No.' He was as short with her as ever. She had thought his face hard before this, now it was stone. 'Do you really want to send for them, Clare—after your involvement in Boy's death?'

Clare remembered her first thoughts when she had found Jeremy's body, and said slowly, 'I suppose you're right—but they ought to know as soon as possible, surely? If they're going to find out who did it, that is.'

Ralph's wave of his hand was both lordly and dismissive. 'Sutton will find him soon enough when he comes home. A few hours aren't going to make any real difference.'

'I suppose not,' acknowledged Clare miserably.

Ralph announced curtly, all impatience, 'We've no time to waste, we must leave immediately. If you begin to feel faint again, hang on to me.'

He fired one more question at her. 'Did anyone see you arrive?'

'I don't think so.' What a beast he was. Not a word of sympathy, just questions and answers shot at her as though she were a private in the Army.

She might have complained, but he was pulling her to her feet, without so much as a 'by your leave', tucking her arm in his and walking her to the door, which he opened with his gloved hand.

'There must be a back way out,' he announced brusquely. 'We'll take it, and hope no one sees us.'

He walked her briskly through the kitchen, where the crockery and cutlery were waiting for a master who would never use them. The backstairs were dark and uncarpeted, and then they were in an alleyway which led to Clarges Street and thence to Piccadilly.

'You can take me to Piccadilly Circus Tube station. After that I can find my own way home,' announced Clare firmly. It was time that she gave a few orders.

'Indeed not.' Ralph's grip on her arm tightened. 'You're coming home with me.'

'What! No, I won't, why should I?'

Ralph turned his harsh face on her and said curtly, 'I haven't time to argue with you here. I don't want a scene, or anything to draw attention to us whilst we're in the street. We're going to my place. I'll explain why when we get there. For God's sake, stop arguing with me and try to behave with a little commonsense—if you have any!'

Even in the middle of her fear and shock Clare bridled at the insult.

'Now look here, Ralph Schuyler—'

'No, you look here, Clare Windham.' He was virtually dragging her along, using all his considerable strength. 'I find you in a compromising position in front of a dead body. I doubt whether you have any convincing explanation of what you were doing in Jeremy's flat that would satisfy any policeman, and like a fool I'm busy trying to save you from scandal and worse. Be a good girl, shut up, and save the silly chat for later.'

Seeing that there was a great deal of truth in what he was saying, Clare did just that. Later, she was to admit to herself that shock and distress had driven all practical considerations out of her head. What she didn't expect was that Ralph Schuyler would behave so ruthlessly and lawlessly in saving her from scandal and suspicion. Recovering a little in the taxi Ralph had hailed, she had to admit that she did owe him a debt of gratitude for doing so—but why was he taking the trouble to help her?

Neither of them said anything on the short journey to Ralph's home in Park Lane. Unlike Jeremy, he owned the whole of a considerable house there, Clare found. He escorted her into a beautiful room filled with antiques—one had to remember that he was one of the rich Schuylers and presumably considered such luxury normal.

Ralph had let himself in, and no servant appeared to wait on them. 'Fortunately, it's my man's night off, and I don't like a pack of other servants dancing attendance on me—they do their duties and leave me alone,' he explained. He sat her down and went over to a Sheraton sideboard to pour her a large glass of brandy.

'Here, this will help you a little,' he said, handing it to her before pouring himself an even stiffer drink and sitting down in another large armchair, opposite to her.

Peace at last, Clare thought, but no, his urgent questioning began again.

'Did anyone know that you were visiting Jeremy tonight?' He held his glass up to the light to admire the liquor in it.

Shuddering a little at the amount she was drinking, Clare responded quickly, 'No, I don't think so,' and then, 'Oh, I forgot. I told Gordon Stewart when I dined with him. I said that I wasn't sure that I should visit a man's flat alone. He said I shouldn't worry. He said that Jeremy wouldn't take advantage of me.'

'Did he, indeed?' Ralph drank the remainder of his brandy in one gulp after a fashion which would have made a connoisseur wince. 'And you told no one else?'

'No one else to tell,' admitted Clare, giving away the loneliness of her life to the observant Ralph, who made a mental note of what this told him about her. He distrusted all women on principle, and knew that he had good reason to, but he thought that what Clare had told him so far was the truth. More important was the fact that Gordon was the only person who knew that she was visiting Jeremy. . . .

Warmth began to steal over Clare, a false warmth created by the brandy. She put down her glass. A precious and valuable antique, she noted—but presumably all Schuyler possessions were precious and valuable.

'May I go home now?' she asked his stark profile. He might be tall and dark, but no one, absolutely no one, could possibly call him handsome. Formidable was the right word with that dominant nose and jaw. He was thinking hard, she could tell. About what? Her and Jeremy presumably.

'What? Go home? Certainly not. Why do you think I brought you here?'

Why had he? Clare couldn't guess.

He enlightened her. 'My good girl, you need an alibi. You had an appointment with Jeremy. He's found dead. The police will probably ferret around and discover from Sutton that Jeremy was expecting you. If I had let you go home from Jeremy's flat, all that you could have claimed is that you were alone all night, after changing your mind about visiting him.

'Think how thin that would sound. If you stay here with me until morning you have an alibi. Me. I'm so respectable it hurts. What are you?'

He was so dismissive of her that despite her distress Clare bristled at him. 'No, I won't stay with you. I'd rather risk suspicion. Please, let me call the police.'

Ralph bit back an oath. He had followed her to Jeremy's flat on a hunch. The hunch had paid off more royally than even he could have hoped. He thought it unlikely that she had shot Jeremy, but he could not be sure of that. He meant to bind her to him with hoops of steel because, whether she knew it or not, she was somehow involved in a major intrigue to which he was determined to find the key.

'Clare, don't be stupid,' he managed at last. 'I'm not going to touch you, I promise. If you stay here, and pretend that we are madly smitten with one another, that will protect us both.'

'Both?' Clare had given up trying to make sense of anything. The temporary warmth had disappeared and she was beginning to shiver again. 'Why both?'

'Because I was there, in the flat with you, and poor dead Jeremy. What might the police make of that?'

'But I should tell them that you arrived later. . .some time after me. . .' Something clicked in Clare's brain and the world began to make sense again.

'Oh, I see what you mean. They might think that I was lying. . . If I stay with you, we are protecting one another, giving each other an alibi.'

'Exactly.' Ralph had thought that Clare was highly intelligent, although since he had found her in Jeremy's bedroom she hadn't shown much evidence of it. He conceded that shock and exhaustion had done their worst with her, and now that she was coming out of it, she was beginning to think clearly again. Mentally, at least, she was recovering, but physically was a different thing. Her shivering was becoming violent, shaking her whole body, and when he leaned over and touched her forehead gently he found it icy cold.

He had seen such a phenomenon before in the trenches, and he regretted that he had needed to speak so harshly to her, but it had been necessary to make her obey him immediately if he was to save her—and give

him a chance to discover what was behind Jeremy's
death.

'You ought to go to bed and try to rest,' he said
gently, as the shivers grew worse.

She looked at him with great wondering eyes, whispering, 'Whatever is the matter with me?'

'Delayed shock,' he told her. 'I'll take you upstairs
and you can have a bath and then go to bed.'

Clare tried to make a little joke. 'Well, your home is
big enough for a spare room I suppose.'

He shook his head. 'Oh, no, Clare. We're going to
share a room tonight. That way our alibi is unbreakable
if the police question us.'

The shivers grew worse than ever. 'Oh, no, I can't. I
won't...'

Such a wave of compassion for her passed over hard
Ralph Schuyler that it not only surprised him, but had
him taking her into his arms simply to hold her against
his warmth and try to comfort her, all thought of his
mission forgotten.

'I shan't touch you, Clare. I'll sleep on the sofa, but
Armstrong must be able to testify that we shared a
room together tonight. Your story is that you changed
your mind and came here instead of going to Jeremy's
place.'

He looked down at her. In some odd way stress had
enhanced Clare's beauty. Strain had highlighted the
good bones of her face — bones which would ensure that
she would remain attractive long after her first youth
had gone.

Altogether she was quite different from the women
he usually associated with, brazen and sure of themselves; women like Eva. Clare had lost her home, her
place in society, and was only just managing to sur-

vive—how, he did not know. To give her her due, her spirit had remained unbroken through all her trials. His compassion grew.

He was surprised at how soft and silken she felt against him, and at the temptation that she presented to him, a man who could usually coldly control his desires and appetites. Perhaps it was her vulnerability which was weakening him, and if so, he must armour himself against it. All the same, he could not prevent himself from kissing the top of her head.

Cursing himself for his passing weakness, for it was essential that he remained as sceptical and clear-headed about her as about everyone, Ralph nudged her gently.

'A bath, I said, Clare, not a good sleep. You can have that later. A long soak in a hot bath will make you feel much better.'

Ralph had said that she would feel better after a hot bath and he had been right. Clare couldn't remember how long it was since she had sat in a bath as big and comfortable as the one in Ralph's luxurious dressing-room. There were large mirrors on all of the walls making her feel that she was an extra in a Hollywood extravaganza—one of Cecil B. DeMille's.

His bedroom had been splendid, too. A man's room full of leather and strong fabrics. His bed, from which she had hastily averted her eyes, was a huge fourposter, big enough for him to have entertained three Eva Chance-Smythes in it at once, being her naughtily irreverent thought at the sight of it.

'Might I suggest that when you have bathed, instead of putting your day clothes on again, you try these,' he had said, and without waiting for an answer he had gone to a large armoire standing against the long wall of his room, and fetched out a pink silk nightgown and a woman's beautiful *peignoir* to match, decorated with peacocks.

Now what did *that* tell you about his private life? was Clare's amused, as well as bemused, reaction.

Her face must have betrayed her thoughts for he gave a short laugh. 'Come on, Clare. I promised you earlier that I wouldn't seduce you, and I meant it. I'm not in the mood. Just accept my word that you'll feel better if you do as I ask you. I promise not to visit the bathroom while you're there. In fact, I'll go downstairs. Cross my heart and hope to die! There, does that satisfy you?'

He could see her distrust of him written on her face and for the life of him he could not blame her. It was his turn to show relief when she gave a small nod of agreement, and picked up the towels, the nightie and the dressing-gown.

'Good girl,' he said approvingly, which was a notable first, thought Clare wryly, seeing that everything which she had said and done so far had appeared to annoy him.

'You'll find some women's bits and bobs in the bathroom cabinet,' he went on. 'Shampoos, scented soaps, lipsticks and creams. Don't hesitate to use them.'

So she did. The shampoo, the soaps, the bath oils, the lipsticks and the creams, both cold and vanishing, were in unopened jars, packets and bottles which were far more expensive than those which Clare bought from the local branch of Woolworths.

She wondered who the other women were who had shared his bed and his bathroom. Eva Chance-Smythe, presumably. She knew that Ralph had quite a reputation as a ladies' man, which was why she was being so shy with him.

Wrapped in the *peignoir*, and wearing a pair of new pink women's mules which she had found on a shelf in the bathroom, Clare wandered back into his bedroom, drying her hair as she went. She was beginning to feel a new woman. The dreadful shivering had stopped and the memory of poor dead Jeremy's body was no longer quite so insistent.

Ralph had been as good as his word: the bedroom was empty. She had hardly sat down in a big armchair by the fireplace before there was a tap on the door.

'Clare? Are you out yet? May I come in?'

Well, she could hardly say no! Not only was it his room but he was insisting that she spend the night in it—with him. She tried not to think of that, and what he would look like with his outdoor clothes off and his pyjamas on. She had another dreadful thought. What if he didn't wear pyjamas! She remembered her cousin Angela, a more forward girl than she had been, telling her that quite a lot of young men didn't wear anything to bed these days. Clare hadn't dared to ask her how she knew.

'Yes,' she called, and then to match his insouciance, 'I'm respectable.' It would not do for him to think of her as a complete rabbit. She might not be Eva Chance-Smythe, but she was no man's doormat, either.

To her surprise, when Ralph came in he was carrying a tray of food, had obviously had a bath, or shower, and was wearing brilliantly hued pyjamas beneath the kind of highly fashionable silk dressing gown which Noel Coward had made popular in his plays.

He put the tray of food on the bed before dragging out and opening a low eighteenth-century gate-legged table and arranging it before her. He placed on it two plates, their contents hidden beneath elaborate silver dish covers, a basket of bread, cutlery, two wine glasses and a bottle of champagne.

'Goodness.' Clare stared at this feast. 'However did you carry all that upstairs?'

Ralph's grin was a genuine one. 'With difficulty, Miss Windham, with difficulty. I must admit that Armstrong usually does this with more panache, but he's not here.'

He fished from his dressing-gown pocket two napkins, and pulled up chairs for them both. 'I don't know how long it is since you've had a meal, but I'm starving.'

Before the food arrived, Clare would have said that she would have found it impossible to eat after all she had been through. Instead, as Ralph lifted the covers off with a flourish like that of every well-trained waiter at the Café Royal or Quaglino's, she found her mouth watering at the sight of two cheese omelettes, each with a small helping of salad.

'Oh,' she cried artlessly, 'how splendid. I didn't know how hungry I was.'

'Then eat,' commanded Ralph, who found Clare's evident pleasure at the sight of this simple meal a great contrast to Eva Chance-Smythe's bored acceptance of everything he offered her.

She needed no second invitation. 'It's good,' she exclaimed, 'it's really good. You must have an excellent cook.'

'Now that,' Ralph told her, watching her from under heavy lids, 'really warms my heart, seeing that the cook is before you.'

Down went Clare's knife and fork. 'You made this? Impossible!'

'Cooking's not difficult,' Ralph said. 'Just time-consuming. I used to cook in the trenches. I found that it interested me. When I came home again I bribed my chef to teach me how to prepare simple dishes. Have some bread. I can't boast that I baked that. And more champagne. Once it's open we can't let it go to waste.'

Sitting there in the quiet room, now lit by pink-shaded wall lamps, Clare forgot her first fear of Ralph, particularly as the champagne, with which he constantly filled her glass, began to do its work. Perhaps he didn't look so harsh after all? When he smiled his whole face softened, and became less stern and forbidding. Because he seemed to think nothing of entertaining her in his dressing-gown, Clare began to forget her own scanty attire.

Not, she thought hazily, that it was all that scanty. Women like Eva Chance-Smythe wore less than she was wearing to go to society balls.

Thinking of Eva Chance-Smythe again gave Clare a vague pain. Had Ralph entertained her like this? And if he had, why should she object? And why was she constantly thinking of the woman?

Clare told herself firmly that she didn't mind how many women Ralph Schuyler had entertained. He was nothing to her. She gave him a vague sweet smile of forgiveness for his philandering. On seeing the smile, Ralph thoughtfully poured her another glass of champagne, noting that she seemed to have forgotten that she disliked it. She was also apparently unaware that he had drunk very little of the bottle which was now almost empty. . .

What he hadn't forgotten was why he had become involved with her at all, although, as she sat there opposite to him, her face soft in the low light, he was in danger of doing so. He brought his wandering mind—and his erratic body—sternly back to its proper task.

As casually as he could, he asked her, 'Was there any

particular reason why Jeremy invited you to his rooms? Or was it just a social call?'

A pleasant buzzing had begun in Clare's ears. She answered him equally casually. 'Oh...he said that he...' she yawned, a pretty yawn behind her hand '...wanted to tell me something I ought to know about Boy...but that might have been an excuse to get me there.'

'Probably,' lied Ralph, who was beginning to see a way through the wood. Was that why Jeremy had been shot? To prevent him from telling Clare something about Boy? A fanciful thought, but a possible one.

'Have you seen much of Jeremy since Boy's death?'

For some reason Clare could not quite understand why Ralph's questions—which were really quite simple—seemed to be getting harder and harder to answer. She concentrated on this one for a moment, before replying.

'No. But that's not strange. I haven't seen any of our crowd since Boy committed suicide and I had to earn my own living. No time and no money.'

Clare yawned again before drinking down the last drops of her champagne. Ralph's dark face was becoming hazy and she was feeling the most intense desire to sleep. The good food and the excellent drink which Ralph had given her seemed to be having an almost anaesthetic effect.

She stretched herself as artlessly as a kitten—the champagne had destroyed all her inhibitions—then said, brightly and clearly, 'I think I could go to sleep now,' put her head on the chair's over-stuffed arm, closed her eyes, and was as immediately dead to the world as a happy and well-fed baby.

Ralph rose and walked over to where she half-sat,

half-lay. The pink shaded lights cast a rosy glow on the porcelain of her face. Her dark lashes shaded her cheeks, and in sleep her mouth had curled up into a Mona Lisa smile. One hand was tucked under her right cheek, the other hung down. The short unpainted nails and the calluses on her fingers and palm were the stigmata of unremitting work and toil with fountain pen and typewriter.

But nothing could dim the delicacy of her face and figure and the shining glory of her caramel-coloured hair, with its streaks of gold. A spasm of desire, so strong that it was painful, so involuntary and unexpected that it shocked him, told him something about her effect on him which he did not wish to know. He must try to remember that she was nothing more than a problem which he must solve.

Or so reason said. Emotion said quite another thing.

And it was emotion, mixed with pity, sentiments usually quite foreign to Ralph Schuyler's hard and usually loveless nature, which had him bending down, lifting her carefully out of her chair and carrying her to the great bed.

Armstrong had pulled back the covers for him before he had left for his night out, so that it was easy to slip her inside the bed, still in her *peignoir*, without waking her. She stirred once, caught at his hand as he carefully withdrew it, and clasped it tightly for a moment, before freeing it.

It was a gesture of such simple trust that Ralph, despite himself, was moved all over again. He wondered for a moment whose hand she thought that she was holding, tried to be cynical about *that*—and failed.

For a moment he stood there, looking down at her, and had the strongest desire to throw off his dressing-gown and climb into bed with her—even if only to lie beside her silken softness all night, both of them as innocent as the child she had, for a moment, seemed.

He shuddered, shook his head, murmured roughly to himself, 'Fool,' dimmed the lights and walked over to the sofa which stood athwart the empty fireplace, and tried to sleep.

But unlike Clare, he found sleep long in coming, and the first streaks of morning were in the sky before he, at last, found peace of a kind.

CHAPTER FIVE

'AND will the lady be requiring breakfast, too, sir?'

Armstrong's voice and manner were as bland as he could make them, and carried neither condemnation, nor approval, for the fact that his master had just entertained yet another woman for the night. And one whom Armstrong had never seen before.

He had first met Ralph in the trenches, knew his little ways, and had long ago guessed his true profession — about which he had been as silent as the grave.

'Oh,' said Ralph. 'You knew I had a guest?'

'Indeed, sir. I found her hat and cardigan on the sofa in the drawing-room. I took the liberty of hanging them up.'

He did not add that after that he had also taken an illicit peep into Ralph's bedroom and seen Clare still asleep in the big bed whilst Ralph, already up, had just finished shaving himself in his dressing-room.

So, the alibi he had prepared for Clare, and himself, was working. Useful and tireless busybody that he was, Armstrong had doubtless already discovered that his master had had a woman in his room all night, and would so testify if questioned.

Armstrong, unaware that he had just been manipulated once again by the master whom he always believed *he* was manipulating, asked suavely, 'And will she require the usual, sir? Or is she one of those who prefers the unusual?'

His master considered a moment. 'The usual, I

believe. Perhaps I had better ask her,' and Ralph retreated to the bedroom where Clare was awake and yawning.

For a moment, on waking, as she saw the dark damask curtains of Ralph's fourposter, so different from her own second-hand brass and iron bedstead, Clare had wondered where on earth she could be—until memory of the night before came flooding in, hard and cruel.

She sat bolt upright. At that very moment Ralph knocked and entered in reply to her hesitant, 'Come in!' He was fully dressed, thank goodness, and looked disgustingly cheerful for a man who had spent the night on the sofa.

'Armstrong wants to know, "Do you require the usual?"'

The usual? What did he mean by the usual? Use your wits, Clare, breakfast, of course.

'I suppose so. What does Armstrong call the usual?'

'Oh, bacon and eggs, kippers, kedgeree, and things.'

Suppressing a desire to demand 'and things', plus a remark that a large part of her time with Ralph seemed to consist of talking about food, or eating it, Clare answered, as demurely as she could, 'Oh, the usual will do.'

'Splendid,' returned Ralph. 'Armstrong would have been so disappointed if you had expressed a desire to breakfast off some strange concoction of alfalfa and other rare fodder.'

'Well, I wouldn't want to disappoint Armstrong,' was her dry reply to that. 'Are my clothes handy? I ought to be getting up.'

Although she didn't know it, Ralph's answer was a

parody of Armstrong's. 'I took the liberty of hanging them up in the closet over there.'

Clare blushed at the idea of him handling her personal belongings. She had gone to sleep the night before, overset by shock and champagne, without a thought for such mundane things as taking care of the few good clothes which she possessed.

'Thank you,' she said, awkwardly and belatedly. Her brain being in good working order this sunny morning, it was beginning to occur to her that she owed Ralph a large debt of gratitude and that part of his plan was already working, seeing that Armstrong was well aware of her presence.

The blush grew. He would, of course, also assume that she was Ralph's mistress. Well, that was no great matter. After today she would drop out of Ralph's life, and no one would either know or care about what she had apparently done last night. The people for whom she worked would have no knowledge or interest in what went on in the sort of Mayfair circles which Ralph frequented.

After she had eaten breakfast she would go home and try to forget what had happened. Oh, the police might come to question her, but Ralph had solved that problem for her—which was a kindness which she hadn't expected and for which she must thank him.

Even sitting in the pretty breakfast-room filled with early summer flowers, and being waited on by a deferential Armstrong was not such an ordeal as she might have supposed.

Ralph seemed rather abstracted, and said little. Armstrong had reverently laid *The Times* out on his right hand, and Clare supposed that, had she not been there, he would have read it between the courses of his

very elaborate breakfast. She found herself wondering
how he kept his athletic figure if he enjoyed his food so
much.

Finally, when Armstrong had left the room to fetch
fresh coffee from the kitchen, she laid down her napkin
and said as prettily as she could, 'I have to thank you,
Ralph, for your kindness to me, but I really think that I
ought to trespass on it no longer, and go home immediately. I have a great deal of work to do, as I am sure that
you have.

'If you will tell me where my hat and cardigan are, I
will leave immediately.'

The stare with which Ralph's amber eyes favoured
her was an inimical one.

'Please sit down, Clare,' he told her in his most grave
voice. 'I haven't finished my breakfast yet, and I would
prefer to do so before I escort you back to. . .Chelsea. . .
is it?'

Clare matched his frostiness. 'Oh, there's no need to
do that. I am quite used to travelling on the Tube, and
going about on my own, and,' she found herself saying,
'I'm not Eva Chance-Smythe, you know.'

It was Ralph's turn to throw down his napkin. 'Now
what on earth has Eva to do with anything?' he
wondered aloud, his heavy eyebrows going up alarm-
ingly. 'I have no intention of allowing a young lady with
whom I am involved to go about London on her own
after she has spent the night with me.'

'But I am not involved with you.' Clare was all
agitation, and failed to notice that Armstrong had
returned with the coffee pot. 'And I didn't spend the
night with you.'

'Oh.' Ralph's eyebrows rose even higher. 'Did you,
or did you not, spend the night in my bed?'

'Ahem,' remarked Armstrong, putting the coffee pot down in front of Clare, to draw attention to his arrival on the scene.

Ralph's smile in his direction was a grim one. 'Ghosting again, eh, Armstrong? How many times do I have to tell you that I like a little notice of when you are favouring us with your presence?'

Armstrong was all greasy servility. 'Oh, I do beg pardon, sir. Forgive me. I was not my usual tactful self, I fear.'

'Indeed, you weren't,' returned Ralph, who was secretly pleased that his man had heard his remarks compromising Clare. He was likely after that to be even more convincing when questioned by the police. 'Never mind, I forgive you, although I doubt that Miss Windham will.'

Clare gave a sigh. Her reputation having gone completely down the drain—or up the creek—she was compelled to put her best face on. 'Oh, I am in the business of forgiving everyone this morning, Ralph, even you.'

This didn't faze him in the least. On the contrary, with Armstrong still gazing benevolently at them, he rose, walked round the table, picked up her hand, and kissed it.

'How very gallant of you, my darling. I do appreciate it, and in return you will let me drive you home, won't you?'

What could she say but yes? She had to play her part in this charade, however little she liked it.

'Thank you.' Ralph gave her warm cheek a chaste kiss. 'In the circumstances it's the least I can do for you. Now, do have some toast and marmalade, and a cup of fresh coffee. Do admit that Armstrong's coffee is a revelation.'

The beam he gave her as he said this was fatuously loverlike, if not to say lecherous. Clare almost choked over her coffee, and resigned herself to futher manipulation by Ralph. Unlike Armstrong, she had no illusions about where she stood with him.

She was not prepared, however, to discover that when they had arrived outside her flat in Camden Place he was determined to go in with her, instead of driving on to the Foreign Office—or wherever it was that he worked.

He handed her gallantly out of his green Bentley with its sporty leather strap: a few lace curtains had twitched interestedly on its arrival. She started off briskly towards the front door, having said a muted thank you to him, only to find that he was following her.

Her hand on the door knob, she said, as distantly as she could, 'There's no need to see me any further, Ralph. As I told you, I am used to looking after myself.'

'I know,' he murmured fondly, dropping a kiss on her head to the scandalous delight of all the watchers. 'But you have me to look after you now. I can't allow my best girl to go about unescorted.'

'Oh!' Clare almost stamped her foot. 'Well, you have escorted me to my very door, so now you can go.'

He laid a hand on her arm, a gesture which looked very tender to their watchers but which, to the annoyed Clare, felt like a band of steel clamped there.

'Do be sensible,' he murmured in her ear, as though he was indulging her with the most amorous endearments. 'We are supposed to be wild for one another, and our behaviour must reflect that if we are to be

convincing. Smile at me, and let me come in with you. I
need to talk to you, away from Armstrong.'

Annoyingly, what he said made sense, but was no
more welcome to Clare for that. Grudgingly, she gave
him a sickly grimace which passed for a smile—from a
distance—and, saying, 'If you must, you must,'
motioned him to follow her up some drably carpeted
stairs. Her flat was on the first floor.

The morning sun shone into a largish room which
plainly doubled as a living-room and a study. The
furniture in it was obviously second-hand, as were the
books on the simple shelving on one wall. A deal table
in the window was being used as a desk. An elderly
typewriter stood on it, surrounded by books and papers.

A small battered dining-table at which two chairs
stood, and a pair of elderly armchairs stationed on
either side of the empty hearth, made up the tale of
Clare's few possessions. Ralph found himself seized by
an untimely remorse for having made her reveal to him
her straitened circumstances. He assumed that the rest
of the flat was furnished equally minimally, and he was
not wrong.

He let nothing show. He knew instinctively that she
would fiercely reject his pity. It was written in her
defiant stance, and the expression on her face. Instead
he said, 'May I sit down? I think that we ought to talk.'

'Of course.'

Clare motioned him to one of the armchairs and he
took the other. Thus positioned, they stared at one
another like two duellists on a proving ground until
Ralph said, 'Clare, do call pax. I'm only trying to help
you. You must understand that it is essential, for the
next few weeks at least, until Jeremy Peele's death

ceases to be a nine day's wonder, that we must behave in a lover-like way so as to disarm suspicion.

'You must be prepared to be escorted by me, not only to evening parties, but also to the kind of events in the day which I would usually be expected to attend with my latest girlfriend. It won't be for too long, I promise.'

Metaphorically Clare lowered her rapier, gave a great sigh, and admitted defeat.

'Yes, I see what you mean, and I will try to be good. But the problem is that I have to earn a living,' and she waved a hand at the crowded table. 'I can't spend too much time away from my work.'

His point gained, Ralph was easy. 'Granted, and I'll take account of that, and keep my demands to a minimum. In the meantime, we must talk freely to one another about our lives so that we don't say or do anything which might give us away.'

For some moments they exchanged confidences. Clare told him of her work and its demands, and he described his daily life at the Foreign Office. The difference was that Clare was telling the truth and Ralph was lying.

'And you promise that Eva You-Know-Who won't be a problem,' said Clare at last. 'I don't want any jealous scenes in public.'

'Well,' answered Ralph with the rather mischievous grin which she was coming to associate with him, 'it might, you know, be rather useful if she did make some—it would seal our supposed affair, wouldn't it? But, alas, she's off to Hollywood this week, so there's no danger of that.'

'Good.' Clare felt strangely relieved on hearing this news, but was giving nothing away. 'Then that's that, isn't it? I needn't detain you any longer.'

The sight of Ralph sitting large and dominant in her small room after seeing him in his own spacious habitat was having an odd effect on her. He was behaving as though he had lived in it for years instead of having only recently arrived as a guest. It was time that she suggested that he was only passing through.

He was having nothing of *that*. Instead, he remarked, 'No, indeed. I haven't finished. You've had a go at Eva. Now I'll ask you a personal question to which I need to know the answer. Why did you jilt Boy Mallory?'

Ralph was not prepared for what followed. Clare, who had hitherto been holding her own with him, went quite white and bit her lip. She spun away from him saying, 'I can't tell you that. Why do you need to know? It can have nothing to do with Jeremy's death. Nothing.'

But Ralph, who was beginning to think quite otherwise, pressed on. 'Come on, Clare, I've been honest with you about Eva. Why make such a secret of it?'

'No!' Clare sprang to her feet and walked to the door. 'No!' She was not prepared, would never be prepared, to tell anyone why she had jilted Boy, two days before their wedding. Her father, her mother and assorted relatives, even the local parson, had badgered her, all to no avail. She was certainly not going to chat about it with Ralph Schuyler, however much he might insist.

They were duellists again. The brief moment of rapport which they had shared was over.

Ralph frowned. 'I'm sorry,' he began—but got no further. There was an insistent knocking on the door.

'Are you expecting anyone?' he asked.

Clare, her colour restored, shook her head.

'I'd better answer it,' she said. 'You might like to go now.' Not that she really thought he would.

The knocking came again, more insistent than before. 'Open up,' a harsh male voice insisted. 'We know that you're in, Miss Windham. Your landlady saw you arrive a few minutes ago.'

'My God,' hissed Ralph hopefully, 'it must be the police.' Better and better, he thought. If I'm here my presence will give Clare the confidence to deceive them.

To Clare's horror he rapidly walked over to her, ruffled her hair, rubbed his cheek against her lipsticked mouth and with one smooth movement undid the two top buttons of her dress.

'Ralph!' Clare exclaimed, horrified. 'What are you up to now. . .?' and then stopped. She knew only too well what he was up to: making them look like lovers. He was now pulling his tie off and undoing the top buttons of his shirt before walking to the door and calling through it in an annoyed voice, 'Yes, who is it? Miss Windham and I are in conference. Very busy, too.'

In conference, what next? And he was right. It *was* the police, as they told him in no uncertain terms. Cursing loudly—to add conviction to the picture of a guilty pair making love in the morning and resenting being disturbed—Ralph opened the door.

Two plainclothes men, one of whom showed Ralph his badge, walked past him into the room to stare at Clare who was looking the picture of unhappy confusion as she tried to repair her dishevelled state whilst Ralph was wrestling his tie back on.

The leading man looked from her to Ralph, and gave a knowing smile. His fellow was openly smirking as Clare continued to struggle with her buttons.

'It *is* Miss Windham, Miss Clare Windham, isn't it?' Number One said. 'We'd like you to answer a few questions, miss, if you don't mind.'

It would, Clare supposed, be all the same if she did. Behind the two men's backs Ralph was smiling encouragingly at her. At least she thought that was what he was doing. In the madhouse which her life had become, anything was possible.

'I am Inspector Malcolm and this is Sergeant Johnson,' he continued. 'We shall try to be as brief as we can.'

Sergeant Johnson, who had, with some difficulty, wrenched his eyes from Clare, was now staring hard at Ralph who was lounging against the wall, the picture of upper-class boredom.

'Don't I know you, sir? It *is* Captain Schuyler, isn't it?'

'Certainly.' Ralph's smile was man to man, comradely, marred a little by the lipstick on his cheek, of which he was apparently unaware. 'With me at Arras, weren't you, Johnson? A corporal then, if I remember rightly.'

'I knew I couldn't be mistaken, sir.' Johnson was all friendly ingenuousness.

'Hmm, Johnson,' intoned the Inspector, 'this isn't a regimental reunion, as I am sure the Captain is aware.'

'Major, actually,' murmured Ralph. 'Although I don't use my wartime rank now I'm in Civvy Street. Plain mister will do.'

'Quite, sir,' replied the Inspector, frowning at his Sergeant to shut up. 'I'm sure you won't mind if we ask the lady a few simple questions.'

'Depends on what they are,' was Ralph's genial answer to that.

'Oh, nothing difficult I'm sure, Mr Schuyler.'

'It was I to whom you wished to speak, I believe,

Inspector,' said Clare repressively, 'and not Mr Schuyler.'

'Indeed, miss. And the first question is a very simple one. Where were you last night, Miss Windham?'

She took a deep breath. Here beganneth the lies.

Clare had rarely lied before. When questioned about her jilting of Boy she had never lied, but had simply refused to answer anyone who questioned her. She had thereby lost everything, or nearly everything, in doing so. She would probably lose all that was left to her if she told the police the truth: that she had been in Jeremy's flat the night before.

When she spoke she was astonished by her calmness. 'Oh, that's easily answered. I was with Mr Schuyler.'

The Inspector consulted his notebook. 'I would advise you to tell me the exact truth about the time when you were with him,' he told her portentously. 'Mr Sutton, Mr Jeremy Peele's man, told us that you had an appointment with him at his flat last night. At seven-thirty. Did you visit him last night, Miss Windham?'

This last question needed a careful answer. Ralph, his heart in his mouth—a phrase which he had always thought was ridiculous, but didn't now—waited for it. Clare mustn't forget that she wasn't supposed to know that Jeremy was dead.

Clare didn't let him down.

'Jeremy's man?' she echoed in a puzzled voice. 'What has he to do with anything? Why haven't you asked Jeremy? And why come to me? Jeremy must have told you that I had an appointment to visit him but that I never turned up. I changed my mind and I went out with Ralph—Mr Schuyler—instead.'

Ralph's sigh of relief was internal. Good girl. She

couldn't have answered the Inspector with more apparent truth if he had had time to coach her.

Intercepting a glance from the Inspector, Sergeant Johnson now piped up.

'You haven't heard what the newsboys are crying on the streets this morning, then?'

'No, Sergeant, I haven't. Why? What are they saying?'

The Inspector, who was apparently in the habit of engaging in a duet with his sergeant, took up the questioning again, watching Clare closely as he spoke.

'Mr Peele was murdered in his rooms last night, some time between seven and eleven o'clock, we think. His man, Sutton, discovered his body when he came home after his night out. It was he who told us that his master was expecting you, and we found a note to that effect in Mr Peele's diary. Are you sure that you didn't visit him last night?'

Ralph thought that it was time that he took a hand. 'Really, Inspector, why this inquisition? Clare, Miss Windham, has already told you that she cancelled her appointment with Jeremy because I asked her to come out with me instead. She agreed, and here we are.'

'Yes, sir. So I see. But I would like the young lady to answer me. If you would, Miss Windham.'

It was perhaps time that she showed the Inspector a little of the distress which she had felt the night before. Clare pulled out her handkerchief, covered her face with it, and sank into a chair. Faintly, through the handkerchief, she muttered, 'If you will allow me to sit down, I will try to answer you. This has come as a great shock to me. Jeremy and I have been friends since I was a small girl.'

'Let me fetch her a glass of water, Inspector.' Ralph

sprang forward. All the gallantry which had been missing from his behaviour the night before, Clare noticed acidly, was now being ladled over her.

'Indeed, Major Schuyler. Were you acquainted with Mr Peele, sir?' he asked as Ralph emerged from Clare's small kitchen, carrying a Woolworth's tumbler full of water.

'Mr Schuyler, if you please,' retorted Ralph briskly as he tenderly handed Clare the tumbler. Her sigh of gratitude was not all a pretence. He was creating a breathing space for her in which she could prepare herself to give the Inspector the least self-compromising answer she could.

'And the answer to your question,' Ralph continued, 'is yes, a little.'

The Sergeant spoke again. 'You haven't answered the Inspector's question yet, Miss Windham. Are you sure that you didn't visit Mr Peele last night?'

Her blue eyes as wide and innocent as she could make them, Clare looked at both men over the rim of her glass.

'I have already told you that I changed my mind.' She took another swallow of the water, and added, 'I was with Mr Schuyler last night, as he has confirmed I never visited Mr Peele.

'And how long was that? That you were with Mr Schuyler, I mean.'

Clare's confusion and its accompanying blush were not entirely faked. Here came the embarrassing moment of truth—or rather, half-truth. She dropped her head a little, closed her eyes, and mumbled, 'We met about half past six, I think.'

'Half past six.' The Sergeant was even more relentless

than his superior. 'And what time did your evening together end?'

Clare's head drooped even further. 'I. . .I. . .don't like to say.' This piece of untruthful embroidery came out so artlessly that she was more than a little shocked at her own duplicity. It was all Ralph's fault, of course. She was merely profiting from his example!

He sprang to her rescue again since the Inspector was showing signs of impatience.

'I think, Inspector, that Miss Windham may find it a little difficult to tell you the truth. Instead of our going to a restaurant, I arranged for us to dine informally at my home in Park Lane. . . It was very late by the time that we had finished our meal, and we. . .er. . .decided to spend the rest of the night together.

'All night?' intervened the Sergeant, again playing the heavy in this double act. 'Miss Windham was with you all night. You're sure of that?'

Clare put her handkerchief to her face again to hide her blushes. Over the top of it she could see that Ralph had put on an expression which, if he were a woman, could only have been described as coy.

'Yes,' he said, softly, and at last. 'I have very good reason to know that we spent the night together—' and then, with a show of remembering something import-ant—he could have commanded a good fee as an actor on the West End stage, Clare thought snidely '—of course,' and now he sounded both triumphant and relieved. 'My man, Armstrong, saw us together, in my. . .er. . .bedroom, first thing this morning.'

'And, after we had breakfast, Ralph kindly drove me home,' added Clare, surfacing from beneath her hankies and giving her supposed bedmate a loving and grateful glance.

'How very helpful of him, miss, to be sure,' was the Inspector's sardonic response to that.

Earlier that morning, hearing of Clare Windham's appointment with Jeremy, and remembering all the *brouhaha* which had surrounded Boy's sensational death, and Clare's involvement in it, he had sniffed great possibilities coming out of an interview with her.

Instead, all he had discovered was that Miss Clare Windham was apparently a lady—save the mark—who spread her favours far and wide, and had thrown over one lover, Jeremy Peele, for another, Ralph Schuyler, whom even the two police officers knew to be immensely rich, richer probably than the late Mr Peele.

Looking around the humble room, the Inspector thought that the lady wasn't asking enough for her services. On the other hand her latest piece of home-work seemed pretty obsessed with her, and she might well end up in a palatial home in Park Lane instead of a squalid flat in the wrong part of Chelsea.

Another dead end, he concluded glumly, avoiding Ralph Schuyler's quizzical stare. Well, he would go out with a flourish.

'Do either of you know of anyone who might wish to harm Mr Peele? He seems to me to have been a most inoffensive gentleman.'

Clare put her handkerchief in front of her face again, mainly in order to avoid Sergeant Johnson's leering inspection of her. At least Ralph had saved her from having to say very much, but she was well aware of what the two men were thinking about her.

She was helped by Ralph again. He came over to where she sat, pulled up a small stool, sat on it in order to take her hand, and stroke it, before replying, 'Most inoffensive, Inspector. I can't imagine why anyone would wish to kill him. Most probably he interrupted a burglar.'

'That was what we thought, sir. But his man assures us that nothing was taken. Most mysterious.'

'Mysterious, indeed, Inspector. May I ask how Mr Peele met his end?'

'He was shot, sir. In circumstances which suggest that suicide was most unlikely.'

'Indeed.' Ralph planted a loving kiss on the bit of Clare's cheek which he could see. 'May I suggest to you that if you have finished questioning us, you might leave us as soon as possible. As you can see, Miss Windham is in a state of shock. I am sure that you would not wish to distress her further.'

'Certainly not, sir. If you could give my Sergeant your own address, I would be most grateful to you. I already have the lady's. Who knows, we might wish to question you further.'

'Oh, I do hope not,' Ralph said earnestly, patting Clare on the shoulder as though she were an unhappy baby who needed comforting.

'You will forgive me if I help the Sergeant, my dear,' and with all the solemnity which the occasion demanded he told the Sergeant his address, which that minion of the law duly wrote down in his little notebook.

'You do understand,' he said, as he showed the two officers to the door, 'if either of us can assist you in any way, we shall be most happy to do so. I have written where I might be found at the Foreign Office,' he told the Sergeant helpfully.

'Very good, sir,' the Inspector said in a dying fall,

before pushing his Sergeant out of the room, 'and you know where to find me, I'm sure.'

The door closed behind them. Clare lifted her handkerchief from her face, and fell back, relieved, against the cushions of the armchair. 'Thank God that's over,' she breathed. 'I don't know what I should have done without you.'

'On the contrary,' Ralph retorted gallantly. 'I don't know what I should have done without *you*. I particularly admired the use you made of your handkerchief. If the Inspector was trying to read your face, he must have been making heavy weather of it!'

Clare began to laugh, then stopped to say mournfully, 'It's not funny, you know. All those lies I told—and Jeremy's death.'

'I know.' Ralph wanted to take her in his arms and comfort her in the most time-honoured way he could think of. He tried not to think of it. He had no business lusting after Clare Windham, precisely because she was his business.

'It's a most natural reaction, as Byron once said, "And if I laugh, 'tis that I may not weep". I saw it often enough in the trenches.'

'I suppose.' Clare sounded dubious, so dubious that Ralph thought a little comfort was in order.

'Do you have anything to drink here?' he asked prosaically.

'Not what *you* would call drink,' retorted Clare. 'Only tea or coffee. I can't—' and she stopped, not wishing to sound as though she were complaining.

'Afford alcohol,' Ralph finished for her. 'Contrary to what you may believe, I don't spend my entire life drinking spirits or champagne. Furthermore, I am also aware that you must have a hard time making ends meet.'

He looked round the room. 'I'd be a fool if I didn't. Tea will do splendidly, and we can have a little conference over it.'

'What, another?' riposted Clare, who was beginning to recover her usual spirited response to life and its trials.

'Yes, another.' Ralph's reply was equally lively. By God, whatever else, the girl's got guts, he informed himself, and then aloud he asked, 'I wonder what the Inspector made of us?'

Walking down the stairs, and out into the early afternoon sunlight, after interviewing Armstrong, the Inspector and his Sergeant were exchanging notes.

'Now, what exactly did you make of that, Sergeant?'

'Well, sir, on the face of it, it was all perfectly straightforward. The pair of them made a dirty night of it whilst chummy was topping Master Jeremy half a mile away. . .but. . .' He stopped.

'But what? Spit it out, man.'

'It's the Major, sir, who bothers me. Slippery cove, Major Schuyler. Cool customer, very. Should have got the VC.'

'Eh, how was that?'

'Oh, it was the usual cock-up. He was only a captain then and I was a corporal. We was told off to attack a strong point—supposed not to be as strong as it was when we attacked it. All a *canard*, as we said in the trenches, a lie.'

The Sergeant knew that his Inspector had sat out the war on the Home Front for medical reasons, so was always careful to make his meaning plain. 'What was worse, we was expected. The Captain, he never turned a hair. Instead he altered the plan of attack and went in on the blind side, if you get my meaning. He led us from the front and took the strong point—was badly wounded and sent home after saving everyone's bacon, including that of the fool who gave us the orders. Never saw him again. I was promoted Sergeant for my part in it, and they said he was sent to another part of the front when he recovered. If he got a medal, I never heard of it. The fool got one, though.'

'But why does that make you a little doubtful about what you heard this morning?'

'Don't know, sir. But he was always a devious devil. The other officers never beat him at poker. And he was a terror with the ladies. He'd bear watching.'

'And this lady, Miss Windham? What did you think of her?'

'Not like his usual bit of stuff, sir; he liked 'em bold. This one's quiet. And that's odd in itself. Another odd thing, he was always discreet about his goings-on. Not very discreet this morning, was he? No, I don't like odd things.'

'Nor do I, Johnson. Nor do I. We'll keep a quiet eye on 'em. Come to think of it, this case was an odd one even before we met the galloping Major. A man murdered for apparently no reason at all. Yes, we'll keep our options open. Find out what he does at the Foreign Office first... No. I don't like Mr Ralph Schuyler.'

'Begging your pardon, sir, but the gentry pronounce it Rafe.'

'Oh, do they, Johnson?' retorted Malcolm, sneering. 'Now how do you know that?'

'His fellow officers called him that sir—and his

batman. Odd, ain't it? They've a lot of names which
sound different from how they look.'

'Tricky lot, all of them,' pronounced the Inspector.
'More reason than ever to keep an eye on him. Funny
ways go with funny names, eh, Johnson?'

'As you say, sir. As you say.'

From behind the net curtains of Clare's bay window,
Ralph watched them walking down the street, while she
made them both a cup of tea in the kitchen. He read
body language accurately. Neither he nor Clare had
seen the last of them, was his rueful conclusion. He
wondered what exactly it was that he and Clare had said
or done—or not said or done—which had caused the
two officers not to swallow their story completely.

On the whole, he considered that it had been a bit of
bad luck that the Inspector's Sergeant should have been
an old soldier who knew exactly what a tricky bastard
Ralph Schuyler was—in every way!

CHAPTER SIX

'HMM,' said Colonel B reflectively. 'I think you did the right thing, Schuyler, although only time will tell.'

Having it both ways, as usual, was Ralph's sardonic internal comment on that. Whatever happens, he can claim he forecast it!

It was the day after he and Clare had been busy deceiving the police. He had spent the time since then reading innumerable newspaper reports and secret files of events around the time of Boy Mallory's death, as well as the reports of the Coroner's Inquest and the police investigation of it. Nothing he had so far come across seemed to disprove the theory that Boy had shot himself because Clare Windham had jilted him. On the other hand, his instincts, as well as the Colonel's, told him that this theory, despite all the evidence, was an unlikely one.

'And you think it necessary to go on keeping a close eye on Miss Windham?'

'Very necessary, sir. I think that she knows something vital about Boy Mallory's death—whether consciously, or unconsciously, I don't know. I shall try to find out. She won't give me any explanation for why she jilted him.'

'Good man. I'm sorry you felt it necessary to mislead the police, but needs must, you know. Don't want their great clumsy feet trampling over everything do we. . .?'

Ralph didn't feel it necessary to tell his superior that he was not sure how much he had managed to deceive

Malcolm and Johnson. Better to let him think that they had swallowed every word which he and Clare had uttered.

Colonel B had picked up a file so Ralph started for the door — to be stopped for once.

'Oh, and Schuyler, I'm sure that I can trust you not to give Miss Windham any inkling of why you are showing such an interest in her.'

However much he winced inwardly at the thought that he was being ordered to behave like a complete bounder to a girl who might well be innocent of anything except knowing some fact which she considered unimportant, Ralph was compelled to nod agreement.

'I'm taking her to the Norton-Norris thrash tonight. That should help to convince everyone that she and I are a couple.'

'Pretty girl, is she?' asked the Colonel artlessly just as Ralph put his hand on the doorknob.

'Pretty enough,' retorted Ralph, and left it at that. For some reason he did not wish to discuss Clare overmuch with his master. He felt enough of a cad as it was, since she apparently believed that he was helping to save her trouble over Jeremy's death out of the goodness of his heart.

She was not to know, and he hoped that she did not soon find out, that Ralph Schuyler had no good heart, only a bad one...

Unaware that she was the subject of conversation in the higher levels of the Secret Service, Clare was busy earning her living by translating yet another light novel from the French. Everyone in it was enormously rich, enormously idle, and spent their time analysing their feelings and emotions in a manner which seemed far removed from the harsh world in which she now lived.

She was having difficulty concentrating because she was worrying about her promise to accompany Ralph to Mrs Norton-Norris's do. The worry was about what she would wear that would not make her look an absolute dowd.

Since her father had told her that she must make her own way in the world seeing that she had seen fit to jilt Boy, not only causing him to lose face, but also a great deal of money spent on preparations for an expensive and fashionable wedding she had bought little in the way of clothes.

Thinking of Ralph and his debonair charms was beginning to make her feel quite light-headed. She could hardly go with him in one of her usual summer dresses, and to wear the Fortuny again would only cause a great deal of unkind comment amongst those who had seen it at Bitsy's party.

She was staring abstractedly out of the window when there was a knock on her door. Opening it, she was confronted by a boy in a smart brown and gold suit with a brown and gold pillbox hat. He was carrying three brown and gold boxes, one large and two small.

'Parcels for Miss Windham,' he piped at her. 'Sign, please,' and he held out a piece of paper and a pencil.

'For me?' Clare asked bewildered. 'You're sure they're for me?'

'Miss Clare Windham, of 5b, Camden Place, Chelsea,' he said, showing her the labels on the boxes and his piece of paper. 'You are Miss Windham, aren't you?'

Yes, she was, no doubt of that, so she signed the

paper and carried the boxes in: they bore the name of a well-known Bond Street dress shop.

The first one she opened contained a small nosegay of the most exquisite deep pink rosebuds, and a card on which was written in a bold hand, 'I hope that you will see fit to wear these flowers tonight with the accompanying evening dress and its accessories. I trust that you will accept them all in the spirit in which they are given. One of homage, not of insult. R.S.'

Homage, not insult! Whatever could he mean? Other than that he was not trying to buy her favours. But homage was going a bit far, surely? Clare didn't know whether to be flattered or insulted as she opened the big dress box. What she found there confused her even more. She had made up her mind to refuse both the flowers and the dress, but as she lifted it out, it took her breath away. It was exactly the sort of gown which she would have bought if she had married Boy, and shared his wealth with him.

It was a model, made by Lucien Lelong, in white crêpe, low waisted, adorned with chenille, ending just below the knee, with fringes of different length, the one on the right descending to the ankle. On the left of the low waist was one single crêpe rose of the same shade as the nosegay which Ralph had sent her, and which would look perfect on her left shoulder.

With the dress and obviously designed to be worn with it, was a cobweb of a shawl, white with small pink roses woven into it.

Clare knew immediately that the dress would fit her, as well as the white evening bag on a silver chain, the white underslip, white kid shoes and white silk stockings which the third parcel contained. She also knew that she would look sensational in them all.

But how had he known her measurements?

Oh, there was nothing remarkable about that. He must have examined her things either whilst she was in the bath, or some time during the next morning whilst she slept.

One half of her said, send them back, either with regrets, or without. The other half of her longed to put them on, to be once again the girl whom men and women had turned round to look at because of the excellence of her taste—something Boy had always been proud of.

Clare was about to put the dress back into its box in order to return it, when temptation struck. There was a longish mirror in the door of the wardrobe in her bedroom, and she could not resist holding the dress in front of her and examining herself in it.

In so doing, she was lost.

Oh, he had no right to tempt her, no right at all! But if she wore the beautiful things which he had sent her she would walk by his side as proudly as a woman could, secure in the knowledge of her attraction—and that she was with one of the most sought-after men in London society.

And then, tomorrow, she would return to him everything but the flowers, telling him that she had only agreed to wear them so that he might not be ashamed of her in the dowdy dress which she would otherwise have had to wear.

He had said that he had sent them to her in homage, so she would pretend that he had. For she knew, from everything which had happened since he had found her in the bedroom with Jeremy's body, that he was the most devious person she had ever met, and that it would be best not to trust a word he said to her. Just look at the cool way in which he had deceived the two policemen!

Clare did not remind herself that she had also played a devious part in that game. She was too busy remembering Ralph's role to question her own!

He had said that he would call for her at seven o'clock. She was waiting in her bay window for him, and when his Bentley came round the corner and roared up the road, she ran down into the hall as quickly as she could, to save him a journey up the dingy stairs.

She had barely reached the bottom of them when the door to her landlady's quarters opened and Mrs Green stood there, her arms folded and her eyes inimical as she glared at Clare in her expensive finery.

'Ah, Miss Windham, I'm glad I've caught you. I believe that you had a gentleman caller in your rooms yesterday morning.'

Clare bowed her head in agreement. 'Yes, that is true, Mrs Green.'

'Then I shall have to remind you, Miss Windham, of one of my rules: no gentlemen callers are to be entertained in my tenants' rooms after six o'clock in the evening. I want no misbehaviour in my house tonight.'

All the subservience in Clare's posture flew away. She became Miss Windham, of Windham Place in Surrey, again.

'You need have no fears on that score, Mrs Green.' Her smile was as sweet as she could make it. 'I have no doubt that Major Schuyler will arrange it so that any misbehaviour will take place elsewhere.'

'Well, I never—' Mrs Green began, to stop when Ralph walked though the open front door. He was looking more splendid than ever in his evening dress.

He wore the star of some order pinned to his jacket beneath a row of medals. He was carrying a top hat, had a white silk scarf around his neck, white gloves in his hand, and altogether looked like the wealthy toff he was.

Clare's landlady did not know whether to be impressed by his appearance, or to be confirmed in her belief that he was nothing but a vile seducer, like the actor whom he rather resembled and who had had his wicked way with the heroine in the film which she had seen at the local picture palace a few nights ago.

He disarmed her immediately with a display of Schuyler magic, sweeping off his top hat, bowing his sleek black head, and saying, 'Good evening, madam,' to her, and 'I see that you are ready for me, my dear Clare,' in such a soothing fashion that to spark at him would have seemed worse than ungracious.

And when he promised, still in a voice which oozed treacle, 'I shall see that she is not too late home, madam, so that your other tenants will not be disturbed,' Mrs Green was quite won over.

His remark to Clare as he handed her into the Bentley was typically dry. 'Old dragon after you about your morals, was she?'

'That was quick of you,' commented Clare, admiringly. 'How did you guess?'

'Body language,' replied Ralph. 'Had she not been there, ready to pounce if I said or did the wrong thing, I would have told you how absolutely stunning you look in that frock. I thought you would. And I am glad you had the sense to wear it, and not throw it back at me, as though I were buying you body and soul.'

'Oh, I wouldn't let you do that,' riposted Clare, 'although I think that I ought to return it to you after wearing it tonight. I couldn't go with you in my dreary afternoon frock after seeing what you had chosen for me.'

'Good. And I meant what I said about homage. So don't send it back. Keep it. It's some payment for the fact that what's been happening is almost certainly slowing down your ability to work at your normal speed.'

Now, how did he know that? But it was true. She had been thinking about either him, or Jeremy or Boy, on and off since he had left her yesterday morning, and it had certainly interfered with her work.

'Know old Mother Norton-Norris, do you?' he went on. 'She's an upper-class version of Mrs Green. More money, but about as narrow-minded. But she throws good parties. If we're seen together there, no one is going to question that we are an item, as the Yankees say.'

Clare remembered that he was supposed to be half-Yankee himself.

'Lord Longthorne will be there, too,' added Ralph, 'giving credence to Nonno's wish to be a political hostess.'

'Nonno?' asked Clare, who no longer knew the nicknames that those in high society gave one another. She wondered what Ralph's was.

'Mrs Norton-Norris,' replied Ralph with a sidelong glance at her as they reached his home where he was leaving the Bentley in its garage; the Norton-Norrises' palace being a short distance away at the other end of Park Lane.

They walked along the red carpet under the canopy which led to the front doors, an arrangement which was *de rigeur* for society occasions. A string of superbly

dressed men and women preceded and followed them.
Many of them tipped their hats or made some kind of
acknowledgment to Ralph, but merely stared at Clare.
They either didn't recognise her or, for the present,
thought it politic not to.

Ralph pressed her arm as they climbed the wide
staircase to where Mr and Mrs Norton-Norris stood to
greet them after an impressively dressed footman had
bawled their names out.

Nonno, as Clare now sardonically thought of her,
pressed her middle-aged powdered cheek against
Ralph's hard, younger one.

'So pleased to see you, and Miss Windham, isn't it?'
She paused, wondering whether her next sentence
might be tactless—decided she didn't care, and drawled,
'I believe your father and mother, and your cousin
Angela, are here somewhere.'

She waved a careless hand as though she couldn't be
sure of how many guests she had or who they were. Her
husband, a small man, as retiring as his wife was brash,
murmured kindly as they passed him, 'I think that they
are in the ballroom. Most people seemed to be going
there. The jazz band is very good, I am told.'

'The Blackbirds,' Ralph whispered into Clare's ear.
'Just over from the States. New since your time. You
don't really want to meet your family, yet, do you?
Enjoy yourself a little first.'

He thought that she might need some reassurance,
and it was essential to his plans that she appear happy
with him. Clare, however, needed no reassurance. If her
family were here, then so be it. If she met them, she met
them: it was all one to her.

The ballroom, as Mr Norton-Norris had prophesied,
was packed. The band were playing a foxtrot, and

Ralph, without waiting to ask Clare's permission, swung her on to the floor. As she might have expected, he was a superb dancer, light on his feet, piloting her skilfully around the crowded room.

Several people waved to him as they swept round a corner, passing in front of the band who were now playing a quickstep, 'Yes, we have no bananas', at twice its normal speed.

Nothing fazed, Ralph changed step, and swung Clare in a series of rapid *chassés* straight down the room, thus ensuring that as many people as possible saw that she was with him.

Excitement and exhilaration gripped her. It seemed forever since she had enjoyed herself as much as this. Boy had been a good dancer, too. Ralph had held her at some distance whilst they foxtrotted, but once the quickstep began he had pulled her to him, and she could feel the length of his hard body against her whilst they moved as one.

What neither of them had bargained for was that he would rapidly become aroused by such a close contact to her. Ralph swore to himself, tried to think of Arctic wastes and cold water being poured over him. Just as he thought that he had his surprisingly errant body under control he looked down at Clare to see her amazing blue eyes looking happily up at him.

This undid him all over again! He had wanted others to believe that he was genuinely attracted to her, whilst remaining his usually aloof self. What he had not bargained for was the effect which she was beginning to have on him—and he knew that she was not even trying to snare him. For all her cleverness, there was a sexual artlessness about her that led him to believe that she and Boy had not gone very far with their love-making, which was going to make his task harder than ever.

The music ended. Ralph gave Clare one last long spin to bring them near to an open window: the room was hot. It also ensured that they were still on the floor when most couples had left it, so that even more people could see that Clare Windham was Ralph Schuyler's latest conquest.

'Oh, thank you,' exclaimed Clare breathlessly. 'I had forgotten how much I enjoyed dancing!'

'No, thank *you*,' Ralph could not help saying. 'You're a pleasure to dance with—unlike some women, you never try to lead.'

He was thinking of Eva Chance-Smythe.

Before Clare could answer him, an acid voice commented, 'Oh, hello, Clare, I didn't expect to see *you* here.'

It was her cousin, Angela Windham, escorted by a chinless wonder whom Clare had never seen before. She was glaring at Clare as though she were her worst enemy.

'I didn't expect to see myself here,' returned Clare, as coolly as she could. 'But Ralph thought that it might be amusing to drop in on Nonno's party.' She spoke as though the last five years had never happened, and Mrs Norton-Norris was an old and valued friend. Ralph gave an inwardly sardonic grin at her *savoir-faire*. He wondered what piece of cattiness such a knowing comment might evoke. He hadn't long to wait to find out.

'Ralph? Oh, yes, Ralph Schuyler,' drawled Angela as though she were one of his oldest friends, instead of a mere acquaintance. 'You're with him, I see. And isn't that a Lelong you're wearing? I didn't know that you could afford him!'

'I can't.' Clare was thoroughly in charge of herself. She laid a loving hand on Ralph's arm. 'Ralph bought it for me.'

This came out as though she had been the *belle amie* of half a dozen rich men. After Jeremy's murderer was found, she could give up this charade and return to a world where no one knew—or cared—about her past or present, so she felt quite safe in being reckless about her way of life.

Angela's eyes widened. Her companion, who had been staring at both Ralph and Clare as though they were strange species of wild life, drawled, 'Don't think we've met, Schuyler. Hear you're in the FO.' Since Angela seemed to have no intention of introducing him to either Clare or Ralph, he added, 'Tim Hallowes— late of the Hussars. Heard you had a good war.'

'Who didn't—if they managed to survive?' riposted Ralph briefly. He had been enjoying Clare's dissection of her cousin, and the calm way in which she had implied unmentionable things in her relationship with him.

His admiration for her grew, and increased when Clare said, as frankly as a boy, 'Happy to meet you, Tim. Nonno's husband told us that Angela was here with my father and mother.'

'Oh, didn't you know?' Angela's jealous eyes glittered. Who would have thought that her disgraced cousin was walking off with Ralph Schuyler of all people!

'After Daddy died, Uncle John persuaded Mummy to let him adopt me legally. Windham Place needed an heir, he said, and with you disinherited, and no male relatives available, he picked on me. Mummy and I live with your father and mother now.'

Once Clare would have felt a pang of sorrow at the news that she had been supplanted, and by Angela whom she had always disliked. Now she felt only indifference.

'I wouldn't go near them, if I were you,' Angela continued spitefully. 'Uncle John hasn't forgiven you. . .'

'And I haven't forgiven him,' Clare returned fiercely, 'so, we are quits. Besides, so long as I have Ralph I don't need anyone's forgiveness. He's all I want.'

She offered Ralph a smile of such dazzling brilliance that even that hard-hearted adventurer was full of admiration for her gallantry. He picked up her hand, raised it to his lips and, his eyes on Angela to whom he had taken an instant dislike, kissed it, then murmured confidentially, 'And you are all *I* want, so you and I are quits.'

By Angela's expression, she was more than ready to run round Mrs Norton-Norris's party telling all and sundry that, of all things, Ralph Schuyler was besotted with Clare Windham—which more than suited Ralph's book.

'You will forgive us, Miss Windham, I'm sure, but the band has begun to play and Clare and I wish to make up for lost time. A tango, too. Clare's tangoing is an absolute dream.'

Bowing goodbye to Angela and her staring escort, he swung Clare round and, stamping his feet and tossing his head, he danced her across the ballroom floor in a whirl of white-fringed skirts.

He had scarcely gone a few yards before Clare murmured, choking with laughter, 'You took a real risk there, Ralph. Suppose I couldn't tango. What would you have done then?'

'No risk,' he told her, stopping dead, and taking a rose bud from the nosegay on her shoulder, he put it between his teeth, but not before adding, 'Anyone who can quickstep as well as you would be sure to perform the tango well.'

His eyes on hers, he held her at arm's length, spun her round, strutted along with her for several steps, bent her backwards in a surprisingly good imitation of Rudolph Valentino in *Blood and Sand* and transferred the rose from his mouth to hers. They moved as one, he found, and what's more he was becoming aroused again, but never mind that. No one looking at them could believe other than that they were lovers—and passionate ones.

So Brigadier Windham thought when, a little later, he accosted his daughter. Ralph had left her for a moment, to sit by an open window to recover her breath after the excesses of the tango.

Her father stared at her with such rage on his face that Clare found herself trembling. She rose to her feet and tried to trade him stare for stare. She had nothing to be ashamed of, nothing. He had wronged her, and not she him. He was so purple with anger that, despite herself, she feared for him.

'Is it not enough for you,' he began, 'that by your disgraceful conduct you drove a good man to commit suicide? Must you now behave like a strumpet and take up with such a notorious lecher as Ralph Schuyler? On top of that, it is being whispered around the room that you are somehow implicated in Jeremy Peele's death. . .' He was so incensed that he ran out of breath.

Behind him, Clare could see her mother looking ill

and frightened. She was clutching the hand of her Aunt Laura, Brigadier Windham's sister-in-law who was busy looking triumphant at the spectacle of Clare's humiliation, an expression shared by Angela who still had young Tim Hallowes in tow.

She wondered, for one delirious moment, what they would all say if she told them the true reason why she had jilted Boy. Commonsense informed her drily: nothing to that. They would probably not believe you and an apparently false accusation would simply add one more to the tally of your crimes.

Instead, she merely said, 'Now, who told you that, Father? Angela, I suppose.'

'Do not call me Father. I am no father of yours, miss. And never you mind who told me. I still have good friends in the Home Office who warned me that the police were investigating both you and your current lover. Are there no depths to which you will not sink?'

It was like being caught in a society melodrama at Wyndham's Theatre, thought Clare despairingly. Whatever next would her father come out with? The strain was beginning to tell on her, but help was at hand. Unnoticed by either Clare, or Brigadier Windham, Ralph had caught sight of the ugly little scene, and decided to end it before the Brigadier's loudly expressed anger created a larger one.

'Sorry I had to leave you, my dear,' he announced, the Schuyler charm once again in evidence; he might have been his cousin Gis Havilland at his most overwhelming.

'Brigadier Windham, isn't it?' he went on, apparently completely unaware of the insults which Clare's father had been hurling at her. 'We haven't been introduced formally. I do hope you will forgive me for speaking to you, but I was so happy to see that Clare was not alone.'

'I have no wish to be introduced to you, sir.' The Brigadier had gone from red rage to icy glaciality. 'Nothing I know of my daughter, or of you, could lead me to have anything to do with either of you.'

Red rage now had Ralph by the throat: the strength of his anger at this insult to Clare surprised him. He controlled himself at the sight of her white face. He took her hand, and said, as genially as his half-brother, Lord Longthorne, did when he was trying to calm an irate House of Lords, 'Then you will forgive me if I take her away. I cannot have the lady who has promised to be my wife subjected to insults from anyone, not even from her father!'

CHAPTER SEVEN

RALPH'S announcement stunned everyone: the proposed bride most of all. Clare stared at him open-mouthed, too astonished to contradict him—which was, she later thought, just as well!

Angela, who had been listening avidly to all that went on, gave a shrill laugh. 'Marry her! Marry Clare! That's rich! Why on earth should you need to do that?'

By now an interested crowd had gathered. The Brigadier, who had never intended that his reproaches to his daughter should form the centre of an open scandal, snarled rather than said, 'You must do as you please, sir. Do not expect me and mine to approve of the conduct of either of you.'

'Oh, I always do as I please,' announced Ralph, whose strong right arm was now around Clare's shoulders, 'and I'm not sure that I want the approval of either you, or of Miss Angela Windham. I might think that I was doing something wrong if I had your support.'

He was going against all the rules of his carefully run life: never to be rude to a lady, never to make an enemy needlessly, and, particularly, never to take part in a public scene. But the sight of Clare at bay, being badgered by a Puritanic fool of a father, and a malicious bitch like Angela Windham, had roused in him a sense of chivalry which he had not known he possessed. Colonel B would be appalled when he learned of his behaviour

All caution, all deviousness, had been leached out of

him. He saw Clare's father open his mouth to rebut the insult to Angela and gave him no time to do so.

'Come, my dear Clare,' he announced, his voice now as hard as iron. 'Mrs Norton-Norris wishes us to meet her American cousin. Nothing must be allowed to detain us.'

He bowed ironically to the Windham party, and to the spectators, then, with Clare on his arm, they processed to where the Norton-Norrises awaited them.

Clare, who had been struck dumb by Ralph's announcement of their coming marriage, found her voice at last. She tried to pull her arm away, but Ralph held tightly on to it.

'Why did you say that?' she cried indignantly. 'You know perfectly well that you have never asked me to marry you, and I would certainly not agree to do so.'

'Too late,' was Ralph's cheerful reply, 'and I don't propose to discuss it here, later will do. Smile at Mrs Norton-Norris. By now the news of our engagement will not only be round her thrash, but all over Mayfair.'

Mocking eyes followed them, to gain a little respect when Mrs Norton-Norris proceeded to make a great fuss of them both. They were the evening's sensation and she thrived on sensation. As for Ralph, he wondered wryly what Colonel B would make of his indiscretions. He had seen him earlier, playing bridge in one of the ante-rooms, surrounded by other old men of power.

Clare began to feel that she had been at the party for ever, so much had happened. Surely she and Ralph could not be the centre of any more excitement? She whispered to Ralph, 'Do you think that we could leave soon?'

'Certainly not,' Ralph whispered back. 'It must not look as though we are running away.'

All the same, when their hostess had finished with them he took Clare into a side-room, away from the bustle, and sat her down on the sofa, a tray of food and a bottle of strong red wine, between them.

'Now, what was your father threatening you with?' he asked her. 'About the Home Office. I only arrived at the end.'

Clare drank the wine gratefully. Being with Ralph was turning her into a toper. She had polished off more drink since she had met him than in the whole of her previous life.

'Oh, someone had told him that the police were suspicious of us both. He was only too happy to have another stick to beat me with.'

Ralph's expression was thoughtful. 'Why was he so angry with you, Clare? I was told that he turned you out after you jilted Boy. Was that true?'

Clare nodded, her mouth so full of lobster patty that speech was difficult. She was also eating better food than she had done for five years—and that was Ralph's doing, too. She supposed she ought to be grateful. Gratitude consisted in telling him a little of the truth about her past.

'It was rather like the old music-hall song where the father turns the erring daughter into the snow because she has done something of which he disapproves. Only it wasn't funny. If it hadn't been for my mother's sister, Aunt Jane Cameron, I don't know what I should have done. She hadn't much money, but she took me in, and paid for me to go to night-school to learn shorthand and typing. Through her friends in the academic world—she was the widow of a professor at King's College,

London—she found me work typing theses and reports, and persuaded a publisher to let me have a go at translating novels from the French. When she died she left me enough to set myself up in rooms, buy a little furniture and have enough over to give me a tiny income each week to add to what I earn from my work.'

She stopped, and then said, 'Why am I telling you all this? I have never spoken of it to anyone before.'

'I have a willing ear,' Ralph replied gently.

He was not only feeling the most enormous pity for her, but also great admiration for her raw courage. Alone in the world now that the kind aunt had died, cut off from everything she must have known and loved, she was displaying a gallantry which was rare for someone who had been brought up in pampered circumstances and who had been waited on all her life. The guilt he felt over deceiving her about his profession grew by the minute.

But he dare not, could not, tell her the truth: that would be to breach his duty.

Nor did he wish to ask her again at this point why she had jilted Boy. To do so would add to the pain which she must be feeling at her father's treatment of her, however brave the face she was putting on.

Something must have shown on his normally poker face for Clare said, almost violently, 'You are not to pity me. And I don't intend to marry you, either. I suppose you said that to thwart Father, and add support to the tales we told the police.'

Ralph nodded his head. 'We can always part later when the mystery of Jeremy's death is cleared up, and say that we didn't suit.'

'I don't think that I ought to jilt you, though,' remarked Clare, a naughty gleam in her eye. 'Once is quite enough. How about you jilting me? Father would say that it was all I deserved. Think how happy it would make him and my Aunt Laura and Angela. . .'

Ralph nodded abstractedly. He was thinking hard. He must have *something* to tell Colonel B, and he must try not to distress Clare by what he might demand of her.

'Would you do me a small favour, Clare?'

'Depends,' Clare replied, licking cream from a chocolate eclair off her fingers.

'Gordon Stewart is here. You said that he knew you were going to see Jeremy on the evening he was killed. I think it might be a good idea if you talked to him—let him know that you were with me, instead.'

'Um. . .makes sense,' agreed Clare.

'And I want you to meet a colleague of mine. George Pryde. More suspicion to be disarmed.'

Clare sighed. 'Isn't conspiring hard work? I have to think so carefully about everything I say. I hope I don't look or sound too unnatural.'

Ralph, who was sitting by her, put his empty plate down, and finished his glass of wine, before moving the tray full of used crockery to the floor. He turned to look at her.

'Not unnatural at all,' he told her, and before he could stop himself he did what he had wanted to do all evening. He took her in his arms.

She slid as sweetly into them as though she had been made to do nothing else. He put a hand under her chin, tilted it towards him, and kissed her. It was meant to be a gentle kiss, but her mouth was so soft and sweet that it soon grew excited. It was like sipping ambrosia on Mount Olympus. The jaded man which Ralph had become felt himself a boy again.

He slid his hand upward into her caramel-coloured mane and cupped the back of her head, prolonging the kiss, which now became even more intimate. He teased her mouth open, met her tongue, and for a moment, each tasted the other.

Clare gave a deep throaty moan. She felt that she was drowning, and as he was touching her she found that she wished to touch him. She put a hand up to stroke his jaw, and at her touch it was his turn to growl something inarticulate.

His mouth still on hers, he slipped both his hands down to stroke her breasts through the crêpe of the dress that he had given her.

The effect on Clare was electric. The sensations beginning to shoot through her were so sinfully pleasant, she thought dazedly, that they must be wicked. Ralph's hard body, pressed against her own, was so different from Boy's softer, slighter one—which she could now hardly remember. From sitting up they began to slide down the sofa, Clare backwards, Ralph above her.

The growing rapport between them was so strong that they each broke away from the other at the same time. But not before the door had opened for Gordon Stewart to find them still in each other's arms.

'Oops, sorry,' he exclaimed with a knowing grin. 'Someone said that you and Clare were in here, so I came along to congratulate you. I take it that congratulations *are* in order? You look as though they are.'

Clare was blushing crimson. Ralph was as cool as a man who again had lipstick on his cheek could be. Unnaturally cool, thought Clare indignantly. Would nothing ever ruffle him?

'Yes,' he told the grinning Gordon. 'You may congratulate us.'

Gordon shook him by the hand and pecked Clare on the cheek.

'Little bit of a surprise, though,' he offered, shaking his head. 'Thought that you and Jeremy were going to be a thing when you told me you were visiting his rooms the other night.'

'Oh,' said Clare unblushingly—she was getting used to being economical with the truth—'that was before Ralph and I found out about one another. Naturally after that I couldn't visit Jeremy. Might have given him wrong ideas—except, of course—' and she heaved a great sigh at the memory of Jeremy's demise. The sigh, at least, was not a lie.

'Good thing you didn't. Might have interrupted something, and gone the same way as Jeremy. Odd business, that. I'll leave you to it, then. *Bon appetit* now and in the future.' His grin was more knowing than ever.

'Oh, we've had that already tonight, thanks.' Ralph's returning grin was there to betray that his *double entendre* was intended.

'Well, 'gratters and all that again. See you at St Margaret's, Westminster,' was his parting shot as he left them.

'Now that was what I call fortunate,' commented Ralph to Clare, who was still scarlet with embarrassment. 'We didn't even have to set it up for him! A nice tit-bit for him to spread round the ballroom!'

'Oh!' cried Clare indignantly. 'You really are a cad, Ralph. What about my reputation?'

'Quite intact, old thing! It's quite in order for engaged couples to enjoy themselves. You heard that Gordon already had the church booked for us. I suppose St Margaret's would be suitable. About time the Schuylers had a grand marriage again. On the other hand. . .'

'I do wish all this wasn't necessary,' fumed Clare.

Ralph took no heed of this *cri de coeur.* 'I shall have to buy you an engagement ring tomorrow,' he murmured thoughtfully.

'It's a good thing that one of us is enjoying themselves,' remarked Clare tartly.

'You should be enjoying yourself, too. It's always a pleasure to know something others don't.' He remembered suddenly how unused she was to a life of deceit and trickery, and said in a low voice as they left the room, 'I wasn't deceiving you just now, Clare, when I began to make love to you. I really meant it. I wasn't kissing you because I hoped that someone might find us, but because I've wanted to kiss you ever since you spent the night in my bed!'

And if that wasn't a two-edged statement, thought Clare, torn between indignation and laughter, what was?

If she had hoped that Gordon's bursting in on them was the coda to the excitements of the evening, Clare soon found that she was mistaken. Everyone, virtually everyone, went out of their way to seek them out and offer congratulations to them.

And so the evening progressed. It seemed to Clare that like it or not, she and Ralph were in danger of being married by popular acclamation, if nothing else! They spent the rest of their time accepting congratulations from those who, yesterday, would not have spoken to her! Finally, Ralph, taking pity on her white face, murmured, 'Time to go home, I think. We are already later than the dragon's curfew.'

She could not remember when anyone had been as kind to her as he had been, and was still being. He was shielding her as much as he could from the curiosity of the other guests. When he introduced her to George Pryde, he took care to do so in such a way that that gentleman thought, greatly to his surprise, that Schuyler really was smitten with his intended bride, even though she was very unlike anyone in whom he had ever shown an interest before.

They were on their way out when a strange thing happened—it seemed that the surprises of the night were not yet over.

A handsome woman came out of one of the doors which opened into the entrance hall. She was dark, erect, of a majestic carriage, and was not dressed in evening wear, but in a black linen afternoon frock so stunningly simple, so well cut that Clare knew at once that it was a model from a Paris fashion house. She could not tell how old the woman was, only that she was no longer young. Her beauty was of an ageless kind, classic and austere. Clare had the curious impression that she had been waiting for them.

What also surprised her was that Ralph, who was placing her shawl around her shoulders, had suddenly tensed. He spoke to the woman who had come to a stop before them and was regarding Clare steadily with her dramatic black eyes.

'Yes, what is it you want?' he asked as curtly as though he were speaking to a recalcitrant servant.

'To speak to you,' the woman said. They obviously knew one another. Had she been his mistress? Clare had the somewhat cynical notion that Ralph Schuyler might not find age a consideration in a woman to whom he wished to make love.

'Then speak,' he told her, still curt.

'I hear you are to marry. Is that true?'

'Yes. My companion, Miss Clare Windham, has promised to be my wife.'

Oh, what a fib, Clare thought. I have promised him nothing. But she kept quiet.

'Then I wish you both happy. But I must also warn you, Ralph, although I am aware that you will take no heed of what I say. Take care. You are following a dangerous line of action at the moment. You are prying into what you should not, and your enemies are powerful. Guard your pretty girl. That is all.'

She did not wait for an answer, but turned her back on them to retreat through the door by which she had entered.

The expression on Ralph's face was unreadable. Clare felt as though she had never known him. Curiosity, and a little fear, provoked her into speech.

'Who was she, Ralph?' And as he did not answer her, she ventured a judgement. 'A discarded mistress?'

He gave a harsh laugh. 'Good God, no. That was my loving mother, the Princess Astra of Carpathia, now the Countess Dumitrescu,' and as she turned on him a face of total bewilderment, he said brusquely, 'I haven't seen her for many years, and I have never lived with her. I am the bastard she never wanted, and that is the end of that. I am being as honest with you as you have been with me.'

So he knew that she had not told him the whole truth about her past—as he was not telling her the whole truth about his.

His face changed and he was debonair Ralph Schuyler again. 'Come on, Clare. Let us forget her, and her message of doom. We must get you back to Chelsea before midnight strikes.'

'And I turn into a skivvy again,' she finished, trying to be as light with him as he had been with her.

'If you like,' he said, cheerfully, and walked her to the door, back to the land where ordinary people lived, worked and suffered. The night was warm and the stars were out. London's streets were emptying and it was pleasant to stroll along Park Lane, towards Ralph's home, her hand on his hard arm as though they were truly destined for the altar and not engaged in a giant pretence.

In the distance they could hear the sound of traffic, and the noise of a car which had been parked just inside the corner into Oxford Street but was now coming towards them, gathering speed.

Ralph, who was more concerned with looking after Clare's well-being than minding his front or back, as he later told Colonel B, only realised at the last moment that the car was being driven straight at them, and was about to mount the pavement and mow them down!

CHAPTER EIGHT

ONE moment they were walking calmly along—Clare
feeling at peace with the world at last—and then in the
next there was a great noise and Ralph was catching her
by the upper arm and jerking her with all his strength
off the pavement and into the road!

The car which had been driving straight at them and
had mounted the pavement where they had been
walking, had missed them by inches as a consequence of
Ralph's manoeuvre. It continued along the pavement
for a short distance before it spun round—to drive
straight at them once more, leaving no doubt that the
original intention had been to mow them down in order
to injure or kill them.

Ralph pulled Clare sideways again not, as the driver
obviously expected, towards the opposite pavement,
but diagonally forward on to the one on which they had
been walking when the car first attacked them. He
dragged her across it, and into a small pathway between
two of the great houses.

Its driver's murderous ambitions frustrated yet again
by the speed of Ralph's reactions, the car roared by on
the opposite pavement, before returning to the road
and giving up the chase. It disappeared in the direction
from which it had originally come. . . .

Ralph's last lunge had been made with such force
that as they reached the safety of the pathway, Clare
lost her balance. She tripped and fell, dragging Ralph

down with her. For a moment, both winded, they lay on the ground, panting hard.

It was Ralph who rose to his feet first, putting out a hand to help Clare up, before pulling her to him, to say into her hair, 'I hope that I didn't hurt you. I'm sorry I had to be so rough so quickly, but I had no choice if we were to escape a messy death.'

It was best, he thought, that he was brutally explicit. It was high time that she realised the danger that she was in, hard though it was for him to say anything which might frighten her.

'Why?' she managed at last, into his chest, her right side aching where it had hit the pavement. 'Why did he do that? Was the driver mad? I thought that he had lost control of the car—but then he drove at us again and that must have been deliberate. But why?'

'Yes,' he told her, as calmly as he could, 'it *was* deliberate, Clare. I think that we ought to have a talk about it. But not here, not now. Let me take you back to my place. You need to rest a little, to recover from the shock you must be suffering.'

No, this was neither the time nor the place to begin a lengthy explanation, as Clare tacitly agreed by a nod of her head. Now that an overt and direct attack had been made on them, Ralph decided that he had no choices left to him. He had to put real pressure on Clare to make her tell him the truth about her jilting of Boy Mallory.

The attack, he was sure, had been made as much, if not more, to kill her rather than him—though killing him might have been regarded as a bonus. He had a duty to protect her, particularly since she was unaware that she had become a target and needed protecting.

The devil of it was that he could not take her back to

Chelsea where she would be an easy victim for a determined assassin. She would be safer staying with him in Park Lane—although to persuade her to do so might be difficult.

All of this passed through Ralph's mind as he held Clare to him, telling himself that there was no reason why he wished to protect her, other than expediency and the demands of the state which he served. He could not afford to allow himself the luxury of falling in love with her—not that he was doing so, of course. Cold-hearted Ralph Schuyler had no intention of falling in love with anyone, least of all Clare Windham.

But as she relaxed against him, and he began to escort her slowly in the direction of his home, he knew that he was lying to himself. From the moment he had first seen her at Bitsy Bentley's engagement party he had been drawn to her, and every time they met her power over him had grown.

No matter how much Ralph told himself firmly that she was not his type, to see her, to touch her, to hold her against him as he had just done, was to undo him. He might tell himself that it was simply lust which moved him, but he was experienced enough to know better. Her very calm, the quiet way in which she walked beside him, not exclaiming or lamenting over what had just occurred, engaged his admiration, and strengthened the strange emotions which she excited in him. Emotions which he had never experienced before.

'Why?' she asked him again, when they had reached the haven of his drawing-room. Armstrong had served them with coffee and sandwiches and it was not until they were sitting relaxed, before a big electric fire, that Clare at last asked him the question over which she had been puzzling ever since the car had driven at them. 'Why? Why should anyone want to kill us?'

Ralph didn't answer her immediately. He merely finished drinking his coffee before he spoke. When he did so, it was not to answer her question. His amber eyes hard on her, he said, as gently as he could, 'I have been thinking, Clare. You need to be protected, and the best protection I can give you is to marry you, as soon as possible.'

If Clare was astonished when she heard this remarkable statement, her astonishment hardly matched Ralph's! He had no idea when he had begun to speak that he intended to say any such thing! It flew out of him, unpremeditated.

Or was it? Had his subconscious mind—Ralph had read the works of the new pundit of the mind, Sigmund Freud, and knew all about the subconscious—been leading him towards the idea of marrying her?

Clare had sprung to her feet, almost more shocked by this sudden proposal than by the recent murderous attack.

'How can you suggest such a thing! I hardly know you. And why on earth should you wish to marry me, of all people? Of course, I shan't marry you. It would ruin your career at the Foreign Office if I did. I thought that the idea was that we would pretend to be engaged, and then break it off when Jeremy's murderer was found.'

This showed what happened when you let your emotions run out of control, was Ralph's despairing inner cry. Much better not to feel anything for anyone— not even one's self. Had he been as coldly sensible as he always was, he would have spent some time preparing Clare for such an apparently outlandish proposal, but all he could think of was that whatever the cost, he must protect her.

Well, the damage was done, and now he must make her sit down, understand the danger that she was in, and that to do as he had suggested and marry him was perhaps the best and safest action she could take—given her present circumstances.

'Please, Clare, do sit down,' Ralph said in the tones of one gentling a frightened horse, 'and forgive me for being so precipitate. Please let me explain why I came out with what must seem something totally outrageous.'

He added the last sentence because she was drawing herself away from him, saying agitatedly, 'I must go home. I need time to think. However could my life have become such a horrible muddle? First I find Jeremy murdered, and then someone tries to kill *me*. I feel as though I am living in a bad movie.'

'If you will only sit down and let me explain.'

All Ralph's normally smooth and superior self-control was disappearing in the face of Clare's patent distress. Not that she was panicking, or being unreasonable. He quite understood why she wished to leave him, to be alone, to try to work out what was happening to her usual safe and eventless life.

Clare stared at him, her eyes wide. So many terrible things had happened to her in such a short time that she really had no idea what to do for the best. Should she trust him? Or should she try to make her way home at this early hour of the morning despite the difficulties and danger that so doing might entail?

What did she really know of Ralph? He had walked into her life precisely at the point where it had started to go mad—which was worrying enough in itself.

On the one hand, he was a wealthy member of a

powerful family with a reputation as a womaniser who had no intention of marrying. Was this whole business simply a complicated way of getting her into his bed? On the other hand, though, there was no mistaking that they had been in real danger earlier on and that he had saved her life—both their lives, she amended. Was the kind way in which he had treated her, the real concern which he had shown every time she had been in trouble, genuine, or did it cover something more sinister?

If only she had time to sit and think, away from his distracting presence, because the most disturbing thing of all was the power he was beginning to exert over her. Never before had she been so attracted to a man; not even Boy had affected her so strongly. What she had felt for Boy was tepid in comparison.

Oh, Ralph was not handsome, nor did he treat her in the honeyed fashion which Boy, Jeremy, Gordon and the rest of their set used towards women. He was brusque, rather.

But if he was not handsome and servile, he was something better. His face had a rough strength in it missing from theirs, and, despite his brusque manner, she was becoming aware that he had an odd respect for her as a person, missing from the almost patronising manner which Boy's friends had always adopted with her, as though she were a little woman to be humoured.

Ralph Schuyler plainly did not humour anyone, even women. She remembered his row with Eva...

Forget Eva, remember the mess I'm in, Clare told herself sternly, and if he wishes to help me, why should I refuse him?

'Very well,' she said at length to Ralph who had been watching with some fascination the play of emotions passing over her face. 'I'll listen to your explanation—but it had better be good.'

Without preamble, and this Clare was coming to recognise was typical of him, he began by asking her a question. 'Clare, I want you to tell me why you jilted Boy Mallory, because I believe that it may lie behind Jeremy's death and the attack on us.'

Clare sprang to her feet again. 'Oh, this is nonsense! What in the world can the reason why I refused to marry Boy have to do with Jeremy being murdered and someone wanting to kill me? Please take me home, at once.'

Before she could make for the door again he was catching her by the arms, saying fiercely, 'Look at me, Clare,' and compelling her to stare into his feral eyes.

'I wouldn't ask you such a personal question if I weren't absolutely convinced that the creature who murdered Jeremy was trying to kill two birds with one stone. To get rid of Jeremy because of what he knew, and make it look as though you killed him so as to dispose of you—because of what you know. Now, tell me the truth, and I might be able to protect you.'

His eyes were mesmeric. She was drowning in them. The heat of his body, the touch of his hands, the male scent of him, his power over her, and, as she was coming to recognise, over others, were doing odd things to Clare. She allowed him to help her back to her chair. He sat down opposite to her, her hands now in his.

'Believe me, Clare, I mean you no harm. And if I think that your reason for jilting Boy has nothing to do with recent events, then I will apologise—but I won't let you go home until I find out what it is that you *do* know, and then only if I am sure that you will be safe there. Trust me, Clare.'

She must trust someone. For five years she had trusted only herself because everyone in the world who mattered to her—everyone except her dead aunt—had rejected her, but now the hard man opposite to her was offering her a strange kind of sanctuary.

'Very well,' she said at length, 'I will tell you what I have never told anyone, principally because I didn't think anyone would believe me, but also because I didn't want to destroy Boy's reputation, particularly after he committed suicide.'

Her eyes were suddenly blind, Ralph saw. Her hands in his were lax: she was reliving the past of which she had never spoken. Time had turned backwards: she was the eager young Clare Windham of five years ago, living in a fairytale world where she was going to marry Boy Mallory and live happily ever afterwards, where everyone loved her and she was always safe, cocooned against the grime and disappointments of the world in which the majority of people lived. . .

Clare parked her sporty little Austin in the mews of Boy's house in Piccadilly. She had spent the first part of the day with her mother, going over the arrangements for the wedding which was to be held in two days' time. After that, she had driven to Richmond Hill in the new motor which her father had given her for her birthday, to visit her best friend, Marjorie Belsize, who was going to be her chief bridesmaid. They had arranged to visit a picture palace that evening, for one last girlish fling together before Clare's marriage changed their friendship for ever.

Earlier that day Boy had rung and asked her to go with him to the Café Royale and then on to the theatre. She had had to refuse him because of her previous

engagement with Marjorie. He said that he quite understood, but had made his disappointment plain.

'Never mind,' he had told her before he rang off. 'We
shall always be together soon. See you tomorrow, my
sweet, but not in the evening. Gordon and the others
are arranging a bumper stag night for me.' Then he said,
oh so tenderly, she remembered bitterly, 'I shall try not
to overdo it so that I don't look too wan on our big day.'

As luck would have it, when she reached Richmond
she saw by Marjorie's pale face that she was in the grip
of one of the migraine headaches which occasionally
plagued her.

'I'm afraid I shan't be able to manage the pictures
this evening,' Marjorie told her sadly, 'but it would
cheer me up no end if you'd stay and have tea with me.
Not that I shall be able to eat much, but you're always
my Florence Nightingale when I'm feeling down.'

They sat and talked quietly together, and drank weak
tea. They agreed that Clare would leave early, after she
had done her good deed for the day by sitting with
Marjorie in a darkened room.

'At least I shall be fit to be your bridesmaid,' Marjorie
said thankfully. 'I have secretly been terrified that I
should wake up on the great day and find that I had
been laid low. No chance of that now, thank goodness.'
Her migraines afflicted her at fairly wide intervals, and
she was safe for at least another few weeks, she said.

Clare was to wonder again and again in the years
which followed how different her life would have been
if she and Marjorie had gone to the pictures together.
Instead, she rang Boy to tell him that she could go out
with him after all, but she could get no answer.

'Call in on him on the way home,' Marjorie suggested
weakly. She was now lying on a sofa, a warm flannel

over her eyes, and her hand in Clare's. 'No need to miss a treat just because I'm out of action. My bad luck is Boy's good fortune.'

Which just went to show, Clare was later to reflect miserably, how ironically wrong one could be if one attempted to foretell the future. She had jumped at the idea, if only because just lately she had felt that Boy had seemed oddly *distrait* when they had been together. So much so that she had once asked him if he regretted their coming marriage.

'Oh, no, old dear,' he had said, kissing her on the end of her nose. 'You're quite the best thing which could have happened to me.' Reassured, she had given him a loving kiss back. Later she was to wonder exactly what he had meant. . .

After leaving Marjorie and reaching Boy's *pied à terre*, she was relieved to see his big Bentley outside, and that he must have a visitor with him for another car, an expensive Daimler, was also parked outside.

She rang the bell impatiently, but no one answered. It was Parker's afternoon off, she remembered, and she debated whether to go home, and ring Boy from there. It was another river crossed, she realised later, but at the time she dithered on the doorstep, before fetching out the front-door key Boy had given her and going in. Boy had sounded so disappointed when she had turned him down that she wanted to tell him as soon as possible that she could go to the theatre with him after all.

It was quiet inside. She considered calling Boy's name, but decided that she would give him a surprise. She looked in the big room at the front, but he wasn't there, so she walked down the corridor to the drawing-room at the back which opened on to a small and pretty garden.

Now she could hear his voice, and that of another man. They were laughing, or, at least, that was what it sounded like until Boy, she was sure it was Boy, gave a small cry. She opened the back drawing-room door, and walked in.

To discover a tableau which made no sense. . .and then made a sense which her stunned mind refused to accept.

A sheet had been flung down on the floor, and cushions. On them were two naked figures. Boy's and another's. Two days before the wedding and he was betraying her with another woman. . . Except that when Boy reared up, to turn and see her, his face a rictus of shame and shock, she saw that the person with him, who had been in his arms, was not a woman, but a man.

He was scrambling away from Boy, pulling the sheet about him, to leave Boy exposed, but there was no doubt about his sex. None at all. He was someone young and dark whom she had never seen before, and hoped never to see again. And then he was gone through the side door to hide himself away, leaving Boy to clutch his discarded shirt to him. . .and face her.

'Clare.' It was plain that he was in agony. 'It's not what you think.'

'Oh, it's exactly what I think.' Suddenly a host of small things had come together in Clare's mind to make a dreadful kind of sense. Even the gentle way in which he had always treated her, saying that they must wait until they were married to make proper love, took on a different, horrible meaning.

She was tugging her engagement ring from her finger to throw it down on the floor in front of him. 'I can't marry you now, Boy, you must see that.'

'No, Clare, no. You must. This was a last. . .' He faltered into silence at the sight of her white face.

'Fling!' she finished for him, her eyes burning with unshed tears. 'Well, so it is, and for me, as well. Goodbye, Boy,' and she turned to go.

Behind her he cried out something inarticulate about her being his salvation, that she could not want him ruined.

Clare closed her eyes. 'I shan't tell anyone why I am not going to marry you,' she managed at last, unaware in her youthful ignorance of life what that promise was going to cost her—the loss of everything she knew. 'What you do with your life is your concern, and not mine or the world's.'

How she stumbled out of the house and into the Austin she never knew. Her own life lay in ruins about her. She drove she knew not where, to end up in a small park where she left her car at the gates, and sat before a pond where rails and ducks ran around her as she shivered and tried to think what she must say when she reached home.

What she had not anticipated was the reception she got when she told them that she had broken off her engagement to Boy and that the wedding would not take place—but not the reason why. Her father and mother's disappointment were only what she had expected, but not her father's white rage and her banishment. . .her five years' exile and her consequent difficult hard-working life. Boy had destroyed her, as well as himself. . .

She finished. Ralph had said nothing, just continued to hold her hands in his.

'So you see,' she ended, 'it can have nothing to do with Jeremy's murder or tonight's attempt on us.'

The amber eyes on her were first soft with pity, and then hard with another emotion.

'My God, Clare,' he said gently. 'They say that women cannot keep a secret, but you have kept that to yourself all these years! You would never have told me if I hadn't bulldozed you into doing so, would you?'

Clare shook her head painfully. 'And now may I go home?'

Ralph shook his head in his turn. 'Oh, no. For you have told me what I wanted to know.'

CHAPTER NINE

'BUT why, Ralph?' It seemed to Clare that she had done nothing but ask, or answer, questions ever since she had first met him. 'Why would Boy being what he was make people want to kill me?'

He could not tell her the truth. Or at least not the whole truth, for to do so would betray who and what he was, and for that his masters would never forgive him. He had to temporise, tell her a half-truth and hope that she would never find out that he was lying to her by omission. For that *she* would never forgive him. Ralph was becoming uncomfortably aware that Clare possessed something which few people did: a core of stern and unbending integrity.

It had sustained her through all the difficulties of her life. If she had broken her word to Boy and told her parents the truth about him, then they would not only have forgiven her for breaking the marriage off, but the Brigadier would have made it his business to see that the police were informed about his unlawful activities.

Which would have meant prison and ruin for him.

Instead, by keeping Boy's secret and retaining her honour, Clare had brought near ruin upon herself.

Ralph had always taken a certain pleasure in deceiving people, in allowing them to think that he was other than he was—the more fool they if they believed everything which was said to them, being his motto. But he had never felt more uncomfortable in his whole life than he did now as he prepared to tell Clare a series of half-truths.

'What you have to understand,' he said slowly, 'is that Boy's...activities...being illegal, and consequently undertaken in secret, he laid himself, and those who shared them, open to being blackmailed for money. And if anyone who was being blackmailed threatened to reveal the blackmailers to the police, then to protect themselves, the blackmailers might resort to murdering not only their victims to keep them quiet, but anyone who might become aware of what was going on.

'Which brings us to you—and to Jeremy. Jeremy was Boy's friend. He had never married. What more likely than that he had male lovers, too? That he was killed to silence him—and indirectly, you? Except fortuitously, I helped you to avoid suspicion, so they resorted to other methods to silence you—and also me—for you might tell me the truth about Boy. Which you now have.'

Ralph fell silent, watching Clare's face grow even paler as he finished speaking. What he did not say was, God forgive me, Clare, for not telling you the whole truth. For it is becoming plain to me that the real reason why Boy—and possibly others—was being blackmailed by the agents of a foreign power was to compel them to steal government secrets, and consequently you are in even greater danger than you might think.

Of course, Colonel B knew of Boy and his circle, but he had no proof. That was for Ralph to find—and so he had, but at what cost to himself and Clare?

'Oh, I am such an innocent,' Clare said at last. 'I knew that behaviour like Boy's occurred—although I never once suspected it of him. I overheard Father talking once about a young subaltern who was compelled to resign, but I never knew that the kind of wickedness which you have just told me of could be going on as a consequence of it. Murder and blackmail! What kind of world am I living in?'

Ralph tightened his grip on her hands. 'Oh, my dear. Do not be too distressed. Think, murder is uncommon, and blackmail, too. There are not fifty murders a year in England! They are like lightning striking. It has to strike someone, or something, but most miss it—the odds are heavily in favour of them doing so. It was your misfortune to love Boy and then to discover the truth about him.'

Clare found his sturdy reassurance convincing. What was more, she was beginning to think that she could trust him. He had saved first her reputation and, earlier in the evening, her life.

'And now,' Ralph went on, 'you can see why you must marry me. Even if the marriage is a sham, it is the only way I can protect you until this whole rotten business has been cleared up and you are safe again. I dare not let you live alone in Chelsea where you would be so vulnerable to attack.'

He was talking sense, Clare knew, but to marry him seemed so extreme. She told him so.

'It is the only way that you can stay here with me and retain your reputation. Oh, I know that you think that because you no longer live in society your reputation does not matter, but one day, things might change, and you might need to be respectable. Once all danger has passed, we can divorce.'

Ralph smiled a rueful smile. 'For people as rich as I am, Clare, there are always ways and means to divorce easily.' He had correctly interpreted the slight demurral she had begun to make. 'We're not bound by the chains which imprison others.'

He paused, then added wryly, 'My chains may be different, but just as real.' He was thinking of his role as a counterspy.

Clare wondered what they were. But she was too overwhelmed to ask him. She was conscious of an enormous tiredness. Increasingly sensitive to all her moods, Ralph saw this, too, but he was compelled to ask her at least one further question before he could allow her to rest.

'Clare, you said the other day that the only person who knew that you were going to visit Jeremy on the night of his murder was Gordon Stewart. How did he come to know of it?'

Astonishment was written on Clare's face. 'Surely, Ralph, you don't think Gordon had anything to do with all this!'

'We can't rule anyone out,' he said patiently. 'It's possible that Jeremy told other people that he expected you, of course. But I would like to know about Gordon.'

Well, it could not hurt to tell him. 'It was at Bitsy Bentley's party. I think that he must have overheard Jeremy asking me to visit him. Jeremy caught me up just as I was leaving. Gordon spoke to me after Jeremy had left.'

Memory told her something else. 'It was a bit odd, perhaps. His making such a fuss of me then, I mean. He had made no effort to get in touch with me after Boy's suicide, although he had been a great chum of Boy's, but he came round to see me the very day after the party to suggest that we have dinner together some time soon. He brought me flowers, too.

'Oh, and he made a point of asking after you, I do remember that. When he did take me to lunch he told me that Jeremy had had a pash for me. I asked him if he thought that it was wise to go to Jeremy's flat alone—it was then I told him that I was going to visit him on the following evening. He said that I'd be safe with Jeremy: he was a perfect gentleman. I'm certain that I didn't mention my visit to anyone else, for there was no one else to tell,' she ended stoically.

If Ralph thought cynically that Gordon had told her she would be safe with Jeremy because he knew that he shared Boy's tastes, he did not say so to Clare. He wondered what Gordon's tastes were.

'He did say that he'd come into money,' Clare added. 'I remember that he used to be quite poor. I thought that he sponged on Boy rather. That's what we all thought.'

Ralph made no comment on all this, but he thought quite a lot. He said nothing further about Gordon's possible implication in the mystery because he would need to make some investigations into his life—and where his new-found wealth had come from. There was no point in worrying Clare about someone who might be quite innocent—although Ralph had begun to doubt this.

'Just one more question, and a short one. You implied that you didn't know who Boy's partner was. Can you remember anything at all about him?'

Reluctantly, Clare dragged her mind back to that dreadful afternoon again. 'Yes,' she said at last. 'Although I had no idea who he was, I gained the impression that he was a foreigner. Why, I don't know.'

'Good girl,' was Ralph's response. 'No more questions now, I promise.' He rose and pulled her to her feet, holding her to him for a fleeting second.

'Time for bed. You must sleep in mine again. I promise that when we do marry you shall have your own suite of rooms where you may be private. No one will think anything of that—it is the common habit among us, as you must know.'

Yes, Clare did know. She had one last important matter to clear up. 'Mrs Green,' she said hesitantly to him. 'We did promise her that I should be home reasonably early, and now I am not going home at all! Whatever will she say when I tell her that I shall be giving up my rooms without notice?'

Ralph was all considerate charm. 'You may safely leave the good lady to me. Tomorrow we shall go to Chelsea to pick up all your things, and I shall give Mrs Green a sum of money which will more than compensate her for losing you. She will regard you as her benefactress, I promise you.'

What it was to be rich! Which made Ralph's reference to his 'chains' all the more mysterious. She would think about that later, when she was in bed.

But at first Clare thought of nothing. It was only as she was drifting towards sleep that something occurred to her with such force that she sat up in bed and stared into the dark. She remembered the strange warning which Ralph's mother had given as they left the Norton-Norrises' do.

Had she known that they were going to be attacked? And if so, why hadn't she warned them properly instead of being all dark and mysterious? It was as though she had suddenly started to live in a thriller by Sapper or E. Phillips Oppenheim, where people popped out of the woodwork mouthing dire threats—only to pop back in again!

She felt that she couldn't question Ralph about his mother, but, knowing him, she thought that he was probably already considering the implications of the

warning she had given them. After that Clare thought
that sleep would be impossible, but she was wrong. It
claimed her immediately, and she knew nothing until
Armstrong arrived to bring them tea, and congratulations on their coming marriage!

It seemed that there was never to be a moment for her
to think about anything. Early the next morning Ralph
drove her to Chelsea where matters went exactly as
Ralph had said that they would. Mrs Green practically
kissed him in her delight at having a large wad of five-
pound notes handed over to her as though they were
half-crowns.

'Such a perfect gentleman,' she enthused to her
cronies that night in the Gate Hangs Well. 'I do hope
Miss Windham appreciates what a lucky girl she is to
land such a toff!'

He had hired a taxi to take Clare's few pathetic
belongings to Park Lane, and then he drove her to
Asprey's, the King's jewellers, where they chose an
engagement ring.

Or rather Ralph chose it, making a charming panto-
mime about doing so, going on as though they were
both passionately in love and pretending that he could
hardly keep his hands off her.

'Nothing large, please,' Clare told him severely as
trays of the most expensive and tasteful rings were laid
reverently in front of them.

'Pity, that,' remarked Ralph, a naughty twinkle in his
eye. 'I had notions of buying you something really huge
and vulgar. You do disappoint me.'

'Something small and chaste would be my prefer-
ence,' Clare riposted.

'Like you,' he returned gallantly, bowing to her.

Armstrong had dressed him in the most dandy style. He was wearing a top hat, morning coat, and pinstriped trousers. An ebony cane with a silver knob, and spats, things which Clare usually hated, but which Ralph wore with panache, completed the *tout ensemble* of a man about town.

'This one,' he announced suddenly, lifting from the tray an exquisitely delicate half-hoop of small diamonds. Clare was compelled to admit that it was exactly what she would have chosen for herself. She put out her hand, and the assistant slipped the beautiful thing on to her finger.

'Perfect,' Ralph said, bending gallantly over her hand. 'It might have been made with you in mind, my dear. Delightfully modest, but rare for all that.' He completed the compliment by planting a butterfly kiss on her palm.

The unexpected frisson of delight which ran through Clare shocked her by its strength. She lifted her eyes to meet his, and saw that he had registered both her delight, and the following shock.

She had already grasped what a hard man he was, which made these sudden moments of empathy seem all the more surprising.

'You like it?' and whether he meant the kiss or the ring, was hard to tell. Clare decided to be as ambiguous back. 'Yes,' she half whispered, and dropped her eyes modestly. The young salesgirl who held the trays for her superior awarded them a sympathetic smile. She evidently considered them an ideal pair of lovers.

Which was a tribute to them both, Clare conceded. Ralph and the male assistant held a whispered colloquy in which no such vulgar item as the price was mentioned aloud. The upshot was that she was to be allowed to wear the ring immediately since it fitted her. Its pretty box was given to Ralph for safe keeping and a decision was made that the inside of the ring would be engraved with their entwined initials after the wedding—'and the honeymoon. Madam will wish to have her ring on the honeymoon, of course.'

'Of course,' murmured Ralph, favouring Clare with a conspiratorial wink which was invisible to both assistants. He hadn't enjoyed himself so much for years. The delicate flush of delight on Clare's face when the ring was slipped on her finger had given him more pleasure than he could possibly have expected. He had grown used to women who were both blasé and bored, and Clare was neither.

Next her finger was measured for a wedding ring, 'which is to be a surprise for you,' Ralph decreed. It was to be ready by the next day. 'For,' he added to the jeweller, 'Madam and I will be getting hitched a week today. By special licence, you understand. We couldn't wait for the banns and all that, could we, darling? Now, how about me buying you this dear little sapphire pendant? No woman can have too much jewellery, they tell me, and you haven't half enough.'

Clare leaned forward to hiss in his ear. 'This is too much, Ralph. I expected something simple and inexpensive if anything at all—and isn't a week from today a little soon?'

'What a dear you are,' was all that *that* evoked from him. 'I have no intention of letting you bully me into something less than my love for you deserves. And a week from today isn't soon enough for me. And we can't change the date now. Armstrong,' and he pulled out his beautiful gold hunter to check the time, 'is now on his way to *The Times* and the *Morning Post*, with the announcement of both our engagement and the coming wedding. That should silence the gossips.'

The deed was done.

She was to marry him, in a week.

There was no getting out of it—even if she wanted to. Or out of everything else which Ralph was so carefully arranging. Their next destination was the Café Royale for lunch where Armstrong had booked a table for them. Several obsequious waiters danced attendance on them from the moment they walked through the door.

Clare had forgotten the nuances of the life of an idle rich girl. It was strange to be waited on again. She was wearing her new pendant with a pale blue linen dress which she had changed into before they left Chelsea, and which, if cheap, was tasteful—as the observant Ralph had already noticed.

After they had ordered, and an aperitif, a glass each of Saint Raphael, had been brought to them, Ralph leaned back in his chair.

'It is imperative that we have a discussion straight-away, my dear. I have to go into the office this afternoon, and there's a great deal to arrange. Your parents must be informed, and invited to the wedding, regardless of what has happened in the past. We must be seen to do all the right things. I have arranged with the parson of St Faith's in the Meadows that he will marry us, and they ought to be there. The dread Angela will have to be invited, too, I suppose, and the wicked witch of the wood, her mother. A pity, but we must disarm suspicion by being very proper, and all that.'

Clare put down her sherry. 'Do we have to? I thought everything was going to be private.' All her newfound gaiety which had given Ralph such quiet pleasure had fled before this unwelcome news.

'I'm afraid we must. And you must arrange that we visit your parents as soon as possible. I promise not to let them bully you. To arrange it *after* the announcement appears in the Press would be the best thing. You can apologise prettily for jumping the gun and put it down to my mad impetuosity. If the deed is done your father can hardly forbid us to marry.' He smiled engagingly at her, the golden eyes alight with naughty mirth.

His mad impetuosity! She had never met anyone less madly impetuous than Ralph Schuyler. Everything which he did seemed so carefully considered. Even this mad wedding had obviously been planned with the most meticulous care.

'And if they quibble about your living with me, then from tonight we shall have separate rooms, and Armstrong can be chaperon, and so you can tell them. Besides. . .' and he stopped, looking, Clare thought amusedly, more wicked than ever, one eyebrow cocked up like Mephistopheles in a bad film.

'Besides what?' she prodded him, seeing that he was so obviously waiting to be prodded.

'Besides, they will be most immensely grateful that I have decided not to seduce you, but to marry you instead. They will almost certainly be in a passion of delight that you are marrying an enormously rich Schuyler, particularly since they will be acquiring the celebrated Lord Longthorne as a relative-in-law—even if he won't be at the wedding. He will, however, be at the reception afterwards.'

'The reception,' repeated Clare idiotically.

'Yes, at the Ritz. And if that isn't respectable enough for everyone, I should like to know what would be.'

Clare was silent for a moment before asking in a

dangerously quiet voice, 'When did you make all these plans, Ralph? If I may ask, that is.'

'Last night. Once you were safely asleep. I'm afraid that I kept Armstrong from his bed until the small hours, and from his duties in Park Lane today. He is amazingly reliable, and will have set all in train.'

'I didn't expect that our wedding would mean all this fuss. I thought that it would be quite private, but I can see that it's important that everyone thinks we are madly in love, and that the marriage is genuine,' announced Clare dolefully, just as their oysters and champagne arrived.

'How odd,' she added, once the waiters had gone—it seemed to need three to serve them, 'that an attempt to run me down would end up with me being bought expensive presents and eating gourmet food.'

'Very odd. I should advise you to sit back and enjoy it,' was Ralph's cheerful comment as he squeezed lemon on to an oyster before swallowing it, and then drinking champagne.

'Enjoy the good food, Clare. "Seize the Day" is my motto, and I suggest that you adopt it, too, and then we shall get on famously.'

They seemed to be getting on famously already, Clare thought. Or at least Ralph was. He appeared to be enjoying himself immensely, so she followed suit, eating her way through sole meunière, fillet of steak, and a peach Melba. She refused cheese and biscuits, but drank the good wine which came with every course, and the tiny demitasse of black coffee at the end.

Well, it was quite plain that so long as Ralph was looking after her, she wasn't going to starve! The big difficulty lay in not wanting to have a good sleep after every one of the delicious meals she was eating with him! How she would be able to do any work once she got back to Park Lane, she couldn't imagine.

She found herself telling him so, earnestly and at some length, tripping over all her consonants. She couldn't work out whether it was the food or the wine which was doing her the most damage.

'Not to worry,' he said soothingly. 'Finish off all the commissions which you have started and then don't take on any more. So long as you are my wife and my responsibility, you won't need to work.'

'But later,' said Clare anxiously, 'later, when this charade is over, I shall have to work again. I can't go on living off you after the marriage is over. And it isn't a proper marriage, so you aren't really responsible for me, anyway.'

'Not to worry,' he repeated. 'Let's think about that when it happens, hmmm? We have enough on our plates at present working out why someone wants to kill us, without worrying about the future. Other than it's time that I took you home, so that you and Armstrong can sort out the rooms I have given you whilst I show my face at the FO. Even a poodlefaker has to show willing at times, you know.'

Of course, why he really wanted to go was to report to Colonel B what Clare had told him, and work out plans for the future.

It was only when she was back in Park Lane, and her head had cleared as her splendid lunch receded into the past, and she was laying out her papers preparatory to finish typing the Professor's academic report, that Clare began to prove Ralph's belief that she was no fool was true.

At the Café Royale he had called himself a poodle-faker, and everyone she knew seemed to think that he had some sort of decorative but fundamentally useless post at the Foreign Office. But—and it was a big but—the kind of questions he had asked her, together with his instant and rapid reactions both at the time of Jeremy's death, and when the car had attacked them, seemed to suggest that such easy judgements were far from the truth.

She was discovering that he was a much more subtle and complicated man than his reputation suggested. But then, he was a Schuyler, and everyone knew what they were!

'Good,' said the Colonel. 'Knew I could trust you to get to the heart of the matter, Schuyler. I suspected, from a lot of bits and pieces coming my way, that Anthony Mallory was part of a homosexual ring, but I had no proof. You winkled it out of the girl, and now we have it. Well done! This man Stewart is definitely involved, too. He keeps popping up, but so far I've nothing on him.

'Mallory was at the FO for a couple of years after the war. When his grandfather died and he came into money, he resigned. Rumour in the dark corridors of espionage suggests that he was blackmailed into betraying both diplomatic and defence secrets, but by the nature of the thing, hard evidence is difficult to come by. Hang on to the girl. Marrying her seems a bit extreme, but you know best. You're sure she's not involved?'

'Quite sure,' said Ralph firmly. He had hated the phrase the old man had used about his winkling things out of Clare—but, after all, wasn't that what he had done? The truth invariably sounded nasty when plainly spoken. All that about the 'dark corridors of espionage' was a bit flowery for Colonel B, but the old fellow was doubtless on his high ropes now that his suspicions had been confirmed.

'Use the girl as bait, eh,' the Colonel went on, 'to flush them into the open? One thing, Mallory was ex-FO, but Stewart was never with us, so commonsense suggests we have a traitor within as well. Another thing for you to follow up. Heard again from Havilland, have you?'

'I'm seeing him at the Hendon Air Show,' said Ralph. 'I'll take Clare along.' Use her as bait, he thought dismally, disliking himself, and the work he did, more and more. He had to remind himself that the safety of his country and its citizens depended on him, to keep himself in countenance at all.

'Good, good. Carry on, m'boy. We're not out of the wood yet.'

'One more thing,' said Ralph. 'Am I to be allowed to be told something of what you already know? Or do you prefer me to scratch around in the dark, wasting time?'

This insolence was bold of him, he knew, but so what, as the Yankee cousins said. Come to think of it, he was a Yankee cousin himself, if origins counted for anything.

The Colonel was not put out. 'Well,' he smiled cunningly, 'it's like this, Schuyler. I'm a bit of a crossword fiend, like you, and if you give another feller an answer to a clue which turns out to be wrong, it's damnably difficult to come up with the right one. The feller keeps falling back on the wrong one. Bit like a sore tooth. Best you don't know too much, and then you'll use your brains to find out what's what, instead of assuming you already know. Right, Schuyler?'

Ralph gritted his teeth. And meantime, he thought, because the old toad plays his cards so close to his chest he keeps putting my life at risk—to say nothing of Clare's.

But he knew that the devious old devil whom he served had the right of it.

He was leaving the room when his master boomed at him, 'Think about Eastern Europe and the Soviets, m'boy—which gives you a devilish lot of ground to cover!'

So it does, thought Ralph, on top of having to protect Clare as much as possible—from Colonel B, as well as unknown foreign agents!

CHAPTER TEN

'I DON'T believe it! Someone must have made a mistake.'

Laura Windham had been reading the column detailing forthcoming marriages in the *Morning Post* and drinking her early morning cup of tea when she came across Ralph Schuyler's discreet announcement of his forthcoming marriage, by special licence, to Miss Clare Windham, daughter and only child of Brigadier and Mrs J. Windham, MC.

So shocked was she that she broke the habit of a lifetime, jumped out of bed, threw on her dressing-gown and rushed downstairs into the breakfast-room of the Windhams' home in Mayfair, and addressed her brother- and sister-in-law, and her daughter Angela, with all the unbecoming panache of a leading lady in a melodrama.

'Have you seen this? Can it possibly be true? Is it in *The Times*?'

'What in the world can be the matter, Laura,' enquired the Brigadier glacially, 'to bring you down at this hour?' He considered his sister-in-law's tendency to lie abed in the morning the only flaw in an otherwise perfect character.

'This!' she exclaimed dramatically, and read the short announcement to them.

Echoing her mother, Angela exclaimed, 'I agree, that cannot possibly be true. The paper must have made a mistake. Clare marrying Ralph Schuyler! What nonsense!'

'No nonsense,' said Sophie Windham quietly. She had risen from the table and picked up the Brigadier's *Times*, which had been ironed and laid out for him on the sideboard. 'The same notice is in *The Times* as well. They cannot both have made a mistake.'

'Let me look,' ordered the Brigadier curtly, holding his hand out for the newspaper as though the words might have rearranged themselves before he had had time to inspect them.

'Hmm. Yes, you are right, Sophie. That is what it says.'

Angela said, 'Gordon Stewart did tell me that Ralph Schuyler was taking Clare about—but then he's taken so many women about. But why Clare? And what will Eva Chance-Smythe have to say?'

The Brigadier laid the paper down as though to hold it any further would contaminate him. 'I might have supposed that such a dubious character as Schuyler would not have the decency either to ask me for Clare's hand, or to have informed me of the proposed marriage before placing such a notice in the public prints.'

For once the worm turned. Sophie Windham said quietly, 'But, my dear, seeing that you virtually threw Clare out of the house, and have had nothing to do with her since Anthony Mallory's death, he probably thought that you would not consider your permission necessary.'

'Then he thought wrongly,' retorted the Brigadier nastily. It would never do to let his downtrodden wife have the last word. 'It is the action of a man who is hardly a gentleman.'

'But he's so rich,' sighed Angela, who like many

others had set her cap at Ralph Schuyler—to no avail. All the more annoying, then, that her disgraced cousin had captured him.

The Brigadier thought of the Schuyler millions— even greater than the wealth Boy Mallory had commanded—and wondered whether some sort of *rapprochement* with Clare might be in order. Even the prodigal son had been welcomed back by his father, although he had brought nothing home with him: a prodigal daughter who had netted one of the richest men in society could surely be forgiven.

These self-serving thoughts were interrupted by the shrilling of the newly installed telephone and the arrival of the parlourmaid to inform them that madam was required to answer it.

At this, Laura Windham, majestic even though in her dressing-gown, rose to stalk to the door to do exactly that.

'No, not you,' said the parlourmaid, shocked out of her usual well-taught prim tones. 'It's the real missis what's wanted. She was particularly asked for.' Most of the staff disliked the second Mrs Windham, as they called her, intensely, and pitied the Brigadier's wife who was bullied by both her husband and her sister-in-law.

'Very well, then,' intoned Laura graciously after throwing the maid a poisonous look. 'You may answer it, Sophie.' She said this as though conferring a favour.

Silence followed. Mrs Laura Windham, suddenly conscious of her *déshabillé* and fuming inwardly that the disgraced cousin should be married before the respectable one, was making for the stairs just as her sister-in-law returned, but stayed to listen instead.

Sophie Windham's face was one smile.

'That was Clare!' she said happily. 'It's perfectly true that she is to be married. She has asked if she may bring her future husband round to be introduced to you. She says that she's rather cross with him because he jumped the gun and put the notice in the paper before he spoke to us, but he's so wishful to be married soon, that he forgot the proprieties. I told her this afternoon at four would be splendid. I know that none of us have engagements today.'

'No gentleman, as I said,' pronounced the Brigadier morosely, 'but he is related to Lord Longthorne, so you were right to agree—although you might have asked my permission first, my dear. I do not like to be taken for granted.'

The worm turned again.

'Oh, I knew that you would not wish me to snub a peer's cousin. I believe that's what he is. He wants us to be at the wedding and the reception afterwards, Clare says. The reception will be at the Ritz.'

'I have no intention of paying for a reception at the Ritz,' announced the Brigadier. 'They will have to make other arrangements.'

By now the worm was positively revolving, it was turning so rapidly. 'Oh, there's no need to trouble yourself, my dear. Mr Schuyler has arranged that, too. Clare says that with the marriage being so hasty he cannot expect you to bear the expense—even though traditionally it is the responsibility of the bride's parents. Most generous of him, is it not?' she finished ingenuously.

'He can afford it,' grunted the Brigadier, Angela and her mother both nodding agreement.

Laura Windham could not resist making one unpleasant parting shot before she returned upstairs to dress for the day. 'I do so hope,' she uttered poison-ously, 'that this marriage is not being undertaken in such haste for the usual reasons. Babies born eight month after the wedding always occasion scandalous comment, do they not? I should hate to see you both have to endure *that* on top of Boy Mallory's suicide!'

Similar comments, some kind, some unkind, were being made all over Belgravia and Mayfair. 'Never thought I'd ever see old Ralph trotted to the altar,' being the usual male remark, accompanied by knowing guffaws. Mothers and daughters, by contrast, mourned the loss of yet another eligible male. And such a rich one, too!

Ralph treated Clare to a running commentary of possible gossip over breakfast the morning the notice was published. She didn't want to laugh, but he was being so acute that he rapidly had her in stitches, coughing madly into her table napkin.

'Pat her on the back, Armstrong, there's a good fellow. Can't have madam choking herself to death before we get hitched, can we? Gently now, gently. That's the ticket. Now fetch her a glass of water, if you would.'

Clare lifted her scarlet face, tears of mirth streaming down it. 'You looked exactly like my Aunt Laura when you said in her voice, "One can only hope that the usual reason for a marriage undertaken in such haste does not obtain."'

'So glad to have entertained my future wife,' mur-mured Ralph. 'I should have added that she actually hopes that that *is* the reason for all the rush, so that she can dance on your poor mother all the way to the christening ceremony. So sorry that we're going to disappoint her, seeing that it's too late for us to do anything about it now.'

This had the effect of starting Clare off all over again.

Ralph watched her with approval. 'Yes,' he remarked, as she subsided at last, 'it *is* rather jolly to know something others don't, isn't it? Wonder what she'd say if she knew that it was going to be a white marriage. Accuse me of being like poor Boy, and you of being of a similar persuasion, I suppose. That'd be the day.'

'Please stop,' Clare begged him. 'At this rate I shall be unfit to do any work this morning, and I have to begin translating Hodder's dubious French masterpiece once I have finished the Professor's report.'

'Then perhaps I ought to go on. No, I don't really mean that; besides, your commissions will mean that we needn't take time off for a honeymoon—but I promise you a bang-up one later.'

'I don't want a honeymoon—' Clare began as Armstrong ghosted in carrying a glass of water for her, and a pile of letters for Ralph.

'I took the liberty of bringing you these, sir. I wasn't sure whether or not you wished to continue your usual custom.'

Ralph took the letters from him, and said to Clare, 'It's been my habit to read my mail whilst drinking coffee at the end of my breakfast. If you would rather I didn't, I will discontinue the habit and retreat with them to my den after breakfast has ended.'

'Oh, read them by all means,' Clare told him. 'I've no wish to disrupt your life any more than I need.'

'What an obliging wife you're going to be, my dear.' He blew her a kiss, which together with his loving manner to her had Armstrong telling cook, the maids, boots, and the rest of the servants that he had never thought to see the randy old devil so sweet on anyone as he was on his future missis.

Ralph was as rapid in his dissection of his mail as he was in everything, Clare noticed, and he possessed a reading speed which was beyond anything which she had met before. He laughed once or twice, and then, after opening a large buff envelope, he frowned, and bit his lip. Something was disturbing him profoundly.

His growing empathy with Clare's moods and emotions was no greater than that which she was beginning to feel for his. Before she could stop herself she said, 'Is there anything wrong, Ralph?'

'Wrong?' he repeated. 'Oh, no. Just some rather sad news about an old friend. Not unexpected, though.' He folded the letter and slipped it back into its envelope.

Why did she think that he was lying to her? She wanted to say something further, but she had already said more than she should, and ran the risk of appearing to pry into his private life. In any case, time was becoming of the essence. She must finish her breakfast and start work.

The door closed behind her. Ralph gave a sigh, picked up the buff envelope, and pulled out what it contained to read it again.

Printed in crude capitals on a sheet of cheap writing paper was the following message: 'Stop meddling with matters which have nothing to do with you, or we'll cut your pretty bird's throat—and yours as well.'

Cold rage welled up inside him. He was getting near to something big and treacherous, no doubt of it: the threat told him so. Bait was the word which the Colonel had used to describe Clare, and there was no doubt about that too. She possessed the only hard evidence which linked Boy Mallory, Jeremy Peele and Gordon Stewart with activities which those who ran them were determined to keep secret.

From now on 'Mind your back' must be his watchword.

And so he told Colonel B when he called in that morning to report progress and show him the letter.

'Proves we are on the right lines, Schuyler,' was all he had to say. 'Carry on the good work.'

'I'm meeting an informant this evening, at nine o'clock,' Ralph offered. 'I contacted him when you first ordered me to watch Clare. He sent me a cryptic note this morning proposing a meeting at a seedy dive in Limehouse.'

'Good man. We progress. I've also some information for you about Gordon Stewart that looks promising. I had a talk with a feller at the Club the other night. Connected with Special Branch. He promised to look into him for me, said the name sounded familiar.'

How fortunate for the Colonel that his narks met him in a West End club rather than him having to cross London in disguise to drink warm beer in a dirty pub whilst being fed dubious confidences, was Ralph's inward response to that!

His master had picked up a small file and was examining it with a frown on his face. 'As a result, this arrived by first post today, marked urgent. Apparently Stewart is on their list of people who would bear watching—for two reasons. The first is that he is known to have some associates of rum sexual habits. The other is that he is connected with some dubious financial goings-on, swindles you might say.'

From what he knew of Gordon Stewart, Ralph wasn't at all surprised, and so he told the Colonel.

'Apparently,' the Colonel continued, 'he suddenly began to throw money around after having been on his uppers ever since he left University. Blackmail, or worse, was suspected. Nothing could be proved, it seems, because the one chap who could have given evidence against him disappeared without trace. He has some odd associates in various Eastern European embassies. Their sexual habits are suspect, too. Diplomatic immunity protects them, though. What price that he is being paid for information, eh? Keep after him.'

'Noted,' said Ralph.

'Heard any more from Havilland? Any developments there?'

'None so far. As you already know, I'm going to Hendon Air Show next week, and I shall be meeting him there.'

This had been arranged with the Colonel, who was now sending Ralph to it in some mysterious official capacity which would require him to be charming to all the world, and look as innocent as a supposed idler could possibly be.

'Good, good, that's all, then—be on your way. You've a lot to do—including getting married.'

'Would you like to be invited to the wedding, sir?'

'You know better than that, Schuyler. What should you and I have to do with one another, eh?'

That was unanswerable and Ralph was grinning to himself as he passed Pryde, patiently working through a set of elderly files to try to find something in them which was out of place and might give someone away.

He lifted his head as Ralph, whistling, picked up his briefcase and hat.

'Still got that bee in his bonnet about there being some sort of gigantic conspiracy to undo us all, eh?'

'Buzzing away,' agreed Ralph, without revealing that he knew enough to prove that the bee might have more bodily reality than Pryde conceded it.

'Sooner you running round trying to catch it than me,' riposted Pryde feelingly.

'Not doing much running. Dawdling, rather. Getting ready for m'wedding. You will come, won't you?'

'Wouldn't miss it. Saw the announcement this morning. Never thought you'd ever get caught.'

'Happens to the best of us in the end.' By now Ralph was at the door, suddenly anxious to be with his 'pretty bird' as the threatening letter had called Clare.

No one seeing Clare and Ralph at her parents' home that afternoon could possibly have guessed that they were aware that they were being pursued by remorseless and unknown enemies.

That they were faced by known enemies was made quite plain by the distant fashion in which Mrs Laura Windham and Angela spoke to them. The Brigadier had relaxed his frigid manner somewhat, and Clare's mother beamed proudly at them the whole time they were there.

Pinpricks, though, there were in plenty. Angela cornered Clare in her old bedroom where she had been told she might powder her nose before being shown into the drawing-room. Leaving Ralph to do so made her feel strangely isolated. Angela's behaviour to her reinforced the feeling that coming to her old London home was like entering enemy territory.

'Think you're very clever, don't you?' Angela's sneer made her pretty face plain. 'Landing Ralph Schuyler, I mean. I suppose all that money makes up for him being so ugly. I must say that your wedding is going to be the surprise of the season!'

Clare did not dignify this nastiness with an answer. She knew perfectly well that if Ralph had proposed to Angela she would have hauled him to the altar in double-quick time!

The Brigadier's nastiness came when Clare was left alone with him whilst Ralph was being shown round her mother's pretty garden: her sole consolation for her unhappy marriage and the bullying of her female relatives.

'A word with you, Clare. I suppose that, considering everything, you are lucky that any man should want you for a wife at all. I'd rather you weren't giving me a lounge lizard for a son-in-law, but any man prepared to take you on is better than none, I suppose — and he is related to Longthorne.'

She had never thought that her father would forgive her completely for jilting Boy, but she had hoped for something warmer than what he had just offered her. Surprisingly, it was not for herself that she was hurt, but Ralph — which was silly, because he would have simply shrugged the insult off.

It was he who had told her before they set out that she must swallow any insult offered. He had said, 'They demean themselves, not you. The magnanimity must come from us, not them. Another piece of knowledge for us to share, to enable us to control life, not let it control us.'

Remembering his advice was difficult when her aunt Laura chose to whisper to her, 'My dear Clare, I do hope everything about this marriage is above board. I should hate your poor father to be compelled to suffer

all over again in a few months' time, if it isn't. He has
had enough to bear, without enduring the shame of an
early birth.'

Clare made no effort to explain or to justify herself.
She would have liked to say, 'But think how happy he
will be to have all his worst opinions about me justified
when Ralph and I divorce!'

But her mother's pleasure, not only in having her
home again, but also that she was marrying someone as
rich and eligible as Ralph Schuyler, was patent.

'What a lucky girl you are,' she exclaimed wistfully,
after admiring Clare's engagement ring and her pendant. 'He's so kind—and I was so surprised that he
seems to know so much about flowers. Not what I would
have expected at all.'

It occurred to Clare that Ralph seemed to know a
great deal about almost everything, and it had taken her
mother to reveal that interesting fact to her!

Sandwiches and tea were being handed around when
the Windhams had a caller. It was Gordon Stewart.

If the welcome for Ralph and herself had been a trifle
chilly, it was more than made up for by the warmth of
the one offered to Gordon. It appeared that he was
Angela's most favoured suitor, something which would
once have surprised Clare, but since he had come into
money he had become something of a catch for a girl
who was having difficulty in snaring a husband.

It must be Ralph's cynicism rubbing off on me, Clare
thought, watching the Windhams dance around
Gordon, I would never have thought anything as cutting
as that before I met him. On the other hand, if I had
been more worldly wise five years ago I might have
guessed the truth about Boy earlier and saved myself a

lot of grief. So, perhaps Ralph is right not to take anything, or anyone, on trust. Even me.

If Gordon was charming to the Windhams, he was also charming to her and Ralph.

'I twigged at once what was going on between you when I saw you at the Norton-Norrises',' he beamed at them. 'But I couldn't have guessed that you'd be tying the knot so soon. Am I invited to the wedding?'

He wasn't, but Ralph, whilst admiring Gordon's gall in pursuing him and Clare, took the opportunity to keep an eye on him—at least whilst he was at the wedding— and instantly offered him an invitation. 'Love to have you, wouldn't we, Clare?'

To say that Clare, knowing that Ralph believed that Gordon was heavily involved in the deaths of both Boy and Jeremy, was surprised at his enthusiasm for Gordon's presence at the wedding would have been understating matters more than a little.

Ironically though, Gordon's arrival served to lighten the atmosphere at the Windhams, and all was sweetness and light when Ralph pulled out his watch and announced that he and Clare must leave. 'Another engagement for us both tonight,' he explained regretfully.

'I didn't know that we were going out this evening,' Clare remarked as Ralph deftly drove her back to Park Lane.

'We're not,' Ralph said, negotiating Hyde Park Corner. 'But I have to. I didn't want to say so. It might have looked as though I were neglecting you. I had enough trouble persuading your father that it wasn't necessary for you to be married from home.

'I explained that you were living in self-contained rooms at the top of my house, and that I was respecting your chastity, contrary to what most people might believe. Seeing that he had allowed you to struggle for a living on your own for the past five years, I didn't think that he had any right to dictate your life to you—but I didn't tell him so!'

Clare glanced sideways at him. Ugly, Angela had said. A lounge lizard, her father had declaimed. Ugly? Ralph ugly? It was true that he wasn't conventionally handsome in the way of a theatrical matinee idol or a film star, but he was better than that surely! The sheer strength of his harsh face was coming to mean more to her than the looks of the Apollo Belvedere himself. Not that Apollo would ever have offered for her!

And lounge lizard? Ralph! Now that really was a joke. Clare remembered the steely determination which he had shown when he had saved her from the attacking car. It had nothing to do with lounge lizardry, nothing at all.

In contrast, her mother had said that he was kind. Was he kind? He was sardonic, cynical, mocking and completely disillusioned. All that being so, could he be kind?

He must have been kind to Mother, and he has been kind to me.

Thinking so, a great wave of feeling swept through Clare. A feeling which was neither of the body nor the mind, but something between the two. An inconvenient feeling. For as Ralph helped her out of the Bentley, one gallant hand on her arm, Clare was aware of one thing, and one thing only.

Not only had she fallen in love with Ralph Schuyler, but she also loved him and everything about him with a passion which made the feelings which she had once had for Boy seem mild in the extreme. It was hopeless,

quite hopeless, because he was attracted to women like
Eva Chance-Smythe, and anyone less like Eva Chance-
Smythe than she was, Clare could not imagine!

Ralph had left Clare in her rooms, busy translating her
French novel. The thought of her so earnestly at work,
fulfilling her obligations, when most of the women he
knew would cheerfully have thrown them on one side
once they were safely engaged to a man as rich as
himself, had Ralph disliking her family's attitude to her
all over again.

No doubt of it, she was a woman who always kept her
word: a woman a man could be proud of. Could he be
proud of her? Yes, he could. He tried not to think of the
word love—that was for other men, not him. But more
and more he was coming to believe that once having
married her, he would not lightly let her go, but would
make her his true wife. The word love intruded on his
thoughts again. He pushed it away.

Our ancestors knew best, he told himself firmly. They
married for common sense, for legal reasons, and
almost all marriages were arranged, and they worked.
What's more, they worked the better because love was
not involved. To love was foolish, to give unnecessary
hostages to fortune.

Clare was a sensible woman, and she would surely
come to see the sense of a marriage such as the one he
wanted. It would be a successful one, he knew it would.

He turned matters over and over in his mind until he
reached Limehouse. He had left Park Lane on foot in
anonymous, but decent clothing, and travelled by Tube
into the respectable end of the warren of streets around
the London docks where he rented two first-floor rooms
in a house which had known better days.

There he had changed into clothing which, like the house, had also known better days. A grubby muffler round his neck, a battered cap on his head, his feet now in cracked and unblacked boots, he bore little resemblance to suave Ralph Schuyler who charmed London society.

The only thing which might give him away were his uncalloused, beautifully tended hands, so to hide them he wore greasy cotton gloves as an apparent gesture to departed gentility.

His nark had arranged the meeting in The Jolly Pirate, a pub frequented by dockers and their families, a dirty, noisy cheerful place where he was lost among the crowd, and where he could sit at a table nursing a glass of ale without anyone giving him a second glance.

He had never been more grateful for his hard bony face. It amused him that he looked as harshly plebeian as his cousin Gis looked aristocratic. He had once told Gis that he, Ralph, was the spitting image of the piratical Captain who had founded the Schuyler family fortunes, as seen in a rare daguerrotype of him in youth.

'True,' Gis had laughed, 'and you've got his morals, too. As I had. But I reformed, and so will you. The women do it to us, it's a family thing.'

'No woman will change me,' Ralph had vowed, at which Gis had laughed even harder, so that his wife, Thea, coming in, had asked cheerfully, 'Share the joke with me, Gis?'

He had kissed her on her nose. 'Not one that you would appreciate, my dear.'

It was Thea who had winked at Ralph, after Gis had kissed her, leaving him wondering whether, if he could find someone like her, he might get married after all.

He looked at the big clock which hung above the bar.

His nark was late, which was unusual. He carried his tankard back to the bar and ordered another drink.

The landlord handed it back to him with the words, 'Seen you here with Gabbing Dick, haven't I?'

'Sometimes,' said Ralph.

'He was in earlier tonight, not long before you came in. Went out again with two chaps I ain't seen before. Expecting to meet him, were you?'

'Not really,' lied Ralph.

'Didn't look very happy,' volunteered the landlord before he turned away, 'but then he never does.'

Ralph gave Dick another half an hour. It passed, and still no sign of him. The hairs on the back of his neck rose. A powerful feeling of something wrong had him walking to the door and out into the mean streets.

It had grown dark whilst he was inside, and the moon was sailing above a bank of clouds. For some reason he didn't want to go home. The feeling of something wrong grew worse. He began to walk in the opposite direction to the Tube station which would be the start of his tortuous journey back to Park Lane and Clare.

He found himself in an alley to—where? He didn't know where. Only that something drove him on. He turned down a road lined with warehouses, which was leading him towards the river. Hearing voices at the last bend in it, he followed the sound to find himself in open ground where coils of tarred rope, deserted capstans, and rusted bits of metal were strewn around.

The voices came from a pair of police constables who were bending over something on the ground. On hearing his footsteps one of them looked up and called to him, 'Hey, you. Come here at once. Police business.'

Giving an inward curse Ralph did as he was asked. He thrust his hands in his pockets and put on his most sullen air. One of the policemen stood up, looked him up and down, and said, 'What's your business here?'

'Haven't any,' he growled. 'Lost m'way. Want to find the Tube.'

'Then you're going the wrong way, chum. It's downstream, not up. That way,' and then, 'Know him, do you?'

He had moved so that Ralph could see that what they had been inspecting was the body of a man lying face down on the ground. The policeman still kneeling seized the man's head by the hair and swung it round so that Ralph could see the distorted face and the sightless eyes.

'No,' he said. 'Never seen him afore.'

But Ralph lied.

It was Gabbing Dick who was sprawled before him and one thing was clear. He would never gab to Ralph, or anyone else, ever again.

CHAPTER ELEVEN

AFTERWARDS Clare was to remember everything about her wedding, and the days leading up to it, as happening in a kind of dream.

The morning after they had visited the Windhams Ralph had seemed most unlike himself. He had spoken brusquely to her at breakfast, had hardly bid her 'Good morning' before he had said, most earnestly, 'Clare, you must promise me one thing. For the present you must never go out on your own. If I am not available and the matter's urgent, I give you leave to take Armstrong with you, but I would rather you waited for me.'

He had looked so serious that Clare had not argued with him but had nodded agreement. 'Of course, Ralph. If you think it is necessary.'

'For the moment, yes, I do think it necessary.'

He had been pleased that she had not argued with him. One more count in her favour. And how pleasant and homely it had been to have her sitting opposite to him at breakfast, Armstrong ghosting around them whilst they had eaten bacon and eggs, toast and marmalade and had drunk their coffee.

His dark mood had made Clare feel that it might be tactless of her to raise a subject which had been troubling her. 'The guests for the wedding,' she had said hesitantly, 'don't include your mother, Ralph. My immediate family will be there, but you won't have any. For form's sake, ought we not to invite her?'

The face he had shown her as she had finished

speaking had been granite-hard. 'Indeed not. She has never shown the slightest interest in me from the day I was born. I cannot believe that she has any desire to see me married. My father had little to do with me, but at least he endowed me with a fortune, educated me, and gave me a good start in life.'

'I think she tried to warn us the other night.' Clare's voice had been serious: she had been thinking about the Countess's cryptic utterance, and had no doubt that it referred to the attack which had followed so shortly afterwards.

'You may be pleased to think so.' Ralph had picked up his coffee cup. 'As a subject for conversation I find her boring in the extreme. If she really wanted to help us, she could have been a little more explicit. After all, to know that an attack on us was planned means that she must be aware of the other elements in the puzzle we are investigating—and that we are both still in danger—but she is doing nothing about that.'

It hadn't seemed advisable to say anything further. Clare had thought that there had been a quality of desperation in his mother's behaviour that night, but with Ralph in the mood he was in, it had seemed pointless to continue.

They had finished breakfast in silence. He had said that they might go shopping together, but instead he had told her, curtly for him, that he needed to go to the Foreign Office; there was unfinished work for him to see to.

Later, on returning home in the early afternoon from his stint at the FO, he seemed to have recovered his usual cheerful spirits, and he ordered his chauffeur to fetch out his big white Rolls and drive them to Bond

Street to buy a wedding dress and everything which went with it.

Clare had learned by now not to argue with him when he wanted to buy her pretty things. It was quite useless and simply seemed to provoke him into a line of lovingly sardonic comment which had all the shop assistants doting on him.

'So easy to see how much he loves madam,' one saleswoman said to another when they first arrived in her boutique to try on models hot from Paris.

On the other hand, she was losing a great deal of fun by obediently falling in with all of his whims. So, apparently, was he. For when, later, she tried on a wedding gown of white silk, low waisted, and falling almost to the floor—'the latest style in Paris, madam. Quite the rage over there'—and made no comment on it, he leaned towards her and drawled, 'The salt of our outing is missing, my love, if you passively accept everything I am buying you without arguing about the price or the propriety of what I am choosing.'

He picked up the skirt of the dress to admire the feel of the material—Clare had already discovered that he was a most tactile man, which had made her naughtily wonder what it would be like to be made love to by him. Rubbing it between his fingers, he added, 'It's a wicked price. You're sure your conscience will allow you to wear it?'

Clare could not help herself, but burst out laughing, a joyful sound which had all the shop assistants smiling at him.

He was seated on a fragile gilt chair, perfectly dressed, his top hat on the floor beside him, his grey gloves inside it, his silver-headed stick between his legs, the very model of the youngish man about town. The

salesgirls' admiration of him grew. He seemed to be
able to make madam happy—a gift not usually found
among the men who brought their women here to buy
them things.

Clare's openly expressed pleasure pleased them,
too—as it pleased Ralph.

He insisted on buying her a trousseau—'But we're
not having a honeymoon,' she said helplessly.

'No matter,' was his grand reply. 'You deserve
something for taking me on.'

It was a good thing they had the chauffeur with them,
Claire thought, to carry the piles of parcels and store
them in the Rolls. 'Proper gone on her,' he told the
servants' hall. 'As you said, Armstrong, never thought
I'd live to see the day!'

Nor did Clare. Standing at the altar in her beautiful
dress, pearls, chosen by Ralph, around her throat,
Angela's jealous eyes glaring at her, Ralph's apparently
devoted ones adoring her, she hardly knew who or
where she was.

Gordon, helped by a sullen Angela, threw confetti
over them as they left the church. A society phographer
snapped them. 'Smile, please, ducky!' A society columnist wrote rapturously of a radiant bride and her
entirely *comme il faut* wedding dress. Clare's mother
wept happy tears over them. Even the Brigadier unbent
a little at the sight of all Ralph's grand friends and
relatives present at the reception. Only a few had been
invited to the wedding ceremony.

Gis Havilland and his wife were there, but only Gis
would attend the Hendon Air Display to which Ralph
and Clare would both be going at the end of the week.

Thea was heavily pregnant, and would find the journey difficult.

Across the road from the church, a black Rolls Royce with diplomatic plates was parked. A woman, attended by a liveried chauffeur, stood there, watching the excitement as they left. It was Ralph's mother. She was beautifully dressed as befitted the mother of the groom in a long dusty-pink coat of raw silk, and a large black picture hat trimmed with giant roses. Had she been included in the wedding party she would have put every woman in it in the shade. Apart from Clare, no one took any notice of her.

She saw Ralph throw her a dark look, saw his lips thin with disapproval, then he was laughing and talking again, his arms around Clare as though they were the most romantic couple who had ever married.

And it was all quite unreal. For the wedding was a sham, had no meaning, and out there, in the harsh world which knew nothing of society photographers and society weddings, someone was stalking them. Seeing that nothing odd or dangerous had happened during the run-up to the wedding, Clare had suggested to Ralph, twenty-four hours before it was due to take place, that perhaps it might not be necessary, after all.

She was astonished by the violence of his reactions.

'No!' he had exclaimed, taking her by the arms, pulling her to him and looking deep into her eyes as though he were trying to mesmerise her. 'No! Believe me, Clare, it is more than ever necessary for your protection. I cannot tell you more than that.'

He had reported to Colonel B the tale of his nark's death, and that he had left a false name and address with the two coppers who had accosted him in Limehouse. He would never go there again, and had given up his rooms in the district, so that there was no trace of his ever having been near the pub or Gabbing Dick.

The Colonel had agreed with him that his nark—Ralph had never revealed his name to him—had almost certainly been murdered because someone had discovered that he had vital information which he was about to pass to Ralph. The report of the police investigation—to which the Colonel later gained secret access—showed that he had not been engaged at the time in doing anything suspicious for which he might have been murdered.

The police, of course, had no knowledge that Gabbing Dick had had access to even more dubious circles than those of East End criminals. Ralph's appearance on the scene had been recorded, but had been dismissed as a mere accident.

The devil of it was, thought Ralph despairingly, that with Gabbing Dick dead, the only way in which they were going to find out who and what were behind the mysterious deaths was through Clare. He also carried the unwelcome thought, through the preparations for the wedding and the day itself, that they might try to dispose of her as well.

Seeing his mother standing there had reminded him that he might be behaving like a fool in rejecting her. If she did know something of the truth of the conspiracy in which he and Clare were enmeshed, then it might have been more sensible to ask her to the wedding, appear to mend fences and try to find out exactly what she did know.

Once in the Rolls with Clare, he had scribbled a note and called on Armstrong who was attending as an usher to take it to 'the lady across the road with the black Rolls'. As his own drove away, he watched Armstrong hand it over, and saw his mother nod her head, before they were lost to view.

He had written, 'My wife told me that I ought to have invited you to the wedding, and so I should have done. Forgive me, and come to the reception at the Ritz where I may introduce you to her. Ralph.'

Perhaps the only person who realised that something was on his mind was Clare. Before she could say anything he turned to her, kissed her gently on the cheek, and said, 'You're a good girl, Clare, and I was wrong last week when I savaged you over your wish to invite my mother to the wedding. It's too late for that now, but when I saw her outside the church I sent Armstrong over with a belated invitation to the reception.'

For the first time Clare returned his kiss with interest. 'Oh, Ralph, I'm so pleased that you did. Whatever lies between you, both now and in the past, she is your mother. From things you have said, I gather that your father is dead, so she is all that you have left.'

How different they were! Clare in her essential goodness, and he in his essential badness, was Ralph's mournful gloss on that. His invitation to his mother had nothing to do with mending fences and everything with trying to find out what she knew. Nevertheless, the kiss left a warm glow on his cheek, and he squeezed Clare's hand in lieu of a lying reply. There were times when he wished that he could have the privilege of speaking the truth! He recalled Gis Havilland once saying something similar.

Like Clare, he had expected the reception to he an ordeal, but, surprisingly, it wasn't. He had to explain why he and Clare were not departing for Cap d'Antibes, or Tuscany, but otherwise everything seemed quite normal. Toasts were drunk, the cake was cut, he made the kind of speech expected of a newly married man, kissed Clare on the cheek to assembled cheers and, with her hand in his, moved among guests growing merry from his expensive champagne.

Torry Longthorne put out a hand to take his when they reached her and Lord Longthorne, who were part of a small group which included his mother. Earlier they had all been photographed again and again, until Ralph had told the assembled Press that there was a room downstairs laid out with food and drink for them if they agreed that enough was enough and left.

'You look lovely, my dear,' Torry told Clare, admiring the lilies of the valley in the bandeau in her hair, on her shoulder and in the simple bouquet which she had carried at the wedding. 'You have excellent taste. Nothing overdone as is so common these days.'

'Oh, Ralph chose everything,' replied Clare playing the part of an adoring bride, and giving him a shy glance, to receive yet another conspiratorial wink back from him. 'Which isn't to say that it's other than my taste, too.'

Lord Longthorne shook Ralph by the hand, and then, to her surprise and delight, kissed Clare's. Ralph's mother, who had stood by silently, watching the passing show, agreed, when appealed to, that Ralph's bride was the very picture-book model of what a bride should be. She complimented Clare again when Ralph introduced Clare to her.

In all the long years since Boy had shot himself, Clare had never dreamed of taking part in such a day, or of having such a triumph. Surrounded by admiration and the men and women of power in British politics and society she could almost feel Laura and Angela Windham's anger at her success.

Like her father, though, they dare not say or do anything to express their acute displeasure when surrounded by Ralph's grand friends and relatives. The Windhams might be gentry, but they had never moved in such circles before. Someone was saying loudly that they had expected David—the Prince of Wales—to be present, but they had heard that because of the short notice, he had a state engagement which made it impossible.

'Ralph,' demanded Clare agitatedly, 'is it really true that the Prince of Wales would have come if he could?'

'Oh, I think it was a bit ambitious of someone to suggest *that*, and given the speed of the business, most unlikely, but, yes, I do know him. Played polo with him several times.'

Another thing she didn't know about her future husband. 'You play polo?' Clare said in hollow tones.

'Used to,' Ralph was brief. 'Not any more. Had to give it up recently. Health reasons.'

Health reasons? What could he mean? He looked the picture of health. Puzzling that out when she had hardly eaten but had drunk a great deal of champagne, taxed Clare's overloaded brain so much that she hardly registered that Ralph's mother had come up to her, saying quietly, 'I would like, if possible, to have a private word with you.'

'That would be difficult,' Clare said, aware of Ralph's eyes on her, and that he would probably not be too happy if she were to show overmuch friendship with his mother.

'Not here, then. Later. I need to talk to you. I understand that you are not having a honeymoon. Can that possibly be true?'

'Yes. I have business commitments to fulfil, so we are postponing it.'

'I see. May I suggest, then, that you visit me at my home in Berkeley Square? My husband is a counsellor with the Rumanian Embassy. Here is my card. Would the day after tomorrow at four in the afternoon be a possibility?'

Clare took a chance. 'Oh, yes. I think I could manage that.'

'Good. I see that Ralph is glowering at us so I will move on.' She paused for a moment. 'May I wish you both well, my dear?'

She looked so beautiful, but so infinitely sad, that Clare did something impulsive. Never mind what Ralph might think—he must learn that she was not to be dictated to. She leaned forward to kiss her mother-in-law on the cheek, saying 'Of course you may.'

As she stood back, she saw that the Countess's eyes were filled with tears. 'My son is lucky,' she said simply, and moved away, to be lost in the throng again.

'Now what was all that about?' Ralph muttered into Clare's ear, a certain urgency in his speech.

'I don't know.' Clare decided to begin her marriage by being honest with him. 'She said that she wanted to meet me—alone.'

'And you agreed?'

She had thought that he would be annoyed, but strangely, he seemed to be eager to hear that she had.

'Yes. I hope you don't mind.'

'Mind!' He gave a short laugh. 'Of course I don't mind. You're a clever girl. Use your head, and she may tell you things to help us that she wouldn't tell me.'

Did he never stop planning and plotting? Clare asked herself wearily. Even on our wedding day! But, of course, our wedding is part of the plotting and planning.

'I hadn't thought of that,' she told him truthfully.

'Then you should have done. Your—my—life might depend on it. For sure, she knows more than she should. Some traitor in the Rumanian Embassy may be in on this for all we know.'

'Surely, Ralph, you can't think that your mother is privy to a plan to kill you!' she whispered fiercely back at him, so close to him now that they were almost mouth to mouth.

Bitsy Bentley, who had been watching the pair of them like a jealous hawk, misread what was happening and exclaimed loudly to Woofer, 'Who would have thought it! To see Ralph Schuyler of all people so besotted that he can't wait for tonight to enjoy himself!'

Several people shushed her loudly, but privately agreed with her, unaware that the newlyweds were discussing murder and sudden death, rather than exchanging loving confidences.

Gordon Stewart, holding a champagne flute, suddenly appeared from nowhere to clap Ralph on the back, before he had time to reply. 'None of this, now, m'boy. Time for it later, not here. 'Gratters to you both again, particularly to Clare. Great to see you land on your feet at last, old girl. Make this pirate mind his Ps and Qs, eh?'

Could he possibly be involved in a plot to kill them? was Clare's inward response to Gordon's jovial hilarity. Or was it someone else in this crowd of laughing people, exchanging jokes, confidences and gossip, coming up to offer them both congratulations whilst wanting to stick a knife in their hearts?

Best to forget all that.

Best to pretend that everything was for the best in the best of all possible worlds.

But it was becoming harder and harder to smile all the time, and Clare began to feel deathly tired. The last few weeks had taken their toll of even her resilience, and she suddenly wanted to be away from it all—even if it meant being alone with Ralph.

Be honest Clare. *Particularly* if it means being alone with Ralph!

Something must have shown on her smiling face. Ralph took her gently by the arm. 'I think it's time we left, Clare. We've done the pretty long enough. Our duty is done. Everyone has had time to see what a devoted couple we are.'

Our duty, thought Clare dully. Yes, that is what this is after all. The shared joke with Ralph about how they were deceiving everyone had begun to pall, and she thought that he had guessed as much.

'Yes, I should like to go home.' In so saying, she was unaware of how much she had given away. Park Lane had become home to her, and Ralph was the magnet which drew her there.

'Very well.' He put up a hand, and shouted for silence. 'My lords, ladies and gentlemen,' he announced in a parody of every toastmaster who had ever presided at a banquet. 'My wife and I are about to leave. She wishes to follow custom and precedent as behoves the wife of a good civil servant, and so she will throw her bouquet to you, and may the next bride catch it.'

He turned to Clare and kissed her, whispering, 'Smile, and do as I ask. It will be expected.'

Everyone cheered as they walked to the doors where Clare dutifully tossed her bouquet into the air—to be caught by Angela, who smiled radiantly at Gordon Stewart as she showed her trophy to him. It was the last thing Clare saw as the door closed behind them, and she shivered at the sight.

Ought she to warn Angela that it might be a mistake

to become too involved with him? But, no! She could imagine Ralph's furious reaction if she did any such thing, and rightly so. They were involved in a game in which they dare not take any risks. The deaths of Boy Mallory and Jeremy Peele were sufficient evidence of that.

Clare was unaware of the deaths of Gabbing Dick and Lance Milford or she would have included them in her list.

'If I said thank God that's over,' remarked Ralph as they reached haven in Park Lane at last, 'you might misunderstand me, so I won't.'

'But you already have,' riposted Clare, her logical brain still working in spite of a hard day and too much champagne.

'What it is to have married a clever woman,' retorted Ralph, ripping off his white tie and throwing it down. 'I see that I shall have to mind my Ps and Qs, as the egregious Gordon suggested.'

'You don't like him, do you?'

'No. I remember him fawning on everyone in the old days, particularly Boy, and now he's offensively hail-fellow-well-met to me, full of charmless *bonhomie*, as though he and I were pals from way back.'

'I don't like to see him making such a fuss of Angela,' remarked Clare thoughtfully. 'It's not like him. He usually goes for girls with pots of money, and Angela will only have a moderate dowry to bring to him, even if Father does leave her all he has, and cuts me out.'

'Two points for Mrs Schuyler to ponder on.' Ralph had now removed his morning coat, and was making for the tantalus on the sideboard, as though he hadn't already spent the afternoon drinking steadily. 'Number one, Angela must take her chances with Gordon. She has never considered you, so you hardly need consider her. Number two, you have no need to worry about being disinherited. When all this is over, and we part, I shall settle such a tidy sum on you that you never need work again. One advantage of being a Schuyler, and as rich as Croesus. What do you say to that?'

'That besides being grateful, and you really have no need to do such a thing, I am full of admiration for the fact that you can say Croesus at all after all the drink you have taken on board.'

She added, with a naughty little giggle, 'Do you think that you could manage Xanthippe?'

'Manage Socrates' shrewish wife? Of course I could, any time, any day, all day. Just try me, my own dear Xanthippe,' quipped Ralph, deliberately misunder-standing her use of the word manage, and before she could stop him he was on her, his mouth on hers, his arms around her, his whisky, which he had not yet tasted, put down to give him more leverage.

Before an astonished Clare could push him away, for she had not expected him to try anything on so rapidly, if at all, she found her hands holding his head while she returned his kiss with interest. For a moment, past, present and future merged, and disappeared. The kiss lengthened. Ralph began to walk her gently backwards, and before she could register what he was doing, he was pushing her down into the depths of the big sofa—which had doubtless been the scene of many previous such encounters.

With a rapid wiggle, Clare broke free before her treacherous body persuaded her to lie beneath him to make their wedding day a reality instead of a sham. He was simply treating her as he treated all his women, and she was having none of it. She loved him, and she would only accept him in love, and not in lust. She stood up.

'I can do without this,' she announced dramatically, staring down at Ralph, who had now cocked a quizzical eye at her. He had ended up sitting on the sofa, looking thoroughly dissolute in his unbuttoned shirt, with his hair dishevelled where she had been stroking his head.

He rose, to move towards her, so that she retreated— to be stopped by the wall behind her.

'So can I,' he said thickly. 'Most inconvenient. Gets in the way of logical thought. Probably that's why I enjoy it so much,' and he was kissing her again.

'Not in the bargain,' she told him, pushing him away again.

'But no earthly reason why we shouldn't enjoy ourselves. After all, we *are* man and wife.' She had nowhere to retreat to, so he kissed her again.

'How can we get an annulment,' Clare asked him, after she had pulled her betraying mouth away, 'if we consummate this marriage—which was only meant to be a feint or a sham to protect ourselves?'

'Easy,' he said, advancing on her again. 'We lie.'

'We lie?'

'Yes, people do it all the time. Hadn't you heard?'

'Gordon called you a pirate. How did he know?'

'Takes one to know one.'

There was no answer to that, so Clare made none. She was too busy fighting a losing battle with her mind and body. Emotion said: Why resist him? You love him. Who would know? You are married to him, after all. Reason said: He's a pirate. He said so himself. He will love you and leave you, and what would that do to you? Haven't you suffered enough as a result of loving Boy? And finally, Can you trust him?

How the battle would have ended, Clare was never to know. She thought that emotion would have won because Ralph's caresses had moved from merely kissing her to the use of his hands and body to rouse her as he was already roused. And he was succeeding, when the telephone rang.

The raucous noise of it did the damage and broke the spell, which would have had her on the sofa, or the floor, doing exactly what he wished with her. Ralph sat up, and growled, 'Damn. Modern inventions are the devil. I'll have to answer it.'

He couldn't say, Because I never know whether or not it's duty calling, for Colonel B would not respect even a man's wedding night if he thought that the security of the state demanded it, for that was not for Clare to know. Leaving her on the sofa, not sure whether to be happy or not that it had rescued them, he took the phone off its hook, and said wearily into it, 'Schuyler speaking.'

Silence followed. Clare straightened her dress—Ralph had pulled one of its shoulders down the more easily to make love to her. Still Ralph said nothing.

Until he put the phone back on its hook, carefully, as though it were precious, and swore below his breath, his expression so menacing that it was frightening. Nothing of the tender man he had so recently been was left.

'Ralph! What is it?'

'I can't lie to you,' he said heavily. 'It was someone whose voice I don't know, threatening to harm you if I don't call off our investigation. It's the second such threat I've received. I didn't tell you of the other one, but we are man and wife now, and I owe you a duty.'

CHAPTER TWELVE

ONE thing the threat did: it removed all desire from both of them to make love. Clare wanted comfort, Ralph wanted to scotch the dangers which threatened her. They talked soberly for a time of their dilemma: that they still had no real idea of who was trying to kill them.

Ever since he had met Clare in Jeremy Peele's bedroom, Ralph had been caught between a rock and a hard place. He had fallen in love with her—the very last thing an agent of his experience should have done with someone who was at the centre of a conspiracy. It was likely, he knew, to spoil his judgement, for he would be thinking of her safety all the time, instead of concentrating on fulfilling his mission. The two things, he thought miserably, might not be compatible.

Colonel B had told him long ago that he would only be safe if he was always in cold control of the events which he was investigating. Even that could not guarantee his safety completely, but would reduce the risks he might run. So far he had always found the advice easy to follow—but then he had met Clare, and forgotten everything. He tried to remember that he must be as suspicious of her as of everyone else, but it was useless.

He only had to see her, to be with her, and the habits of a lifetime disappeared. His one aim in life was to protect her, and the thought that the Colonel saw her as bait designed to lure the villains into betraying themselves was anathema to him, because it meant that he ought to be putting her in a position of danger—and he could not.

His one prayer was that she would never discover that he was a member of the Secret Service, that this whole affair would end in such a way that she would never have need to doubt the purity of his motives in becoming involved with her.

The bitter irony of his falling in love with a woman of great integrity, the absolute opposite of Eva and all his previous loves, did not escape him. Sardonically, he saw it as his punishment. He had denied love, denied involvement, denied all responsibilities in life except those connected with his career as an Army officer in the Great War, and after that with his duties in the Secret Service of his country—and then this happened.

Perhaps God might be trying to tell him something!

'No man is an island,' John Donne had said three centuries ago, and it had taken Ralph Schuyler thirty-five years to discover that he was not exempt from the poet's dictum.

Let this be safely over, and he might make a new life for himself with Clare. For the first time he thought of children, Clare's children, his children and remembered Gis Havilland's joy in his son. He had watched Gis's pleasure with wonder, remembering the wild life which his cousin had lived, until he had surrendered himself to domesticity.

Something of his somewhat superior and dismissive thoughts must have shown—or Gis had used his notorious intuition. 'Until you love someone who is not yourself,' he had told Ralph, holding small Rickie in his arms, 'really love them, then you will always lack true fulfilment—as I did until I met Thea. And the final seal on our happiness was this,' and he had kissed his sleeping burden. 'Not that it's easy, mind. It's damned difficult, for selfishness will keep creeping in, but life is barren if the centre of our universe remains our solitary self.'

Gis had not said, 'You won't understand what I am telling you, until you have experienced it for yourself.' He had not needed to.

And now he knew what Gis meant. He had no business telling Clare that he loved her before all this was over and he could be honest with her. He should not have tried to make love to her until he could be honest with her—but drink and excitement had undone him. The ringing of the telephone had saved him, saved them both.

Thinking so, he fell asleep at last.

He was not the only one whose sleep was disturbed that night. They had agreed to sleep apart: Clare in the room he had given her when she had moved from Chelsea, and he would join her in the morning before Armstrong woke them for the day.

'Give him something to gossip about,' Ralph had told her with one of his more satanic grins. Clare was not such a paragon of all the virtues, he had found, that she did not enjoy his jokes and innuendos. She also contributed a few of her own. Thank God that she was not mealy-mouthed, being his verdict.

That night, however, as the alcohol disappeared from her body, and the excitement of the day began to die, Clare found herself prey to strange fears. She remembered that her aunt, who had been a chemist, had told her that strong drink was a depressant, and when its first excitement had worn off, it could leave the mind oddly sad and downcast.

Something like that seemed to have happened to her. Lost in her new-found love of him, she had stopped questioning Ralph's motives in helping her. She had been swept along by events, and by Ralph himself, who barely gave her time to think when she was with him. Away from him she had been too busy working, trying to fulfil her commitments, to question what was happening to her.

Now, in the middle of the night she found herself using what her aunt had called 'the dread word, Why?' Why was Ralph helping her? From the moment he had met her in Jeremy's bedroom he had done nothing else, putting himself in danger by doing so. Was it kindness?

Yes, he was kind, beneath the cynicism. But could she believe that his kindness was so altruistic that it had led him to put himself into a position of great danger solely in order to protect her? Something else nagged at her consciousness. He had not been in the least surprised by the attack on her, or by the fact that she had been set up to take the blame for Jeremy's death. More than that, he had displayed an instant appreciation of what to do both when cleaning up Jeremy's flat, talking to the police, and during the attack when his cool-headedness had saved her life.

On the other hand, if it were not kindness which moved him, what was it that did? It all came back to trust. She loved him. Did she trust him? Could she love him if she didn't trust him? Was it possible that he loved her? Or was it the simple lust which he had felt for Eva and the others which moved him? It was all too much like one of the logic puzzles which her aunt Jane, used to try to solve when you were given a great many different statements about an event and had to work out what had actually happened—frequently failing to do so.

As sleep began to claim her, the puzzle of Gordon Stewart, the deaths of Boy and Jeremy Peele, together with the enigma of Ralph Schuyler, all began to swirl around in Clare's brain. When at last she did sleep, her dreams were shot through with blood and death and fear, until running down an unknown street, in an unknown land, she saw Ralph waiting for her, arms outstretched to take her into them... But as she reached him, she awoke...and the cold light of dawn filled the bedroom.

'Good morning, sir, madame.' Armstrong beamed avuncularly at them as they ate their breakfast.

He had gone to Ralph's room at the usual hour, found him missing, guessed (correctly) where he was, and had tactfully knocked on Clare's bedroom door, murmuring discreetly through the panels, 'Your morning call, sir,' before ghosting off downstairs.

'Damn!' exclaimed Ralph, sitting up in bed beside Clare. He had arrived in her room about half an hour ago, had sat in an armchair until they heard Armstrong coming up the stairs, when he had leaped into bed beside her.

'Who'd have thought the old devil would have gone away without surprising us. Most unlike him. I had quite counted on it. Never mind,' he went on, stirred by being in such close proximity with a Clare who was wearing very little, 'let's take advantage of his discretion, eh?'

All the good resolutions he had made during the night had disappeared. Maddened by her perfume, something innately and particularly Clare, he leaned

over, took her in his arms and began to kiss her
enthusiastically.

Clare's resolution held. It was her turn to leap. Out of
bed, and not into it. 'Really, Ralph, you seem to have
only one idea in your head these days where I'm
concerned.'

He was now leaning lazily back on her pillows, his
arms crooked behind his head, the very picture of
combined sexual invitation and indolence. 'But it's a
jolly good idea, Clare! Do confess!'

'Nothing of the sort.' She began to pull on her
dressing gown, and said crossly, 'Do go, Ralph. We've
successfully hoaxed Armstrong, and that should be
enough.'

'Not for me, it isn't. I want to see madam prepare
herself for the day.'

Clare, who had picked up her sponge bag preparatory
to taking herself into the adjoining bathroom, showed
him eyes full of alarm.

'Behave yourself, do. This wasn't in our bargain,' for
he was now getting out of bed, was walking by her into
the bathroom, and had begun to turn on the taps. His
pyjamas, she noted hazily, were as predatory as he was,
being covered with flame-breathing dragons.

'Whatever do you think you're doing, Ralph
Schuyler?' Now her voice was full of alarm.

'Preparing your bath for you, Mrs Schuyler,' was his
easy reply. 'Which bath salts do you prefer, Jasmine or
Lemon?'

'Lemon,' she answered him before she could stop
herself. 'No, Ralph. I really don't need you to help me,
I'm quite capable of running my bath myself.'

'Spoilsport,' was his only answer. He left the taps
running and put a hand out to lift the caramel-coloured

fall of her hair, so that he could kiss the nape of her neck.

Such a shiver of delight passed through Clare that her legs almost failed her. What on earth would it be like if she ever let him make proper love to her, if such a light kiss could do such dreadful things to her?

But of course, he was a masterly lover—or so rumour said. Why had she ever doubted it?

Almost absent-mindedly he was now kissing her neck all the way up to her ear, and had turned her head towards him so that he might kiss her cheek.

'Stop that,' she said smartly, slapping at his hand. 'The bath will run over.'

'So it will.'

He was not so far gone in lust that he wanted that to happen was Clare's acid response as he moved away from her to turn the taps off. He tested the water, then, to her surprise, began to unbutton his pyjama jacket. 'How about having our baths together, this one's big enough for two?' he offered.

His amber eyes were as wicked and merry as a man's could be. She had no doubt that he was fully roused— and, to her horror, so was she. The thought of them, naked together, in the big bath, was too enticing, too wicked. Ralph's dark, powerful body with its dressing of coarse black hair, her own, creamy white, the caramel hair, falling about her shoulders, too short to hide her. . .Clare banished the vision firmly. Wife or no wife, she was giving him nothing until she knew what his true intentions were. He had made a bargain with her and he would have to keep it.

'If you don't leave immediately, Ralph,' she told him as he began to pull his pyjama jacket off, 'I shan't have a bath at all. You can have one, if you wish—but on your own.'

'We could have such fun,' he said, his jacket half-on, half-off, managing to look like a small boy whose stern mother had deprived him of a treat.

'No doubt.' Clare was now at the bathroom door.

Ralph slipped his pyjama jacket on. 'It was worth a try,' he told her wickedly.

'So you apparently thought!' was her tart rejoinder.

'And Armstrong and Co. will probably think we enjoyed ourselves here anyway. . .'

'If that is meant to persuade me, it has failed.'

'Cruel,' he murmured mournfully, as he closed the bedroom door behind him. Enjoying, if that was the word, her solitary bath, Clare could only imagine glumly what form Ralph's fun would have taken if she had agreed to share it with him.

Being sensible was a rather boring and lonely thing.

One thing was sure. Married life with Ralph was never going to be dull.

Nor was it. Halfway through breakfast the police arrived again.

'No peace for the wicked,' Ralph drawled at Armstrong. 'Put them in the drawing-room, there's a good fellow. Give them something to drink. If they don't want liquor at this hour, or have scruples, offer them tea or coffee—in the best china. I don't want any complaints that we stinted our welcome.'

'I don't like this.' Clare was not half as insouciant as he was. 'What can they want now?' They had heard nothing from Scotland Yard since the day after Jeremy's death, and Clare had begun to feel safe. Wrongly perhaps.

'As our late Prime Minister H. H. Asquith said,

"Wait and see",' was Ralph's contribution, and he refused to say more on the subject. 'Eat your breakfast like a good girl, Clare, nothing to worry about.'

Clare bit back another tart reply to the effect that she didn't like being patronised, because she could sense that for all his apparent carelessness, Ralph was a trifle worried.

No one would have guessed it, as he walked into the drawing room, Clare on his arm.

'Good morning, Inspector Malcolm, Sergeant Johnson. No need to stand up, we'll sit. I hope Armstrong kept you well supplied with whatever tipple you wanted. I'm sure that you didn't mind waiting whilst we finished breakfast. Always wise to start the day right, eh?'

He was giving off an ineffable tinge of the Bertie Woosters, P. G. Wodehouse's hero who was busy entrancing people in his latest series of adventures, *Carry On, Jeeves*, presumably in the hope that the Inspector would think that Armstrong was the brains of his establishment.

What the Inspector really thought was not very evident. He had fetched out his notebook and was studying it as though it were Holy Writ.

'Sorry to trouble you both again, sir, and you only married to your lady yesterday, but we need to clear a few things up. Mrs Schuyler, Miss Windham as was, told me that she hadn't visited Mr Peele on the night of his murder, and you confirmed her statement saying she was with you. Quite sure about that, are you, sir, madam?'

Ralph said, putting an arm about Clare, 'I think that you have distressed my wife, Inspector, by asking a question which seemed to doubt her veracity. Of course, I am sure, and so is she. Look it up in your notebook if you are not. It should be there.'

'Indeed, sir, it is. But, at the risk of distressing her further, I must ask your wife to answer me as well.'

Fearful she might be, and lie she didn't want to, but Clare could not prevent herself from giving a small artistic sob. Ralph was rushing to the rescue again, all concern for his bride. He tightened his grasp and planted a loving kiss on the top of her head. If the Inspector only stayed long enough, who knew what might happen?

Clare peered at the Inspector from the haven of his arm, half whispering, 'I changed my mind about visiting Mr Peele and went out with Ralph instead.'

The Inspector found his notes more interesting than ever. 'Then, Mrs Schuyler, how do you account for the fact that just before seven-thirty, the lady who lives in the house opposite saw a person answering to your description enter Mr Peele's flat? She did not see this person leave.'

'Well, I can't account for it at all, Inspector, except to say that she must be mistaken.'

'Then you wouldn't mind taking part in an identity parade, madam?'

Oh, yes, she would, but she couldn't say so. 'Whenever you like, Inspector.'

'Tomorrow morning, then, at the Yard. At ten-thirty.' He nodded his head at his Sergeant who had remained silent, rose and walked to the door—to Clare's infinite relief. Except that when they reached it, the Sergeant turned and addressed Ralph, not her.

'Oh, by the way, Mr Schuyler, I wonder if you could account for the fact that when we examined the room of a man who was murdered in the Docklands last week, Richard O'Hare, also known as Gabbing Dick, we found a piece of dirty paper with your name on it, and the words, nine o'clock, 18th June, The Jolly Pirate.'

Mr Schuyler couldn't. For starters, he had not thought that his real name was known to Gabbing Dick, and he wondered rapidly and frantically how Dick could have found it out since he had gone to great lengths to keep his identity secret. Well, his cover had been well and truly blown, but by whom?

'Questions about yet another murder with which we have nothing to do, Sergeant! What next? I have never heard of, or met, Gabbing Dick. Is the fact that the paper was dirty significant?'

'You tell me, sir. Two murders, sir, of people whom you knew—or who knew you. We do know that Gabbing Dick went to The Jolly Pirate, but left shortly before nine with two men. The landlord now thinks that he didn't go willingly.'

Ralph's stare was so haughty that even the Sergeant flinched. 'Are you really trying to suggest that I was one of the two men, Sergeant?'

'Now that we're not sure of. For another man, whom Dick sometimes met there, turned up just before nine o'clock and waited for him for some time before leaving. Was that man you, Mr Schuyler?'

'Me, Sergeant? I assume that this is some sort of bad joke. Can you possibly imagine that I should be meeting a low criminal in a Limehouse dive?'

This didn't put the Sergeant out one whit. He returned doggedly to his task of trying to corner Ralph.

'Could you perhaps tell us where you were, if you *weren't* at The Jolly Pirate, that is?'

Now this was a real facer, and something which Ralph had never expected to have to explain. He opened his mouth to make some sort of answer, but his bride, who had guessed that he was in trouble, was there before him.

She gave a great sob, clutched at Ralph, put her handkerchief to her eyes, and said, 'What evening was this, Inspector?' ignoring the Sergeant as though he didn't exist.

It was the Sergeant, however, who replied. 'Last Wednesday, madam, six days ago.'

'Last Wednesday.' Clare gave a relieved laugh. 'Oh, then, no need to worry my husband. I'm afraid that last Wednesday we spent the night...anticipating the wedding. By nine o'clock we were in bed.'

Quick-witted as well as clever, was Ralph's stunned reaction. His new wife had grasped in an instant that he was having trouble in answering the Sergeant, and had interceded to save him, as he had once saved her. For she roared on, 'I'm sure that is why my husband didn't rush to answer you. Having compromised my reputation once on the night of Jeremy's murder, he didn't want to seem to be doing it again. Caught out twice, dear. What a good thing we're safely married now and may do as we please.'

'Indeed, Mrs Schuyler.' The Inspector had taken up the tale again. 'Can anyone else confirm this?'

'My man, Armstrong. The one who brought you coffee.' Ralph knew that he was safe in saying this. Armstrong had a nice line in hedging and ditching which had served him well in the Army. No need to worry about that, though, for Clare followed the Inspector and Sergeant into the kitchen and before they could stop her, cried ingenuously at Armstrong, 'Oh, Armstrong, the Inspector wants to know where Mr Schuyler was last Wednesday. I told him that he was at home, alone with me.'

'Last Wednesday,' mused Armstrong, putting on his most thoughtful face. 'Was that the night you retired early, after a light supper?'

It wasn't. It had been Tuesday. But Armstrong gave a perfect picture of a man trying to catch an elusive memory; having caught it, he offered it to the two policemen like a splendid fish, carefully landed.

'Yes. It was Wednesday. I remember now. The night that Jack and Claude Hulbert were on the wireless. Great stuff, Inspector. Never miss them.'

The exasperated Sergeant and the even more annoyed Inspector were almost sure that Mr Schuyler, his wife and his staff were running rings around them. What more to say? For the moment, what more to do? Nothing but to leave, baffled, and hope that something would turn up to prove them all liars.

'Oh, what a trump you are!' exclaimed the delighted Ralph, kissing his wife on the nose, and congratulating Armstrong on his masterly performance as a second Jeeves, aiding and abetting his stupid master. 'I can't thank you enough for helping me out of a hole.'

'Think nothing of it, sir. Always ready to be of service,' and Armstrong ghosted out again.

'Very true, and very kind of you to say so,' commented Mrs Schuyler to Mr Schuyler after Armstrong had gone. 'But two questions still remain to be answered.'

'They do?' returned Ralph, trying to look innocent and failing as usual.

'Oh, indeed. If you were meeting—Gabbing Dick, was it?—in Limehouse, what on earth were you doing there consorting with a common criminal? And secondly, if you weren't at The Jolly Pirate, what Jolly Place were you really at?'

CHAPTER THIRTEEN

OF COURSE, Ralph never gave Clare an answer which made any kind of sense. Instead, he offered her some fairy story about going to meet an old wartime comrade for a drink. Which was nonsense, because if he were telling the truth then all that he had had to do was to give the Inspector his friend's name and address and the whole business would have been cleared up without delay.

Clare knew perfectly well that Ralph had gone out that night without explaining where he was going, and she also remembered that he had been in an odd mood the next morning. It was, however, impossible to believe that he had been wandering about Limehouse keeping an assignation with a criminal called Gabbing Dick!

The very idea had her stifling laughter. Suave Ralph Schuyler would have looked so completely out of place in the East End. Unless he had been disguised. Memory, on the other hand, reminded her of something which she had almost forgotten: on the evening when Ralph had found her in Jeremy's flat he had been wearing rough clothes, quite unlike his usual smart attire.

This thought, which popped into Clare's head from nowhere, only served to baffle her further. Why on earth should Ralph be doing any such thing? She gave up. She had work to do. Ralph had said that he needed to make an urgent telephone call and had disappeared into his study. The call was either genuine, or invented as a ploy to stop her questioning him: Clare wasn't sure which.

But she knew that she was going to ask him again, obliquely and tactfully, about where he had been and why the police should now be after him, as well as her. Only suddenly, it seemed, they weren't... Which was another puzzle...

Malcolm and Johnson spent the morning in Limehouse, following up further leads. Neither of them could think of any reason why Gabbing Dick should have made an assignation with Ralph Schuyler—if that was what the paper meant.

Their real suspicions arose from the masterly performance put on by all three principals in the investigation that morning. 'As good as a play, wasn't it, guv?' Johnson had said glumly to Malcolm on the way to The Jolly Pirate to ask further questions. 'Do you think that they'd rehearsed it?'

The Inspector shook his head. 'No, I don't. For one moment, when I asked him about Gabbing Dick I could have sworn that Master Ralph Schuyler was genuinely shocked, and put off his stroke a little.'

'But the way his missis jumped in...'

'Oh, I think that surprised him as well as us. And then he was away. First a double act and then a threesome, with that man of his taking part. They ought to go on the halls. Laughing at us, they were. But we'll have him yet if he did for Gabbing Dick. Though why he should, beats me.'

Something else was to beat him. They had scarcely had time to hang their coats up, back at the Yard, before they were sent for.

'Commissioner wants to see you both. Immediately.'

They looked at each other. What for? being the two words which sprang to both their minds. It didn't take long to find out.

'Ah.' The Commissioner looked at his watch, 'Good afternoon to you. Glad to catch you so early. It's about this Peele business, and Gabbing Dick's murder. I understand you went to interview Mr and Mrs Ralph Schuyler this morning. Right?'

'Right, sir.' The Inspector answered the question. Johnson stood at a loose sort of attention.

'It's like this.' The Commissioner leaned forward. 'I'm putting both cases on hold for the moment. There are certain important considerations, delicate ones, involved in both murders. Besides, you have a lot on your plate. That thieving down at the docks, for example. I'll let you know when you can get going again.'

'Oh no, sir! And let the trail grow cold? I've arranged for Mrs Schuyler to attend an identity parade tomorrow morning. We have a witness who thinks she saw her entering Mr Peele's flat that night. . .'

'Then unarrange it, Inspector. You heard what I said. You've a good career ahead of you. Don't endanger it by arguing over your orders.'

'Yes, sir. I mean, no, sir.' The Inspector wasn't sure what he meant. But there was one thing he had to say. 'This man, Schuyler, I mean. He's a big pot, I know. Has he being putting any pressure on the Yard over this?'

'Who? Schuyler? Certainly not. Never met the man, never spoke to the man. Nothing to do with him. Orders from on high, Inspector. Let that be enough.'

'Yes, sir. Thank you, sir. Wouldn't like to think that you could be leaned on by such as Schuyler, sir.'

For a moment he thought that he had gone too far.

'That will be enough, Inspector. Now go, both of you, and mind you do as you're told.'

Once they had left the room the Commissioner passed a silk handkerchief over his sweating face. Good man, Malcolm. Pity to do this to him. Damn Special Branch and the Secret Service, too!

The call from the Inspector came just as Clare was putting the finishing touches to the first part of the novel she was translating. She listened to him with mounting astonishment and relief.

'So you don't require me to come to an identity parade tomorrow morning, Inspector. I want to be quite sure that is what you mean.'

'Yes, Mrs Schuyler. The parade is cancelled—for the time being, anyway. I'll let you know if we need you in the future. For the meantime, our inquiries do not involve you and Mr Schuyler.'

And then he rang off, without any further niceties. Clare stared at the phone. He had sounded sharp and angry. She looked at her watch. It was three o'clock, not many hours since the Inspector had told her with such glee that she was to report to him in the morning.

Alice in Wonderland came to mind again. Curiouser an curiouser. More and more it was like being trapped in one of Aunt Jane's logic puzzles. What was it that Sherlock Holmes had said of the dog who didn't bark in the night? That that was the odd thing. Well, here was another—that the Inspector, so eager for her and Ralph's blood, should suddenly give up the chase.

Everything connected with Ralph seemed odd.

Thoughtfully, Clare returned to her work. One thing was growing plainer and plainer. Ralph Schuyler was certainly more than a bored idler who did a nothing job at the Foreign Office. And if he wasn't, what exactly was he?

Another bit of the puzzle. Perhaps one day they would all come together and make sense of what was happening to her life. Until then, as one homespun philosopher had said, Shuffle the cards and deal again. Which roughly translated meant, Get on with your work. So she did.

Ralph wasn't surprised by the news that the police were temporarily letting them off the hook, Clare noted. She was beginning to watch him carefully—and trying not show it. There was so much he wasn't telling her. He looked tired, and that night he made no effort to seduce her. This was a real disappointment, Clare found. She enjoyed his mocking high spirits and the innuendos which went with them. Surely poodlefaking didn't take as much out of a man as Ralph had seemed to lose that day.

'I can't do any real investigations until I have the police off my tail,' he had told Colonel B when he reported to him. 'I'm certain that Masters is going to have me followed.'

'Hmm, can't have that,' agreed the Colonel and reached for the telephone. 'I want you to go to Roehampton and have a talk with Simmons. He's been monitoring radio transmissions from Moscow, and coming up with some strange stuff. You might be able to make sense of it. He can't.'

It was the last thing Ralph wanted to do. But he went to the small villa which housed a group of operatives hung about with wires and earphones, and read Simmons's transcriptions—and made a little sense of them. They proved that there was a spy ring hard at work, but what it was involved in was vague—deliberately so. The code which was being used was simple and personal, which made it difficult to crack.

On the way out he had spoken to Pryde, who never seemed to be used as a messenger boy to all and sundry—or get the hard assignments either. He knew that the Colonel rated his talents more than Pryde's, but that was a two-edged sword, he had found.

'Busy, old man?' Pryde exuded false sympathy.

'You might say so,' grunted Ralph. He had been looking forward to leaving early and persuading Clare to visit the Tutankhamen exhibition with him.

'Having a hard time these days, are you, what with getting married and losing Gabbing Dick as an informer?'

'Um. . .' said Ralph absently. He was fidgeting about in his desk trying to find a lost document which might be useful at Roehampton. Most inconsiderate of the Colonel to send there him at this juncture. He gave another uncharacteristic, ungentlemanly grunt, and dashed out. The sooner he got to Roehampton, the sooner he would be home again with Clare.

Alas, what he found there meant that he had to dash back to work, to discuss matters with the Colonel. 'The only real fact we winkled out was that the Air Show next Friday is somehow involved.'

'Keep a watch when you get there, then. The girl will make a useful blind.'

The girl! The girl! She's my wife, dammit! Ralph wanted to roar, but he said nothing. The sad truth was

that all those years ago the Colonel had been right.
Loving someone took the edge off an operative's skill.

What the Colonel told him next took the edge off
Ralph's anger with him, and was responsible for his
strange mood when he arrived home.

'You'd better know, Schuyler, although I'm telling no
one else yet. We've had another blow, and a bad one.
Campbell's disappeared. Someone blew his cover and
we're pretty sure he's ended up dead in the Lubyanka's
cellars. We have a traitor in our inmost ranks, Schuyler,
and I haven't the faintest idea of who it can be. Probably
the same man who is leaking information to the ring
you're trying to track down. Go carefully and say
nothing of this, or what you're doing, to anyone. The
less cross-information there is, the better.'

Ralph had known and liked Angus Campbell, who
was attached to the Prague Embassy in Czechoslovakia.
To think that he had ended up being executed in the
Soviet Union's vilest prison was horrific. The day was
clouded enough for him without that news.

For once, the Colonel showed him a little sympathy.
'Some good news for you, though. You won't be
troubled by the police any more, or your lady, either.
That's one complication out of the way. Any idea why
your informant wanted to see you—or why he ended up
dead, for that matter?'

'No idea at all,' confessed Ralph. 'If I were a fanciful
type, I should say that I feel that I'm staggering around
in a dark wood at midnight trying to find a path which
doesn't appear to exist. Every time that I think I've
found it, it turns out to be another dead end.'

'Um,' the Colonel grunted. 'Fancies like that not
often useful, but sometimes they are. Carry on,

Schuyler. I sometimes think that you're the only person I know that I can trust.'

Ralph wasn't sure whether to believe him or not. But for once he took his unhappiness home with him, instead of leaving it at the office door. Added to his worries over Clare was something which nagged at the back of his mind: something he had heard or seen which was out of place, and which he should have taken notice of. Something important. Like a sore tooth in the mouth constantly found by an errant tongue, he had a sore tooth in the brain which his mind kept touching.

'Tired and overworked today, were you?' was Clare's somewhat sardonic comment to him as he lay back in the armchair opposite to her after dinner, nursing a brandy and soda, worrying gently. He didn't, she had already noticed, much like spirits, which suggested that something was disturbing him.

The yellow eyes he turned on her were lustreless. 'You might say so.'

She found herself saying something surprising. 'Care to confide in me?'

'Oh, it's all very dull. I don't think confiding would help.'

'But then, you never do. Confide, I mean.'

He showed his usual spirit at that. 'And what am I supposed to infer from that?'

'I would have thought it a plain enough statement,' Clare retorted.

'Not plain enough for me.' Now he did something surprising. He stood up, pulled her from her chair, so that she dropped the copy of *Vogue* which she had been leafing through on to the floor, and dragged her to him.

'I've no mind to play difficult intellectual word games

with you tonight,' he told her, before kissing her fiercely
on the mouth without so much as a 'by your leave'.

Clare dragged her mouth away from his, and said
sweetly, 'Ah, you prefer simple physical games with me
instead?'

'Nothing simple about this,' was his answer. He
resumed where he had left off, and this time his kiss was
more gentle and Clare found herself responding to it,
and to the urgent stroking of her body which accompanied it.

Ralph wanted to forget everything in her arms. In
some way he didn't quite understand, he needed absolution and only Clare could provide it. She seemed
the one decent thing left in his dark world, a beacon of
light, or a shining star above the tangled wood of which
he had spoken to the Colonel.

'Love me, Clare. Oh, yes, like that,' for she had begun
to stroke his jaw, an innocent form of caress which was
having the strangest effect on both of them. His beard
was so strong that he usually shaved when he arrived
home in the evening, but tiredness and sadness had
taken their toll of him and he had neglected to do so.

The feel of his stubble under her soft fingertips was
oddly erotic, Clare found; even more so was his tongue
in her mouth and hers in his. He was stroking her with
one hand, whilst unbuttoning her dress with the other,
urging her to the door as he did so.

'Come to bed with me, Clare. I need you,' he
whispered, his demanding mouth against her velvet
cheek.

Earlier in the evening Clare had been disappointed
that he had shown so little interest in her. Now that he
most definitely did, she found herself responding to him

enthusiastically instead of holding him off as she had previously done.

Afterwards she was to ask herself why this was so, and had concluded that it was because for the first time he had shown himself vulnerable, less than confident, whereas always before he had been lazily dominant, sure of himself.

She had no idea what had brought this about. Only that he was sad and low and she wanted to comfort him, to restore him to his natural self, however much that natural self had often infuriated her.

Seeing that she made no resistances but clung to him the harder, Ralph walked her to the door. Reaching the bottom of the stairs, he made matters easier for her by throwing her over his left shoulder in a fireman's lift.

Armstrong, emerging from the butler's pantry which served as his little office, gazed benevolently at them. Clare was laughing, the caramel hair hung down and she was beating his back with her fists.

'Let me down, Ralph, you'll do yourself a damage.' A cry which Ralph completely ignored.

Neither of them saw Armstrong, who watched them until the stairs turned. He had no doubt at all about what would follow as he heard Ralph's bedroom door open and close.

A sly smile burgeoned on his lips. 'And about time, too,' he muttered, retreating to his pantry to sample some of Ralph's best single malt whisky, purloined from the drawing room. Ralph and Clare might have deceived the whole of society by their behaviour, but Armstrong had watched their little games with a paternal smile and a heartfelt wish that they would get down to business and have done with it!

* * *

Clare woke up in the morning wondering where she was and what she had been doing to give her such a strange feeling of hard work successfully accomplished, and satisfaction achieved. Muscles which she had not known she possessed were aching gently. She flung out an arm—which connected with another body in the bed with her...

Memory came flooding back. Of Ralph carrying her upstairs, throwing her on the bed, wrenching off his clothes as though they were burning him and then flinging his superbly muscled body on to the bed beside her, before treating her clothes as cavalierly as he had treated his own.

And she had objected to none of it! One moment they had been sitting opposite to one another as quiet and gentle as an elderly couple after a hard life, never mind a hard day, and in the next, without warning, they had set upon one another as greedily as two small boys let loose in a sweet shop.

How long had that been coming on? Clare asked herself, trying to roll over, but being unable to do so because one of her legs was trapped between both of Ralph's. Ever since they had first met at Bitsy Bentley's party was the only correct answer, if the truth were to be told.

Gentleness and ferocity were so mixed in his love-making that Clare had found him more of an enigma than ever. He had known, she was sure, that she was inexperienced, and he had initiated her slowly into the delights of loving. But as she had grown bolder in her responses, kissing and stroking him in response to what he was doing to her, his caresses had grown stronger and stronger until, a mass of sensation, Clare had allowed him to do to her what he would.

And what he had wanted to do was so thrilling, so satisfying that she had found herself crying to him not to stop when they had reached the central core of the behaviour of a man and woman in love.

'I must,' he had panted, 'or I shall be of no use to you.' His desire for her had been so great that he had been almost a boy again, so excited by the first contact with the beloved that consummation was on him immediately—and to be resisted.

The days of living together had taken their toll, but if he were to satisfy her, to give her what he wished—and she deserved—then he had to hold back a little, or he would be spent and she frustrated. His pleasure was nothing to him if it were not shared—a new sensation for him.

Clare had known nothing of this, but instinctively had known that she must trust him, and when she had sought to hold and stroke him—there—and he had shuddered away, saying, 'Not yet, Clare, but soon,' she had given herself up to mindless sensation, until, like runners breasting the tape together after a long race, they had achieved consummation—to lie gasping, afterwards, bodies still entwined although passion was temporarily spent.

Ralph had made love to her so considerately that the breaching of her virginity had been achieved without undue pain; something which Clare had earlier worried about, having heard from several of her more experienced friends what a painful disappointment a first sexual encounter could be.

All fear, all false shame, had disappeared, she had found. Ralph had been panting with effort, his broad chest heaving in the aftermath of love achieved, as though he were truly the runner who had pulled her along with him to victory. What to do but reward him with kisses?

'Oh, thank you!' she had breathed fervently between them. 'Thank you! That was lovely. I wouldn't have believed that I could share such pleasure with anyone.'

Ralph had rolled towards her, astonishment written on his face. He had never been the subject of such gratitude before. Eva, indeed, had been given to complaining that he had not satisfied her exactly as he ought to have done. And, if the truth be known, she had never satisfied him as much as Clare's intuitive response to him had.

'I should thank you,' he had murmured. 'I was worried that I might hurt you if I let myself go.'

'Hurt me? No, not at all. Quite the opposite. Oh, Ralph, I hope you don't regret what we have just done.'

'Regret? Of course not. We are man and wife, and we have just celebrated that fact in proper form.'

A feeling had passed over him as he had said this such as Ralph had never experienced before. Not a feeling like the spasms of ecstasy which they had both just experienced, but one of the tenderest love, blended with the most powerful desire to shelter the loved one from all harm. It had been both more, and less, than passion. Perhaps, more accurately, it had been so different that the two could not be compared.

It had Ralph taking her in his arms again, and inevitably that led to something else, and the something else led to. . .and they had been one again for those brief moments which lovers steal from time.

After that they had slept.

And now, looking down at Ralph's quiet face, Clare wondered where the wildly passionate woman had come from who had at last shared his bed with him. She had not told him that she loved him, and that last night had been for her, the proof of that love, for she did not want to lay an obligation on him. What he felt for her she did not know, but ultimately she hoped that he would tell her.

He moved against her. His questing arm sought and found her. 'Clare?' he whispered drowsily, relieving her of the fear that he might address her by another woman's name.

'My dear,' she said, boldly giving him another kiss.

'I thought I had dreamed you.'

She gave a small laugh. 'Indeed you didn't. Physical games not mental ones, you said, and you finally had your wicked way with me.'

'Not so wicked, seeing that we are married.'

The smile which accompanied her next words robbed them of their sting. 'We had a bargain which denied fulfilment.'

'Oh, that,' he said. 'Come here, woman,' and he wound a fist in the fall of her hair and gently pulled her towards him. 'Allow me to prove to you that the bargain was a mistake.'

'Willingly,' she said, 'willingly.'

So he did.

It was like heaven, Clare thought later that morning, being your husband's wife in the only way which mattered. She was translating from the French with a rapidity which surprised her. Some of the excesses of the book she was engaged on seemed less excessive now that she had enjoyed the joys of love.

Much to Armstrong's secret pleasure, she had kissed Ralph goodbye when he left for the Foreign Office after breakfast. She had also removed the evidence of her first lovemaking, by parcelling up the bottom sheet, to dispose of it privately, and fetching a new one from the linen cupboard to replace it.

'Anyone would think that we were guilty lovers instead of respectably domestic,' Ralph had said with a grin.

Clare had gone bright pink. 'I was thinking of a possible annulment,' she replied demurely.

'Naughty,' he had said, wagging a finger at her like a reproving schoolmarm.

She tried to recover her wandering thoughts. She really must get on if she were going to spend the afternoon visiting his mother. On the other hand, her mind kept dwelling lovingly on the night before, particularly her first sight of his strong body.

The only thing which marred it were the heavy scars on his upper torso and on the shoulder above his left arm. She knew that he had been wounded in the war, but not the extent of it. He must have been an invalid for quite a long time and she wondered how a man as vigorous as Ralph had endured being inactive whilst he recovered. Was that why he had given up polo?

When she knew him better she would ask him how he had come by them, but for the moment she would say nothing. During their lovemaking she had kissed him there, as gently as she could: a tribute to both his suffering and his bravery.

Enough was enough! She must get on with her work. . .

'My dear, I am so glad that you came. I know that you are not having a honeymoon yet, but, even so, it was good of you to find time for me.'

The room into which Clare had been shown was as

beautiful as the Countess herself, full of antique furniture in an Eastern style. There were ikons on the walls—priceless things, glowing in the room's dim light. The Countess was wearing an afternoon frock from the atelier of the new Parisian designer, Coco Chanel. A delightfully simple number in a deep beige which suited her dramatic looks and her pallor.

Tea things were set out on a long low table with a mosaic top. The Countess busied herself with them to give Clare time to feel easy with her.

After some idle conversation, the Countess put her cup down and said, 'Now, I must talk to you of serious matters. I do not wish to frighten you, but I must ask you to take a message to my son. You do know that Ralph is my son—very few people do, but I am sure that he has confided in you.'

'Yes, he has.' Clare thought it politic to say no more.

'So, but I am also sure he has told you little else.' She sighed. 'You know that he resents me for what he sees as my desertion of him. But consider. What else could I do? I was eighteen when I met his father, who was also Lord Longthorne's father, Joris Schuyler. I am told that when he was a young man he was very fat, but when I met him he had just recovered from a serious illness, had lost a great deal of weight, and looked like a cross between Lord Longthorne and Ralph. Like his two sons he was not handsome, but powerful and attractive to women.

'Enough. Despite the difference in our ages he swept me off my feet. He said the feeling was mutual. I was not then regarded as a beauty and he. . .he. . .dazzled me. The result was Ralph—and catastrophe. My parents were devastated by the news. I must bear the child in secret—and give him up to his father who would provide for him. At eighteen, what else could I do but submit? I could not marry Joris, he already had a wife. That is my story—and Ralph's. But I still love him, and now he is in danger because of his work.'

Clare nearly echoed, 'His work?' but prudently kept quiet.

'It is dangerous enough that he is a member of this country's Secret Service, involved in perilous missions, but until now he has never become concerned in matters which will lead to his death—and yours—if he does not tread carefully.'

In her agitation the Countess's good English had begun to fail her. Her accent had become guttural. She coughed, passed her hand before her eyes, continued, 'Do not ask me how I know this, but there are those who are determined to kill him because he has foiled them before. And since you and he are in this together, your life is at risk.

'Tell him he has an enemy inside his own organis-ation, who hates him and wishes to destroy him. One he thinks of as a friend. Tell him also that the man who pretended to be the friend of both Anthony Mallory and Jeremy Peele is also heavily involved in this business. They know that you are both going to the Hendon Air Display. Use every caution if you do.

'I can say no more. I have no wish to betray my own country, so I must tread as carefully as you must. Now, drink your tea, or have some cognac. You look pale.'

And no wonder, was Clare's bitter response. Ralph is a secret agent! He has been cruelly deceiving me from the moment he met me. Pretending that he was looking after me out of the goodness of his heart, and not because I was a decoy leading him to his enemies. No wonder I feel faint.

What a fool I have been.

She remembered so many things which should have told her what he was. His behaviour on the night of Jeremy's death. His determination to find out why she had jilted Boy. . .oh, the list was endless. It included his lack of surprise on the night they had been attacked. Even his ready response to it was explained.

And last night. . .last night. . .he manoeuvred me into his bed.

That was the final betrayal of all. The Judas kiss which sealed me to him. I thought that he loved me, as he has made me love him.

How she sat there, calm, without betraying to the Countess the turmoil she was in, Clare never knew.

All the way home she sat in a kind of daze. Armstrong, letting her in, thought that she looked ill. He offered her tea. First she refused it, and then called after him, 'Please, Armstrong, I will have a cup—and make it strong.'

Now, what's gone wrong? he thought mournfully. Just as everything was going right, dammit; his intuition, as well-developed as that of his master, told him that it was something to do with Ralph.

Ralph might possess intuition; he didn't, however, possess the ability to foretell the future. Afterwards, he thought wryly that if he had not spent the day in a kind of euphoria brought on by loving Clare, he might have recalled the odd thing which had troubled him the day before—which would have saved them both a lot of grief. Nor did he guess that trouble might be waiting for him at home.

As it was, he came home full of beans, whistling happily as he walked into the house, a bad habit of his for which Armstrong had frequently rebuked him. 'Not the action of a gentleman, sir.'

Ralph always made the same reply. 'You should know by now that I'm not a gentleman, Armstrong.'

That Armstrong *didn't* rebuke him that night for saying so should have told him something, but didn't.

Claire didn't rise to greet him. She wasn't in the drawing room. 'Tsk, tsk,' murmured Ralph. 'Working late. Can't have that.'

He took the stairs to the top of the house at the run, flung open the door to her workroom, crying, 'Hubby's home, darling,' like an actor in a bad stage farce, which should have had her laughing, but didn't.

Clare stopped typing and turned round to face him. 'Yes, Ralph? What is it?' Her voice was icy again—the one she had used on him when they had first met.

'That ought to be my question, darling,' he said in his normal voice. 'Why are you still working, at this late hour?'

'Because I need to, Ralph.'

'Not now you're my wife, Clare, you don't.'

The eyes she turned on him were cold and steady. 'Oh, and why am I your wife, Ralph? Why did you really marry me?'

'Why?' He was puzzled, and showed it. That there was something wrong should have been plain to him from the moment he had entered the room, but the joy of last night's lovemaking was still with him, and he had thought of being with her more often than he should throughout the day. Her manner to him now that he was with her at last was such that it was as though she had thrown cold water over him.

He pulled up a chair and sat by her. 'What is it, Clare? What's wrong?'

His voice was so kind that it nearly undid her. She blinked tears away. 'I asked you that, Ralph, because when I met your mother this afternoon, she told me something that I ought to have heard from you.'

He knew! Immediately he knew. He resisted the urge to jump to his feet, and wring his hands.

'What did she tell you, Clare? Anything of use to us?'

'I'll come to that in a second, Ralph.'

All the joyful spontaneity with which she had responded to him last night was gone.

'She told me that you are a member of this country's Secret Service, so I must assume that the "nothing job" that you do at the Foreign Office is a blind for your true activities. How could you deceive me so cruelly? I thought that you were protecting me, looking after me out of kindness, and all the time you were using me. First for information about Boy and Jeremy, and then as bait.

'I believe this because ever since your mother told me what you were, I have been thinking very hard about the last few weeks we have spent together. *That* is what I should have been doing from the moment I met you in Jeremy's bedroom, not trusting you, blindly believing every lying word you uttered. You are not to blame her for telling me. She assumed that I knew, and I let her think that I did.'

The worst of it was the coldly desolate way in which she spoke. She obviously saw what he had done as one more betrayal of her in a life already filled with betrayals. If she had screamed and ranted at him he could have taken a noble line, but being so cold and sad, she left him nowhere to go. . . .

He leaned forward in his chair, and tried to take her hand. At first she resisted him, and then gave way. It lay cold and icy in his, although the day was warm. A kind of terror filled Ralph. Last night he had found true love and tonight he was going to lose it. To lose it so soon, soon...

'Look at me, Clare. Listen to me, my darling. It's true I am a secret agent. It's true that when I found you in Jeremy's bedroom I had been following you—because those were my instructions. It was my duty.

'That was how our relationship began—but that was not how it went on. For me, to come to know you was to love you. What began as duty rapidly turned into something very different. I truly wanted to protect you, not because of what you knew, or because I wished to use you as bait, but because I loved you. I would never willingly endanger you. You must believe me.'

'But I believed you before, Ralph, when you were singing me a different song, pretending to be the idler, willing to help a poor girl in trouble. So why should I believe you now? Where you are concerned, where does truth begin and lies end? That is your profession— and your duty—to lie.'

Clare's eyes filled with tears as she finished.

Her last accusation touched Ralph on the raw. He let go of her hand as though it had stung him.

'Why do I have to lie, Clare? Let me tell you. I am a counterspy, dedicated to tracking down foreign agents and traitors in our own country, one of the guardians of the safe, innocent world in which you live. Where murder is a rarity, and violence is hardly known. Where women can walk safely down the street, day or night, without fear of assault. I, and those like me, are the invisible preservers of your liberties from those who would destroy them. And there are many who would do so—as you have already found out.

'Now I have become visible to you—and you reproach me. When I was a soldier, and was visible, I was honoured. I am no less a soldier than I was. Many of my friends have perished in the silent war we fight. It was my duty, Clare, my duty to say nothing to you. As it was your duty not to tell the world what Boy Mallory was because you had promised him that you would not. Honour binds me as well as you.'

He was moving towards the door, his fists clenched by his side. He loved her. He had feared that this moment might arrive, had feared her response to it, and his to her, if she ever learned what he was.

At whatever cost he must leave her before either of them said anything unforgivable to the other. Beneath her sweet exterior she was as stern and strong as he was, and to clash might destroy anything good and true which might yet lie between them.

Duty prevailed on him even as he reached the door to leave. He turned. 'One thing, Clare. You said that you had a message for me from my mother. What was it?'

'I will try to repeat her exact words,' said Clare, through numb lips. '"Tell him he has an enemy inside his own organisation, who hates him and wishes to destroy him. One he thinks of as a friend. Tell him also that the man who pretended to be the friend of both Anthony Mallory and Jeremy Peele is also heavily involved in this business. They know that you are both going to the Hendon Air Display. Use every caution if you do." That is all.'

'Boy and Jeremy's friend must be Gordon Stewart. I was sure that he was part of a Bolshevik spy ring. It fits. But the other, my false friend? Now, that could be any one of half a dozen.'

He paused, looked at her white face. Something he had said to her earlier had apparently struck home, had already caused her to question a little her anger at his deception of her. He gave her a strained smile, a parody of his usual openly cheerful one.

'Thank you, Clare, you did very well—although I bitterly regret that I consented to your visit to her. Do I expect to see you at dinner?'

He was giving her a chance to stay away to avoid him, to play the coward, now that she had challenged him. All the rapport that they had shared, even before last night's joys, had disappeared. They were strangers again.

Clare's head went up proudly. 'Yes, I shall be there. I had thought of going back to Chelsea, taking off my wedding ring. But I will do my duty, Ralph, as you are doing yours. I may not be a soldier but I am a soldier's wife.'

Her words lit a small flame in the ashes of his heart.

CHAPTER FOURTEEN

'I'M SURE that, like all women, you'll fall for cousin Gis. But it's quite hopeless—he's the happiest married man I've ever met,' Ralph said as he drove Clare in his Bentley towards the Air Show. They were passing through one of the less built-up parts of Hendon which in recent times had changed from being a village to a suburb of London. It was a centre of aviation with a flying school and an airfield.

He and Clare were still speaking to one another—to Armstrong's great relief—although the blissful rapport which they had briefly enjoyed after their lovemaking had not yet been restored. They had spent the night apart.

'I knew of him,' Clare replied. 'That he was very wild, that is. He must be greatly changed.'

'It's a family trait,' Ralph returned looking sideways at her, 'that the Schuyler men are rakes in youth, but once married, never look at another woman.'

Was he trying to tell her something? Clare hoped so, but couldn't resist saying, 'That was not true of your father, Ralph.'

'Oh,' replied Ralph carelessly, taking no offence. 'He wasn't a true Schuyler in that respect—or so I was always told.'

After that Clare concentrated on looking about her at a part of England which she had never visited before. Ralph had left the crowded main road which led to the Air Display and they were now driving on a lonely byway through a lightly wooded area on the edge of the house-building which was joining Hendon to London.

A Bentley, similar to Ralph's, had taken the same short cut and was rapidly gaining on them. Despite his daredevil wartime reputation Ralph was not a road hog, and he moved to the nearside of the road to allow it to pass them. Instead of doing so, however, the driver remained just behind Ralph, and began to nudge him off the road altogether.

If at first Ralph had thought that this was accidental, he was soon disabused. The driver, his face obscured by his goggles, grew bolder, and it soon became apparent that, quite deliberately, he was trying to run Ralph off the road, either to kill them both, or to injure them. Clare let out a little cry as their pursuer's purpose became apparent, and Ralph increased his speed to try to escape being forced into the ditch which ran along the byway.

To no avail. The other car was as powerful as his own—which left Ralph with only one thing to do. He allowed their attacker to run side by side with him, then increased his own speed to pass him, at the same time half ramming him in such a manner that the hub of the rear wheel of Ralph's Bentley engaged the hub of the front wheel of the other car. . .

They were travelling at such high speed that, as a result, instead of Ralph being forced into the ditch, it was his attacker who lost control of his steering. He careered across the road, bumped over the opposite ditch and hit a tree, which not only telescoped his Bentley's bonnet, but left him draped, stunned, over the wheel. The biter bit.

Ralph braked, stopped dead, then jumped out and ran across the road, calling to Clare to stay where she was. By the time he reached the stunned driver he was already beginning to stir, groaning gently as he did so. He tore the other man's goggles off to reveal a face that he had never seen before. The man swore at him in an East End accent so thick that Ralph could barely understand it.

Quite remorseless, Ralph seized the dazed man by the throat, swearing back at him, before shouting, 'Who paid you to do this?' for he was suddenly sure that his enemy, whoever he was, had hired some thug from the docklands to try to kill, or injure, him and Clare. If they had been run off the road and killed, their deaths would have looked like a road accident. If, however, they had been only injured or stunned, they would have been finished off with a heavy steel wrench, or anything else handy.

He was also certain that Gabbing Dick had wanted to warn him that one way or another his death had been ordered—and that he had been killed for his pains.

Good luck—and his driving skills—had saved them.

'Don't know, guv'nor. Gawd'strewth,' the injured man gasped. 'Some bloke wot I've never seen before paid me 'andsome to follow you and finish you orf on the way to Hendon—left the Bentley for me to collect. Said it din't matter if I finished it orf as long as I did for you and the tart wiv you.'

Only Clare's presence prevented Ralph from finishing *him* off. Instead, 'Were you to meet him again? To collect your pay?'

Miserably the man tried to shake his head, and winced as he did so. 'You've done me a mortal 'arm, guvnor. I was to pick it up at a drop tomorrow, if I was successful, that is.'

'And what did he look like, this mysterious hirer of murderers?'

'Don't know much o' that, eether. About your height. Sandy hair. . .I fink. Dirty face, dressed like a mechanic, like me. Spoke like you, though.'

Well, Ralph hadn't expected him to be dressed like a gentleman of leisure out for a stroll in Piccadilly. Whoever had arranged this attempt at an assassination must have known that Ralph was driving to the Air Display, and that his non-arrival would mean that he had been 'done for'—and Clare as well. He could only imagine what his would-be killer would make of his survival. . .

He examined the miserable specimen before him who was now trying, but failing, to extricate himself from behind the twisted steering column. By his pallor, and his difficulty in moving, he was more seriously hurt than had at first been apparent.

He had one more question to ask. 'And Gabbing Dick. Who did for him?'

The man's shifty eyes roved away from him. 'Gabbin' Dick, 'oo's he?'

'Liar,' said Ralph pleasantly, thanking God he and Clare had left early for the Display. He now had to decide what to do with an injured would-be murderer— he couldn't leave him where he was, either from common humanity, or the knowledge that he might escape to kill, or maim, again.

'Ralph, what's happening? Was he trying to kill us?'

Clare, tired of sitting in the car, had disobeyed Ralph and come over to them, and was now staring down at her would-be assassin.

'Well, he wasn't indulging in a little light racing,' returned Ralph negligently.

Feeling more than ever like someone in a thriller—
one by Sidney Horler this time—Clare's biggest surprise was to discover that the man trapped behind the
steering wheel seemed so pathetically ordinary. Usually
in novels, would-be murderers looked like evil incar-
nate. Her next remark surprised Ralph by its practi-
cality. 'Where on earth did he get a Bentley from?'

'Provided,' said Ralph briefly. 'Part of the job. Do
you think that you could help me to winkle him out,
Clare? I think that's he's done something serious to his
back.'

'Not I,' groaned his victim. 'I din't do it. It was you
wot done for me.'

'Oh, splendid!' Ralph was more sardonic than ever.
'Not responsible for our actions, are we? Could you
hold him still, Clare, whilst I try to manoeuvre him?
Good girl, that's right.'

'Does he have a name?' ventured Clare. She couldn't
feel sorry for the man but his face was ashen, and he
was obviously in growing pain. Even an animal in a trap
of his own making was to be pitied a little, she thought.

'Sid, miss. The name's Sid Jones. He's a hard man,
your bloke, and no mistake. Nobody warned me of
that.'

'Hold on to my hand, Sid,' she said, 'if this becomes
too painful,' for he had begun to moan under Ralph's
none-too-tender ministrations.

Somehow they wriggled him out. Only to find that he
couldn't stand, and they had to support him across the
road to lay him down in the back of their Bentley.
Ralph was only too thankful that they were on a
deserted byway, and that there were no spectators. He
wanted as little publicity as possible.

* * *

'Here at last,' Ralph said as they drove into the car park at the Air Display. 'Let's hope that Gis hasn't given us up, and that we shall be able to find him in this mob.'

They had taken Sid to a cottage hospital just outside Hendon. By then he had been barely conscious, and Ralph had (anonymously) rung Scotland Yard to tell them where the possible murderer of Gabbing Dick was to be found, and that he had been in a car accident—and where to find the car. One thing was sure, Sid wasn't going to tell the police that he had tried to kill Ralph Schuyler and his companion, and he, Ralph, wasn't going to tell them, either.

Clare's belief that life with Ralph wasn't going to be dull had certainly proved to be a correct one! What had impressed her most of all was the coolness with which he had tackled every attack made on them. When Sid had tried to drive them off the road to their deaths he had reacted so swiftly and surely that it was Sid who was lying on a bed of pain with a damaged back, and not she and Ralph.

And now she was to meet his cousin, the fabled Gis Havilland, pilot and plane designer—to say nothing of exemplary husband and father. She wondered whether she would find him as handsome as everyone said he was. Ralph had told her that she was not to be fooled by his easy manner: that he was remarkably clever beneath the charm.

Typically, as Ralph said afterwards, it was Gis who found them. 'Where have you been, Ralph? I expected you ages ago.'

'What d'you think, Gis? Dodging death, of course.'

This was lightly said, but wasn't a true reflection of Ralph's feelings. What was beginning to move him and was partly causing his unaccustomed taciturnity was the knowledge that Clare was in as great a danger as he was. Even the threats on her life over the telephone had not angered him as much as the reality of the attack on them.

He didn't faze Gis. Nothing, Ralph had once thought, ever would. 'Tell me all about it,' he said coolly—as though dodging death were an everyday thing—so Ralph began the story of Sid's attack on them. But he didn't get very far with it.

Clare, after registering that Gis was as handsome as rumour had said, had been looking eagerly about her, at the crowds, at the massed cars, and the big stand in the far distance where the King and Queen were seated. They were surrounded by officials including Sir Hugh Trenchard, the Air Marshal and the Secretary of State for Air, Samuel Hoare—or Sammy, as Ralph had called him. Quite unexpectedly in the midst of the bustling throng she saw a face which she knew—and hadn't expected to see again.

They were passing a group of uniformed air attachés from foreign Embassies who were walking towards the seats in the stands assigned to them when she clutched at Ralph's arm exclaiming, 'Look! Look! That officer over there. The one in the fancy uniform. He's the dark young man I found with Boy that day.'

Ralph asked gently, 'You're sure, Clare? After all, you said that you only saw him briefly. Answer me under your breath. It's possible that we're being watched.'

'Quite sure.' She shuddered. 'His face is engraved on my memory. Who is he? Do you know him?'

'By sight. He's an air attaché at the embassy where my mother's husband works. Very often another name for a spy.'

Clare was quick to see the inference to be drawn. 'And he was Boy's secret lover. Does that mean that Boy really was connected with a spy ring? That he was being blackmailed because of *him*?'

'Very likely. A man is known by the company he keeps. Eh, Gis?'

Gis nodded inscrutably. A man who liked to talk, he also knew when to keep quiet — as now. He didn't know Clare's story.

'Oh, Ralph! What ought we to do if I'm right? Who ought we to tell?'

Ralph stopped to look into her eyes, forgetting Gis, forgetting everything. He had so nearly lost her, lost his life. Oh, damn his life. Clare was what mattered.

'Nothing, Clare. We tell no one, other than my master when I next see him. What we have found is merely a possible link between Boy and a spy ring, seeing that five years ago they were lovers. What's more, he's a link with my mother — which makes her warning more plausible. Now we can have him followed. We become, at last, the hunter as well as the hunted. And all because of your good memory.'

He dropped his previous resolution to be stern with her because of her mistrust of him; forgot the trouble which had lain between them, and kissed her. 'Whatever you think of me, Clare, you bring me luck. Smile, and look frivolous, as though you hadn't a care in the world. It's important that no one thinks that we're at work!'

She smiled back at him. 'As we were when the police questioned us about Gabbing Dick! About whom, like everyone else connected with your work, I know nothing.'

All her reservations about him, and his secret life,

were beginning to disappear. Three times he had saved her from death or disgrace, and even if she had not loved him, for that alone he deserved her trust. But since she did love him nothing must come between them. True love asks no questions, makes no reservations, but puts itself unconditionally into the hands of the loved one.

What she did not know, and Ralph could not tell her, for he could scarcely believe it himself, was that for some strange reason, even as she had spoken to him of Gabbing Dick, Ralph had remembered what it was that he had heard which had troubled his subconscious mind for the last few days.

The way through the woods, of which he had spoken to the Colonel, was suddenly plain, sadly plain. Even so, he must go carefully, for he might be mistaken. In the meantime it was agreed that the three of them must be on the qui vive. Who knew what they might discover? The day was full of surprises.

On the way to the numbered benches where they were to sit, they had passed the stand where the Air attachés sat, which provoked yet another sardonic comment from Ralph. 'Only the best for our enemies!'

This brought a quiet laugh from Gis and the gloss from him that, 'I thought that we might have had seats in the Royal Enclosure with their Majesties and the Nobs.'

'Well, I was offered that,' Ralph replied, 'but I convinced my master that it would queer our pitch too much if we were sitting in the Royal Enclosure, and then found that we had to start chasing whoever it is who is after us!'

'Will secret agents really be here?' asked Clare

doubtfully. She was just beginning to understand how little she knew of what formed the staple of Ralph's life.

'Oh, they're always present on these occasions.' Ralph was cheerful. 'Hoping, among other things to pick up some information about what Gis, among others, is up to these days, isn't that right, Gis?'

Gis nodded. 'Yes, and it's a really big day today. It's the first time in history that people on the ground have been able to talk with pilots in the air, via radio-telephony.' He said nothing of his own secrets. Not only walls have ears, being his motto.

And wise men have eyes, he might have added, for like Clare, he suddenly saw among the crowds walking by them a face which he had not thought to see again.

Smiling as though he were passing on an excellent joke, he murmured softly to Ralph, 'Follow me, old fellow. I've just seen the missing mechanic, Watson, of whom I told you earlier in the year—the one who gave a false address and disappeared. I think we ought to follow him. My bones are whispering that something is up.'

He directed their attention to a shortish, sandy-haired man who was walking purposefully away from them.

'Yes, but with the proviso that Clare comes with us—for her safety,' Ralph said. 'We can't leave her alone.'

So she walked between the pair of them through the excited crowds. They were so physically unalike that it was difficult to believe that they were related. Gis was as fair as the morning and astonishingly handsome, and Ralph was as dark as the night, his face as angularly harsh and shuttered as Gis's was apparently open, yet they were as one in every other way which mattered.

Where they met and became two sides of a Janus,

God of light and dark, was when they talked to one another. In the short time since she had met Gis it had become plain to Clare that he and Ralph saw the world through the same eyes, shared the same sardonic sense of humour, and had the same fundamental seriousness beneath a mask of idle amusement. They are the brothers Gemini, the twin star, she thought, and how dangerous that makes them!

Above and beyond them the Air Display continued. Gis stopped them once when their quarry halted, and said, pointing upwards, 'Watch! The King is going to give the order to the planes in the air, and they will change formation.'

Clare looked up—to see the biplanes above them turn and wheel in the sky like so many seagulls readying themselves to fly over the ocean, before they landed on the grassy field before her.

The man they were following had obviously paused to watch as well, and then he was off again, walking towards the edge of the field.

Here the crowds had thinned a little, and Gis said softly, 'There!' and nudged Ralph to look over to where their quarry was now talking urgently to another. He had been on his way to an assignation.

Clare recognised the second man immediately, as did Ralph. 'Gordon Stewart, as I live and breathe,' he muttered.

'You know who Watson's with, then?' Gis, being five years or so younger, had not run with the crowd which had included Boy Mallory, Ralph and Jeremy Peele, and had never met Gordon.

'He was Boy Mallory's toady. As I told you earlier, all three of them were sexually compromised and consequently became part of a major spy ring. I'm not yet sure who is running them. Boy, I think, was bisexual, but I suspect that Peele and Stewart were not. Both of them, for different reasons, pretended to be interested in Clare.'

'So, my belief that Watson was the man who tried to steal the plans is almost certainly correct.'

Ralph nodded. 'And we've smoked Stewart out as well. Now, rightly or wrongly, I think that he's only a messenger boy, not a major player, but I could be wrong.'

It was Gis's turn to shake his head. 'I don't think so, Ralph. You have a built-in lie detector—you know that the Yankees have developed a machine which is supposed to tell whether a man is lying or not?'

'Yes. But I have the feeling that a resolute liar could cheat it. One like you, Gis?'

Gis threw back his handsome head and laughed aloud. Clare thought that anyone watching them would assume that they were exchanging idle badinage and not engaged in tracking men who were putting the country's safety in danger.

'Or you, Ralph. If I may return the compliment. When these two part—if they do—I'll follow Stewart who doesn't know me; likewise, you and Clare can safely follow Watson.'

'Agreed.'

Alas, when Gordon and Watson went their different ways they learned nothing more. Gordon walked to the Royal Enclosure where he spent a blameless afternoon among several important personages, and Watson joined a youngish woman who was sitting on the grass on the airfield's perimeter. By her appearance and behaviour she was his wife and had been expecting him.

Ralph and Clare watched him from a distance for some time, but it was plain that, his meeting with Gordon over, Watson was simply enjoying the show.

To Clare's great relief, the rest of the afternoon passed without incident—if RAF planes travelling at 150 miles an hour and blowing up a mock-up of a battle-cruiser hidden among tropical vegetation could be so described!

'What did you think of Gis?' Ralph asked Clare as he skilfully negotiated the Bentley through the streaming crowds leaving Hendon.

'That he is all that you—and rumour—said.'

Ralph nodded thoughtfully. 'And that you are very like him,' Clare added.

'Like him? I would have thought that we were very unalike.'

'In looks, yes. But in character, no. When we were following Watson, you were like a pair of matched greyhounds straining in the slips.'

She could see that he was pleased, but he made no further comment until they were driving down Oxford Street. 'Would you mind if I dropped you at Park Lane, and then left you? I promise not to be too long before I'm home again.'

He knew that the Colonel would be at his Club, the Travellers', in Pall Mall and it was urgent that he speak to him. Lives might even depend on it, he said to her, without mentioning who it was he was going to see.

'It's your work, isn't it, Ralph?' she told him. 'Of course, you may. After this afternoon I promise never to be stupid about it again. It's your duty.'

He wanted to kiss the earnest face which she had turned towards him. It was she, who by her reference to

Gabbing Dick, had jogged his memory, and opened up a whole new line of thought—about which he needed to consult the Colonel.

Another thought struck him. 'Our friend Sid—if you can remember that far back—might provide the blood-hounds of Scotland Yard with another chance to have a go at me—unofficially. Officially, they've been told to lay off me. I wonder what it is they think I'm up to! I should like to find out why Malcolm is being so determined to nail me—that's why I rang to inform him about Sid.'

Inspector Malcolm didn't know what Ralph was up to. Only that he was up to something.

When the message about Sid Jones came through to him, he called to Johnson who was sitting glumly at his desk catching up with paperwork, 'That's it. Leave that bumph, man. We're off to Hendon. An anonymous call saying that Gabbing Dick's possible murderer is in the cottage hospital outside Hendon. Injured in a car accident.'

'Come on, guv'nor,' whined Johnson. 'You know as how we was told to lay off the Gabbing Dick murder.'

'Oh, damn that for a fairy tale, Johnson. I'm not ignoring a gift from heaven like this just because Special Branch leaned on the Commissioner. What's the betting that our little playmate, Mr Ralph Schuyler, is mixed up in this, somehow?'

He thought so even more when later the woman at the hospital who had admitted Sid described the man and the woman who had brought Dick in. They had departed without leaving their names.

'Dark, stocky gent, natty dresser, drives a Bentley, the woman a pretty blonde! What did I say, Johnson? It's *him* again.'

He had hoped to interview Sid, but he was unconscious. Sid's back was not broken, but he had been filled
full of painkillers, and couldn't be roused until the
morning. Meantime, a local police constable was told
off to watch by his bed. Johnson and Malcolm examined
Sid's Bentley, still crumpled against the tree, and which
told them a little of the nature of the accident which had
hospitalised him.

'Another interview with Master Ralph in the morning,' announced Malcolm gleefully to a disenchanted
Johnson, who saw his chances of promotion going down
the drain as his guv'nor banged about London like a
loose cannon!

CHAPTER FIFTEEN

'MADAM is waiting for you in the drawing-room,' murmured Armstrong when Ralph let himself into the hall much later that night. 'She told me to have coffee and sandwiches ready for you, sir, when you returned in case you needed them. A most thoughtful lady, sir, if I may say so.'

'Indeed you may,' replied Ralph wearily, shrugging himself out of his suit jacket and ripping off his tie, allowing Armstrong to give him the usual pitying stare which he always adopted when Ralph abandoned any show of formality in dress.

'Would you allow me to fetch your smoking jacket, sir, and a silk scarf, seeing that you have left off your tie? Madam might be disconcerted at such a breach of etiquette.'

He didn't add, 'You are not living alone now, sir,' because he thought that he didn't need to.

'No, to your question, and no she won't to your statement. I have found that very little disconcerts madam.'

'If you say so, sir. I will serve the coffee in the drawing-room as soon as possible.'

Madam wasn't disconcerted. Clare rose when Ralph entered, saying, 'You look very tired, Ralph. It has been a long day for you. Armstrong is going to serve us coffee and sandwiches. Would you like a brandy first?'

He gave a slight shudder. 'Heavens, no. The Colonel has been plying me with drink for the last few hours.

Coffee will be splendid.' He did not add how comforting it was to come home to a pretty woman who was so careful of his welfare. In such a situation, Eva would have been petulantly making demands on him from the moment he had walked into the room.

Nor did she badger him about his interview with the Colonel. He lay back in his chair, closed his eyes, and only opened them again when Armstrong had come and gone and Clare was pouring out the coffee.

'I'd no idea that I was so hungry,' he told her, picking up a ham sandwich and beginning to devour it.

'Not surprising, it's hours since you ate. I don't suppose that you had anything at the Travellers'.'

'Only drink, as I said.'

He rose and walked to the sofa where he patted the seat beside him. 'Come and sit by me, Clare. I need a sympathetic body nearly as much as food. Which reminds me — I hope that you have had something to eat.'

'A little,' she said. 'And you? Has Armstrong brought you enough?'

'It's not really food I want,' he said slowly. 'Although I'm grateful to you for providing it. It's comfort. Let me hold you, Clare. Just hold you. I need to know that there is someone true and honest in the world.'

Something was seriously wrong, she knew. Earlier in their relationship she would have questioned him, but she said nothing — just allowed him to put an arm around her shoulders, and lean her back so that both their heads were resting on the sofa's back. There was nothing overtly sexual about anything he was saying or doing.

'I suppose,' he began slowly, 'at my age, and after my experiences in the war, I shouldn't be surprised at anything human beings can do to one another. But there is a form of treachery so vile that killing in war seems clean beside it. That is when a man not only betrays his country, but also sends his friends, who have absolute trust in him, to their deaths.'

Clare said nothing. He needed to talk without interruption. He was showing her the serious side of him, all mockery gone. He sat up suddenly, and let go of her. 'I can't prove it, Clare, even though I know that I'm right. And because of that, a lot of other men may be doomed—and you and I, too. You, because of what he thinks you might know.'

He could tell her no more. The less she knew, the safer she was—though now that might not even be true. He had found the Colonel at his Club, and one look at Ralph's face told his master that Ralph thought that he had discovered something important.

Alone in a small private room, Ralph had said urgently, 'Confirm, sir, that I have never told you the name of my East End informant.'

'You know you haven't, Schuyler. Separate boxes, no leakage from one to another.'

'So, I have told no one who he was and now you are confirming that I have never let slip his name to you. Right?'

'Right, Schuyler.'

'In that case, how did George Pryde know not only his name—but that he had been murdered? Something which I have never told anyone but you.'

The Colonel tugged at his greying moustache. 'I suppose that he might have found out quite legitimately. Remember that he's in a box of his own as well.'

Ralph shook his head. 'I'm sure that he couldn't have

known. My informant had a nickname like Little John's was. It seemed to mean that he talked—but he never did. Only to me. That I know for sure. The only way in which Pryde could have known of him was if he had had me followed.'

'You're hinting that Pryde is our unknown inside traitor, eh?' admitted the Colonel at last. 'Let me put it to you another way. Why shouldn't *he* follow *you*?— thinking that you're the traitor.'

'Oh, I know I'm not,' said Ralph, 'and my life has been twice attempted recently because I'm getting too near this unknown spy ring. Has Pryde's?'

The Colonel shrugged. 'Boxes again. Who's to know? Have you any other evidence? This you claim to have is a bit thin. Couldn't put a man I know and trust in the Tower and shoot him for that. Bring me something more substantial than this. How, by the way, did he give himself away? Admit he knew?'

'He didn't admit anything,' Ralph said. 'It came out in careless conversation when I wasn't even attending to him. It was the day I went to Roehampton and I was in a deuce of a hurry. Clare said something to me today at Hendon which brought it back. I realised that I had heard something wrong lately, but until then I couldn't remember what it was—that Pryde gave himself away by twitting me about Gabbing Dick's death. Of which he wasn't supposed to know.'

'Still damned thin, you must admit. You might not even have heard correctly. I couldn't entertain such an idea about Pryde. Like believing the Prince of Wales is a traitor! Say no more to me or anyone until you have some hard evidence. This is nothing—flimflam.'

Ralph tried to convince the Colonel by reporting the day's events to him, including Sid's attack. He had to admit that he had nothing to link Pryde in any way with Boy Mallory, Jeremy Peele, Gordon Stewart, or Watson, Gis's mechanic, or any missing secrets. Even with Gordon and Watson, as the Colonel pointed out, he was running more on intuition than evidence. Even quoting Gis Havilland made no dent in the armour of the Colonel's belief in Pryde.

'Knew Pryde's father at Sandhurst,' reminisced the Colonel. 'Killed on the Somme. Left Pryde strapped for cash. Both good men—only too happy to have him with me. Some other feller letting us down, I'm sure of it.'

Gis had spoken of his bones telling him something, and that he always believed them. Ralph felt the same. He left the Colonel feeling dazed and empty. His master had offered him drink and he had not liked to refuse. Worse, he had the distinct impression that by even querying Pryde's patriotism he had made a *faux pas* of enormous size.

So he put his arm around Clare and tried to think of some means of proving what he was sure was true before any more deaths could be laid at Pryde's door. He sighed, such a sigh that Clare said as gently as she could, 'I know something's troubling you, Ralph. Is it very important?'

'Very.'

'And you can't tell me?'

'You're in enough trouble as it is, Clare. I can't put you in even more danger.'

She couldn't argue with him. It was strange that they were now more physically close—outside of the act of love, that was—than they had ever been, and yet the emotion which ran between them had nothing to do with sex and everything to do with compassion and friendship. It was almost as though they had been married for years and sexual union was no longer necessary to bind them together.

Clare thought of something her aunt had told her, and which had always worked for her.

'Ralph,' she said, and her voice was hesitant, for his experience of the harsh realities of life was so vast and hers was so small that she was reluctant to advise him. 'My aunt used to say that the best thing to do with a vexing problem if you wished to solve it, was to let it go, to forget it. Then, and only then, did light break in on it—and afterwards you wondered why you found it so hard to solve. It worked for her, and I found that it worked for me. . . That's all.'

Ralph sat up energetically. 'I'm sure you're right. But it's the forgetting bit that's hard. Oh, God, I don't know what to do!' For the first time, the eyes which he turned on her were appealing to her for assistance. The strong man was turning to his woman not simply for absolution, but for help as he swam in the deep waters of life, being pulled down by the undertow.

'Bed,' said Clare simply. 'Bed—to sleep—or not—as you wish. It has been a long and hard day for both of us. My aunt also said that sleeping on a problem helped to solve it. Who knows, that might work for you.'

'Bed it is then,' Ralph returned. 'Although I am not sure how much use I shall be to you in it tonight.'

'No matter,' Clare said. 'I feel that I could sleep for a week.'

Sleep visited them both immediately but not for a week. In the early hours, before dawn broke, they both woke at the same time. Ralph turned to Clare, and the passion that had been suppressed the night before in the aftermath of his feelings of failure and helplessness was revived more strongly than ever.

The act of life—for that is what true love is, Ralph was beginning to find—restored his faith in himself. When Clare fell asleep in his arms, 'the lineaments of satisfied desire' written on her face, Ralph was sure that somehow or other he would solve his problem to his own satisfaction.

Not that he thought so when, as they were finishing breakfast, Armstrong came in to tell them that the police had arrived again and wished to question them both.

'Well, Inspector, I can't say that I am glad to see you at this hour,' was Ralph's opening gambit, 'but at least you don't arrive at dawn to haul us off to the dungeons, as I am informed that they do in the Soviet Union.'

'You will have your little joke, sir,' returned Malcolm, stone-faced. Clare was dismally sure by his manner that he thought that he had something on them. She wondered how wise Ralph had been to inform Scotland Yard about Sid. Nothing else but that could have brought them here so early.

If Ralph was worried, there was nothing to show that he was. Even when Malcolm refused a seat, coffee, breakfast even, in tones which showed that he considered Ralph to be a number one enemy of the state, Ralph remained as insouciant as his cousin Gis usually was—a feat in itself.

'Where were you and your lady yesterday, Mr Schuyler? It is important that you give me a truthful answer. Both of you—and that man of yours as well.'

'Oh, dear,' said Ralph sweetly. 'Now why should I lie?' He turned to Clare who was trying to look innocent and succeeding remarkably well. 'If, by chance, I tell the Inspector an untruth, you will correct me, won't you, sweetheart? My one aim is always to help the police.'

Sergeant Johnson couldn't help giving a suppressed snort of laughter as this blatant untruth was gaily shot at both of them. If possible, Inspector Malcolm became even more stone-faced.

'I would like an answer, sir.'

'And you shall have one. In company with about a hundred thousand others I was visiting the Air Display at Hendon. A most remarkable event, Inspector. If you weren't there you should have been. Truly historic, it was.'

Holding back the giggles as Ralph did his imitation of Bertie Wooster was taxing all Clare's strength of will: it was the Inspector's patience which was being taxed.

'No doubt, sir. I am supposing that you went in your Bentley, sir, and took your good lady with you. Did you stop anywhere on the way, or become involved in an accident?'

'Oh, you suppose right, Inspector. But I am at a loss as to why my itinerary yesterday should be of such burning interest to Scotland Yard. We made good time to Hendon where we met my cousin Gis Havilland and spent the afternoon with him. In the evening I visited the Travellers' Club in Pall Mall, and stayed there until late.'

'It is your journey to Hendon with which I am concerned, sir. A man answering to your description, with a female companion answering to that of Mrs Schuyler, delivered a semi-conscious man who had been in a road accident at the cottage hospital outside Hendon. They arrived and left in a Bentley similar to yours.'

He consulted his notebook. 'At roughly the same

time someone phoned into the Yard that a man named
Sid Jones who had been left at the hospital was involved
in the murder of the minor criminal, Gabbing Dick,
about whom I questioned you some days ago. Were you
that man, Mr Schuyler, and was the lady with you your
wife?'

'Now why,' asked Ralph melodramatically, 'should
you suppose that?'

'Because you were on your way to Hendon at that
time. You drive a Bentley and you were involved with
Gabbing Dick.'

Ralph turned to Clare, who was now wondering by
what legerdemain he could get them out of this. 'Now,
my dear, let me see if I can explain to you the logic of
the Inspector's questions—because for the life of me I
can't make sense of them.

'Yesterday, I, in company with a hundred thousand
others, quite a few of whom were driving Bentleys, and
had a female companion with them, drove to Hendon
Air Display. The Inspector accuses me of being
involved in a road accident with a man who was
somehow involved with a criminal named Gabbing
Dick—whom I am supposed to have known—although
the Inspector has no proof of any of this. I am then
supposed to have driven him to the hospital, left him
there, and for some strange reason telephoned Scotland
Yard about him.

'Who is the madman here—he or I?'

He clutched his brow melodramatically.

Johnson thought his guv'nor, faced with such impu-
dence, was about to burst.

Malcolm said, his voice dripping vitriol, 'We could, of
course, ask the receptionist at the hospital if they can
identify you and Mrs Schuyler.'

This time Ralph was openly smiling at him. 'I think not, Inspector. To do that you would have to arrest us. And what grounds do you have to do any such thing?'

'I would like to question your wife now, sir.' Malcolm' patience was fraying rapidly.

'Oh, I think not.' Ralph was as charmingly carefree as a man could be. 'You have questioned me, and I have given you an answer. My wife's evidence in a case involving her husband is not evidence, as you well know. If you do have any further questions to ask me, I hope that they are based on more evidence than a supposed identification at second hand. If not, then I must ask you to leave.'

The dam burst.

'You're all the same, the whole damned lot of you,' Malcolm roared, ignoring Johnson who was tugging at his arm. 'You think that you gentry can walk on poor devils like me doing their proper job. And you aren't even men, damn you. I know your sort. You pansies are protected all the way—Foreign Office nancy boys, every one of you. Oh, I know what Boy Mallory was, and Peele. No wonder that they were murdered. And that pal of yours, George Pryde, he was lucky not to be sent to prison all those years ago when he was picked up in Hyde Park with a couple of guardsmen. How he got away with it, I shall never know.

'Oh, yes, I've been investigating you and your dubious friends, Mr Schuyler, sir. And what about you? Swing both ways do you, like Boy Mallory, or are you a hard case like Pryde? I only know about him because the Inspector who arrested him was so disgusted he disobeyed orders and didn't destroy the papers relating to his case.

'Chickens coming home to roost, Mr Schuyler, sir.

Are you one of the birds I'm going to down? Do you like Hyde Park for a walk or do you get your jollies picking up the likes of Gabbing Dick in docklands...?'

By now Malcolm was purple in the face, frothing at the mouth, and Johnson was pulling at him, 'Sir, sir, leave it. It's not worth destroying your career to put him down, sir.'

'No, don't stop, Inspector.' Ralph's harsh face was, for once, showing his true feelings. 'Do go on. I find this fascinating. I could bring certificated evidence that I am so violently heterosexual that I'm a menace to good society, but I won't.'

Inside he was bubbling over with joy. Here was the link, the one thing which bound all these men together. And, as he had thought, Pryde was part of it... The evidence had fallen into his hands like a ripe fruit—or rather, a rotting one...

Later, when the Inspector had gone, staring mute threats at him as Johnson mildly took over the questioning—trying to mend matters, Clare supposed—she remonstrated with Ralph over the manner in which he had spoken to the Inspector.

'I know that it's annoying for you to be hounded by the police, Ralph, but you were a trifle harsh with the poor man, weren't you? I'm not surprised that he attacked you so violently at the end. It was almost as though you were goading him into losing his temper.'

'Clever girl,' said Ralph, kissing her on the nose. He was full of *joie de vivre* again. 'That's exactly what I was doing. Oh, I'm not proud of the way I treated a poor devil who was only trying to do his duty, but I did it with a purpose. I had to know why he was chasing me with such mad zeal. And it worked—as you saw. What's more, in his anger he told me something which he didn't intend to, something which he thought that I knew—but I didn't. . .'

'That George Pryde was involved in Boy's secret goings-on,' Clare offered.

'Exactly. Yes, you are a clever girl, Clare, and clever girls get their reward—but not now, not yet—later.' His amber eyes glowed promises at her.

'I had no idea that Pryde's tastes ran that way. He's not married, but he's had girlfriends, quite a lot of them. But guardsmen—in Hyde Park—and caught by the police—and let go by orders from on high—that's worrying.'

He was pacing up and down, his mind now far away from her. He had become a bloodhound, sniffing on the trail. Did the Colonel know? Or suspect? Ralph could not believe that he did. Pryde was the son of his old friend, a gallant soldier, dead in the service of his country—and therefore above suspicion. There was a weakness there, and one that Ralph had not suspected.

How many men had died because of it? And now Ralph had a problem. For there was always the slight possibility that the Colonel himself had become involved in treachery, and because of that Ralph dare not go to him with what he knew. He was on his own, now. Colonel B had suddenly become a liability—not an ally.

What was worse was that Ralph—a true Schuyler in his clear view of the world, free from illusion—suddenly saw that the day of men like the Colonel was over. The Great War had created a new world in which the values of the Colonel and his kind had become outdated, even dangerous, for they assumed that men still adhered to a code of honour simply because they belonged to a particular class. And this was no longer true.

The Colonel had gone to school with Pryde's father, had known Pryde since he was a child, and those two facts meant that he considered Pryde as above suspicion.

But Ralph stood between the two worlds, the old and the new. His honour was grounded first in himself, and then in those whom he served, and he took nothing for granted. He judged those around him by what they said and did, not by what they were, or claimed to be.

He was alone in a world whose foundations were shaking.

He stopped thinking, saw Clare looking at him, her whole expression a testament to their love—and for the first time in his thirty-five years he understood that he was using the wrong tense to think of himself.

He *had* been alone, but was alone no longer. He had Clare, and what had been for him simply an affair, even though they were married, was also no longer true. Loving Clare had transformed things for him forever. He was engaged with her in an affair of honour, the first and last of its kind he was ever to share with anyone. His duty to his country and his duty to Clare were two sides of the same coin. He must be faithful to both.

Which, he knew, put him in a cleft stick, because it was his duty to protect Clare, and that might yet compromise his duty to his country; although he prayed not.

He also knew something else. That his carefree days were over. That, like his cousin Gis, who had found his true love when he had been so much younger than Ralph, he was committed to another, body and soul, and his world was turned upside down.

Clare read him correctly. Saw him close his eyes, and came over to where he stood, transfixed.

'What is it, Ralph?'

'Nothing. Something,' he said, putting his arms around her and hugging her fiercely to him. 'Oh, Clare—' and he buried his face in the scent of her neck '—be with me always. When this is over, continue to be my wife—all loose talk of annulment forgotten. Whatever I said to you before we married, I could not bear to lose you. I think that when I proposed to you I meant what I said at the deepest level of my being, even if the terms I offered you seemed far from that. I love you, Clare. I have loved you from the moment I first met you at Bitsy's party.'

They stood for a moment without moving, entwined. Clare twisted free from him, to look up at the dark harsh face above her soft fair one. There were tears in his eyes. She had never thought to see him so moved.

'You must know that I love you, too, Ralph. From the beginning, as you said. Which was so strange, because I thought that I hated you on sight.'

He laughed tenderly as he nuzzled her neck. 'Oh, I was my usual domineering self with you, Clare. I'd grown too used to the Eva's of this world to know how to deal with pure gold.' He tightened his grip on her.

'I've always dodged commitment, Clare, and now it frightens me. They say that your children are hostages to fortune, but I am fearful that now I have you, *you* might become a hostage. Pray God that this trouble we are in will soon be over—and that we can forget it and live normal lives again.'

At last he loosened his grip. The busy treacherous world in which he had lived for so long was claiming him again—but not for long, for a new world was opening up before him.

Before he left her, Ralph had not needed to tell Clare that he was now on his own, sailing uncharted seas. Something resolute in his demeanour, the stern set of his mouth, his walk, as though he were wearing uniform once again, were all as revealing to her as mere words. She was almost frightened of her ability to read him when she had not been able to read Boy at all. It simply proved to her how little she had really loved Boy, how inexperienced she had been when she had known him.

She was not, therefore, surprised when shortly afterwards, Ralph sent for her to join him in his study. She found Armstrong with him, looking serious for once. Ralph spoke to them both as though he were addressing his troops, without preamble.

'It is more imperative than ever, Clare, that you never go out without Armstrong accompanying you. And Armstrong, I expect you to be her bodyguard in every sense of the word. I shall make sure that you are armed. You understand me? I'm relying on you to protect her.'

He said this as coolly as though he were not suggesting something quite outrageous—that London's streets were no longer safe for Clare to walk in. But what he was about to do was dangerous, not only for himself, but for those whom he loved.

'A bodyguard for me and armed. . .' Clare exclaimed. 'But what about you, Ralph? Who is to guard you?'

'Myself,' he said, unsmiling, 'as I have always done.'

Neither of them argued with him: Armstrong, because he owed his life to obeying his Major's orders, and Clare, because the events of the last few weeks had shown her that beneath the apparently calm surface of the world in which she lived lay a boiling volcano of hate and treachery, ready to erupt at any moment. In any society the crust of civilisation is thin, and its guardians—like Ralph—constantly risk their lives to preserve it.

After Armstrong had gone, he rang Gis Havilland and talked to him for some time. For a reason she did not understand, Clare had walked out of the room when he did so. Whatever else, she was not going to be the kind of wife who insisted on being in on all her husband's secrets. If Ralph wished her to know what he and Gis were discussing, he would tell her.

Ralph also wrote a long letter, with the words 'Only to be opened in the event of my death' on the envelope, to be delivered by hand to his half-brother, Lord Longthorne. He had spent some time over the doing, quite unlike his usual rapid mode of work.

Some little time after he had left for the Foreign Office, a special messenger delivered a letter for him marked MOST URGENT. Clare called in Armstrong, who was now her faithful ally, to help her to decide what to do with it. They finally agreed that Jack, the boy of all work, should deliver it to Ralph by hand.

'For,' as Armstrong said, agreeing with her, 'who knows how important it might be? And if it isn't, madam, nothing lost, eh,' and he gave her a conspiratorial wink. 'Best put it in another envelope with a message from you inside, if I may so advise. Under the circumstances—and the Major is plainly troubled about something—MOST URGENT might be a bit of a giveaway, might even end up in the wrong hands. The Major knows your handwriting, and that what you are sending on to him must be important.'

Not for the first time Clare realised that Armstrong was more than Ralph's servile, if somewhat cheeky, man. Ralph didn't even need to tell Armstrong any details of what he was doing. He seemed to know them by osmosis!

All the way to the Foreign Office, Ralph was thinking of what Gis had advised. 'Go carefully, Ralph. You have Clare to think of now, but I agree that you are on your own until you have evidence that those above you are clear of suspicion. That Pryde *is* your man seems plain to me—but everything else is dark. Guard your back, little cousin, and God bless.'

He had approved Ralph's plan of action, even though he agreed that it might be dangerous '—but failing support from above, there seems little else you can try.'

There were letters and papers on his desk. Ralph was almost too distracted to read them. He must not burst in on Pryde and go off half-cock. He knew that Pryde was in his room, and was likely to be there for the rest of the day—new orders from the Colonel permitting. He was trying to work when Jack delivered the message from Clare to him. Reading it, the last brick in the wall of suspicion surrounding Pryde was cemented into place. It also told him something else which left him feeling surprisingly and strangely sad.

He looked at the clock. Eleven. Pryde would be drinking tea brought to him by one of the junior female clerks. Ralph rarely drank tea in the morning but decided to do so today. It gave him a useful excuse to visit his enemy. He put his head round Pryde's door. Yes, he had a china tea cup in his hand.

'Time for a chat and some tea?' he enquired politely.

Pryde waved his cup at him. 'Always, old chap. I'll ring for a cup for you.'

'Thanks,' Ralph said, sitting himself down in a chair

placed at an oblique angle to Pryde's desk. 'Wanted your advice. Delicate matter. Don't want to trouble the Colonel yet. Forget about boxes for once, eh?'

'Fine by me,' said Pryde. 'What's the problem?' He was leaning back in his chair: a handsome man in the same style as Boy Mallory—an effete version of Gis Havilland, Ralph thought, studying him more closely than usual. Fair, rather willowy, civilised and polished enough to hurt.

'It's like this.' Ralph leaned forward confidentially. 'You know that the Colonel has had me on the trail of a supposed spy ring, which was set in place some five years ago. He thinks that they had an informant in our ranks then, and that he's still with us now. Worse, he belonged to a circle of homosexual friends who were blackmailed into giving their secrets away when they worked for us. Boy Mallory and Peele were among them.

'I believe that they didn't know that he was giving our enemies, the Bolsheviks, their names. They probably thought that he was another victim, as they were. In fact, I'm not sure why he turned traitor. I can't believe that he's a Bolshevik, someone who thinks that the Soviet Union is paradise. I rather think that the money they must have been paying him is the attraction. Are you with me, Pryde? I'm not going too fast for you, am I?'

Pryde's eyes on him were as steady as his voice—betrayed nothing but polite interest. 'Not at all, Schuyler. Most lucid. Do go on, this is deeply interesting.'

'Indeed. For some reason, shame possibly, Boy Mallory committed suicide. Our traitor lay low for some time, then started up again. Imagine his horror when another member of the group told him that he feared that Peele was going to tell Clare Windham the truth about Boy's death, and his own involvement in the spy ring.

'So Peele had to die, and Clare, now my wife, was set up to look like the murderess. Fortunately for her, she and I had become acquainted and she never turned up for the rendezvous, meeting me instead. So our traitor still couldn't be sure that he was safe, and when Clare and I became engaged he tried to dispose of both of us. Twice. He also had one of my informants killed in case he knew more than he should and tried to tell me of it.

'Now, I believe that I know who the traitor is, and my problem is that I'm not sure that Colonel B isn't somehow involved. You see, when I discovered the connection between our traitor and Mallory and Peele I also found out something else. He had been arrested for homosexual behaviour—and the police had been ordered to let him go. I believe that mistakenly, the Colonel won't move against this man because he thinks that he couldn't possibly be a spy.

'So, what do you advise me to do?'

He leaned back, smiling ingenuously at Pryde. He had to hand it to him. Pryde had never so much as blinked whilst the tale of his treachery was unfolded, which was in itself surprising. He should have been full of horror at discovering that one of his colleagues was selling secrets to the Russians and arranging the murder of his friends.

'I could help you more,' Pryde offered coolly, 'if you told me the traitor's name. Or, rather, the name of the man you suspect to be a traitor.'

'Couldn't do that, old man.' Ralph shook his head. 'Just wanted your advice as to what to do, seeing that I

can't tell the Colonel of my suspicions. I don't want to
be accused of blackguarding a common friend.'

'I see.' Pryde rearranged some papers on his desk.
'How strong is your evidence, if I may ask that?'

'Oh, very strong.' Ralph's tone was almost careless. 'I
first suspected him when I realised that he knew about
my most secret doings—even though I hadn't told him,
the Colonel, or anyone else of them. I know who his
underling is, as well. The man who does some of his leg
work for him. I *can* tell you his name. It's Gordon
Stewart.'

'Now, that doesn't surprise me,' mused Pryde. 'Not a
reliable feller at all, I agree. Pity you can't tell me more.
Have you told anyone else?'

'Well, that's it, Pryde. Perhaps I ought to confide in
you more. I've written a letter to Lord Longthorne, my
distant relative. He's to open it in case anything unto-
ward happens to me. He has the ear of our ultimate
masters, you know.'

'Yes, I do know that, Schuyler. As usual, you seem to
have covered everything. Anything else I ought to be
aware of? So that I can help.' This last came out
casually.

Ralph stood up. 'Only that I am close to making a
complete case against him. Get him cornered. Nowhere
to go.'

The double-edged conversation was almost over.
Pryde knew perfectly well that Ralph was speaking of
him, knew that he was the traitor. He must also suspect
that Ralph was not as sure as he sounded about being
able to make a strong enough case against him to put
him at risk.

He was being challenged by a man who was as clever
and ruthless as he thought himself to be. A man who

would stop at nothing in his determination to expose him for the traitor he was. He had only two lines of action open to him. He could stay where he was and defy Schuyler to do his worst—a situation fraught with danger, for he had no illusions about how strong Gordon Stewart might be if faced with detection and a traitor's death by firing squad. Turning King's evidence was the best he could expect from *him*.

Or, he could bolt—which was what Ralph was goading him to do, to save scandal. He had a cottage at Broadstairs, and a small yacht in which he could sail to France and from there travel secretly to the country which had been paying him so handsomely since the end of the war. It little mattered that he had no idea what might await him in the Soviet Union. He was no believer in Bolshevism, but ruin, and most likely a shameful death, was his fate if he stayed. To go, he hoped, might be better than that.

And in the going, if he were cunning, he might deal that swine Schuyler a mortal blow. One which would leave him wishing that he had not meddled with George Pryde. But he had no time to lose. . .

He picked up the telephone and rang Gordon Stewart.

CHAPTER SIXTEEN

THE thing Clare hugged to her heart was that Ralph had told her that he loved her. It was something which she had never expected. Oh, she knew that she loved him, but she had thought that it was a doomed love. He was so self-sufficient, so much in command of himself that she had never hoped that he would admit that something controlled his life other than his own indomitable will .

To tell her that he loved her was in some measure to surrender all that he had previously lived by. That lust was the mere meeting of flesh, never of minds, that lust was barren, but love was joyful, was perhaps still a lesson which Ralph had to learn. It would be a pleasure to teach him: it would give meaning to his sexual expertise, change it from some feat, like doing the long jump, into a celebration of life and its mysteries.

Merely thinking of it made Clare unable to work. Her translation was nearly finished, but she could not put her mind to it: it seemed meaningless beside the enormous thing which had just happened to her. Around lunchtime she was still contemplating the fact that she was blessed among women, when Armstrong rapped on the door to tell her that Miss Angela Windham was on the telephone and wished to speak to her.

Now this *was* a surprise. Even more of a surprise when Angela positively cooed at her.

'I do hope that I'm not interrupting anything, Clare,

but we—I, that is—wondered if you would care to come round to tea today. There might be some news which would interest you.'

Clare couldn't imagine what Angela could have to tell her which was of the slightest possible interest, but as usual she did her duty, and said resignedly, 'Of course. What time?'

'Oh, early,' sighed Angela. 'You do know the way?'

Seeing that Clare had lived there on and off for twenty years before Angela had taken up residence with her parents, this was a somewhat redundant question.

Nevertheless, she reassured Angela that she did know the way to her family's London home well enough to instruct Armstrong to drive her to it. 'No use asking Ralph, I suppose,' Angela said, immediately before ringing off. 'Gordon tells me that he is extremely busy these days.'

'Very true.' Clare was dry. 'I don't expect him home until late this evening.'

She forbore to add that Ralph would not exactly be overjoyed to visit the Windham ménage again. She wasn't exactly overjoyed at the prospect herself but since her family was seeing fit to wave olive branches at her the least that she could do was to let bygones be bygones and take them from their limp fingers.

Early probably meant about three o'clock, so promptly at that hour Armstrong, in his role as body-guard, took over from the chauffeur and drove her to South Farm Street at the back of Berkeley Square.

At first he refused to go in with her. 'Not fitting, madam. In any case, a visit to your family can hardly be regarded as dangerous,' a remark he would later rue when he faced a distraught Ralph.

Clare, thinking of Ralph's anger if Armstrong was less than totally vigilant, assured him that the kitchen staff would be only too happy to entertain him. Thus encouraged, he gave way, parked the Rolls outside and introduced himself to the small servants' hall where Cook served him the same tea which the drawing-room was about to enjoy.

If Clare had had any doubts of the warmth of her welcome, they disappeared as soon as she was shown into the front drawing-room. Her mother, her eyes full of tears threw her arms around her, and even Angela and her aunt offered her small conciliatory smiles. The Brigadier's flag of truce consisted of a gruff, 'You look well, Clare. Marriage seems to suit you.'

But it was the fourth person in the room who constituted something of a surprise, and not a welcome one. Jumping to his feet as she entered, Gordon Stewart, dressed nearly as nattily as Ralph himself, thrust a welcoming hand at her when her family had finished celebrating the return of the prodigal daughter.

'Hullo, Clare. Your father is right. You do look fit.'

Giving him the smallest smile she could, Clare found herself wondering what on earth he was doing being present at all. Knowing what she did about him, she thought for a moment of feigning faintness and calling on Armstrong to take her home at once.

Apparent common sense took over. What on earth could he do to her, here in her parents' respectable home? She must be sensible, not develop a persecution mania where, as the saying had it, every bush became a bear. A dreadful thought struck her as Gordon next took Angela's arm possessively and tenderly sat her down. Could it conceivably be that Angela had asked her to be present to hear Gordon announce their engagement?

She was so stricken by the very idea that she almost missed her father asking her how she was finding life now that she was married. She took refuge in small talk, certain from the way in which they were all behaving that her belief was correct. And knowing the rituals of the Windhams' lives, the announcement of the engagement would be made over afternoon tea.

In the words of the marriage service: could she possibly forbid the banns even before Angela and Gordon reached church? She couldn't knowingly allow Angela to become engaged to a man whom Ralph and Gis thought was spying for the Bolsheviks. Hysterical laughter bubbled inside her at the very thought of her family's disbelieving reaction if she told them the truth about him.

No. The thing to do was to keep quiet. Otherwise she might compromise Ralph. Once again the sheer difficulty of knowing secrets and being unable to do anything about them struck her. First it was Boy Mallory about whom she could say nothing, and now it was Gordon Stewart.

Her mother was speaking again. 'I have put some of your things in the back drawing-room, Clare,' she was saying. 'Things that I thought that you might like to take away with you. Your father and I thought that you might like to look through them before tea is served. We also thought that you would prefer to be alone.'

Now this was thoughtful. When she had first been exiled Clare had had to leave behind her all her many treasures, the memories of her childhood and youth. She leaned forward to kiss her mother's cheek and thank her for her consideration.

'I'll send for you when tea comes in,' her mother added, smiling at Clare's evident pleasure.

The back drawing-room was prettier and more informal than the front. Her mother's canvaswork stood there on a stand. French windows revealed a small yard-cum-garden where brilliant flowers blossomed in terracotta urns. Berkeley Square could be glimpsed beyond the mews at the back of the house. It brought back happy memories to be in the room at all. Memories of the days when she had been her father's darling before the dreadful business of Boy Mallory had changed her life for ever.

Clare picked up her old doll from the cardboard carton in which her belongings had been placed, and held it to her. She couldn't prevent the tears from falling. Slowly she put it down and began to sort through scrap books, old exercise books, even a small box which held the few pieces of jewellery which she had been given from the age of five onwards. Nothing was of particular value, but everything had meaning and memories for her.

She had just finished replacing it all in the carton when the door opened and Gordon Stewart came in.

'Oh, hello,' she said, more for something to say than because she really wanted to speak to him. 'How convenient. I have just finished sorting through everything, and deciding that I want to keep it—for the time being at any rate. Tea is ready, I suppose.'

He made no reply, just kept on walking towards her until he was so close that she began to retreat from him, surprised by the expression on his face: one of grim determination.

'Oh, I've not come to take you in to tea, Clare, nor have I come to propose formally to the lovely Angela, whatever she and the rest of them think. The lovely Angela has no attraction for me at all—other than that I was able to keep in touch with you through her and persuade her to invite you here this afternoon. I've come to take you away.'

So saying, he caught her by the arm with his left hand, and pulled her to him, at the same time pressing something in his right hand into her ribs. Clare opened her mouth to protest, to shout, but he forestalled her.

'I'm holding a pistol on you, Clare, because you're going to come with me. That damned Yankee husband of yours has done for me and George Pryde, but the game isn't over yet. You're a pretty little pawn we're going to put into play. But make a sound and I'll kill you.'

He was pushing her towards the French windows. Clare gasped at him in a hoarse whisper, 'You can't mean this, Gordon. You can't mean to kill me. Besides, you know that Ralph will follow you to the ends of the earth if you do.'

'Oh, but I do mean it, Clare. Now be quiet.'

Out of sight of the house he began to run with her until they had passed the mews and were in Berkeley Square. There he stopped, and whispered fiercely, 'We're going to be arm in arm, Clare, until we reach Pryde's flat, but I'll still have the gun on you all the time.'

'If I see anyone,' Clare whispered defiantly back, 'I'll scream, I promise you.'

'Not likely at this hour,' Gordon returned. 'Everyone's at tea. Besides, we're going by the back way. We shall only be visible for a few minutes. Now be quiet. I hate chattering women.'

'From what I hear,' Clare hissed back at him, 'you hate all women, chattering or not.'

He said nothing but squeezed her arm cruelly, causing her to gasp with pain, and then they were winding a way through deserted back streets and mews until they reached George Pryde's flat off Bruton Place.

Angela Windham had watched Gordon leave to fetch Clare for tea after the parlourmaid had laid it out reverently on a small table in front of Clare's mother. She had offered to go herself but Gordon had leapt gallantly to his feet, seeing a golden opportunity to make off with Clare suddenly presented to him on a plate.

Crying, 'Now darling, allow me,' he was out of the door before she could argue with him.

'Such a gallant man, Gordon,' said Angela's mother sentimentally. 'Not at all like poor Clare's husband...' Her sentence was allowed to hang in the air, leaving her hearers to guess exactly what Ralph's lack of gallantry consisted of.

Time passed. Clare's mother picked up the silver tea-pot, and said doubtfully, 'I suppose that Clare hadn't quite finished yet. Do you think that we could start without them?'

'Certainly not!' Her sister-in-law glared at her. 'I understand that Angela and dear Gordon have a most important announcement to make before tea actually begins. We can surely allow them a few more minutes under the circumstances.'

The older Mrs Windham meekly put the tea-pot down. She had no idea that the iron rod with which her sister-in-law ruled her life and home was shortly to be wrested from her by events which neither of them could have foreseen.

'Very well, dear. If that is what you wish.'

The Brigadier opened his mouth to say something, but judged it inapt. More minutes ticked by. Angela's mother tapped her foot irritably on the floor.

'Whatever can be keeping them?' she snapped. 'Most unsuitable. Angela, dear, do go and remind Gordon that he must not allow Clare to detain him for so long. She was always an inconsiderate girl.'

Angela jumped up eagerly and shot out of the room. Silence fell again, until suddenly, in the distance, Angela could be heard screaming. The screams grew louder, then suddenly stopped. Angela appeared in the doorway, her mouth set in the square position as traditionally represented by the masks in Greek tragedy. She seemed bereft of speech.

'Good God!' Forgetting all niceties of language before ladies in the face of his niece's hysteria, the Brigadier sprang to his feet.

'What on earth's the matter, Angela? Speak, girl,' and he slapped her face, hard.

This had the desired effect. 'They've gone, they've disappeared,' she wailed. 'Clare and Gordon. They've eloped. I know they have. He was always talking about her. Oh. . .' and she gave vent to a series of animal howls.

The once quiet drawing-room suddenly resembled the stage at Drury Lane in the crisis scene of a high society melodrama. The two Mrs Windhams, greatly agitated, both began to speak at the same time. The Brigadier shouted for silence.

'Be quiet!' he bellowed. 'Whatever do you mean, girl? They've gone. How can they have gone? Talk sense.' He was talking to Angela as though she were some dim-witted private soldier who needed to have sense drummed into his head. 'Answer me.'

'They're not in the drawing-room. The doors of the French windows are open. I'm sure that they went out that way. Go and see.' She collapsed sobbing on to the sofa, and hid her face in one of the cushions.

By now the noise had reached the servants' hall. First the butler came running, to accompany the Brigadier into the little back drawing-room—to find it empty, the carton abandoned on the floor and the French windows swinging open.

This sent the Brigadier charging into the hall, Angela's mother wailing after him.

'Oh, the wicked girl. I *said* that you should never have forgiven her, had her back. Look what she's done now!'

'Be quiet,' snarled the Brigadier before calling up the stairs, 'Clare! Stewart! Are you there?'

No answer being forthcoming, he shouted at the butler, 'Go upstairs, man. Look for them.'

He had hardly finished speaking before a white-faced Armstrong arrived on the run. Forgetting all considerations of rank, he grabbed at the Brigadier's arm, forcing him round to face him.

'What's this I've just heard? Is it true that Gordon Stewart has disappeared with Mrs Schuyler?'

The Brigadier tried to dodge away from him, but Armstrong hung on, roaring, 'Answer me, man.'

Trying to retain some vestige of dignity with his women wailing round him like so many members of a demented Greek chorus the Brigadier returned stiffly, 'It appears so.'

Armstrong released him, and staggered back, whispering, 'Oh, Gawd, the Mayor will never forgive me. Where's the telephone, and quick about it? I should have known that she wasn't safe anywhere, not even here.'

It finally struck home to the Brigadier that something serious was well and truly up. Brushing the women aside, he led Armstrong to the telephone. Before he began to use it, Armstrong bawled at him, 'You can stay, but get rid of the women first.'

Angela, who had abandoned the sofa, howled shrilly at him, 'All this fuss because Clare has run off with Gordon...' to have Armstrong round on her, shouting, 'Someone take the bitch away before I kill her.'

And then he told Ralph his terrible news.

Ralph arrived at South Farm Street to find that Angela had been sedated and put to bed, insisting to the last that Clare had run away with Gordon. Armstrong had refused to tell the Brigadier anything other than that he had had orders to protect Clare from attack—but not from whom—and that he had failed to do so, letting the Major down for the first time in his life.

Before he left the Foreign Office Ralph had checked that Pryde was no longer in his room. He had gone out a little earlier, an aide told him to visit Downing Street, he had said. This Ralph privately begged leave to doubt.

His well-trained face betrayed nothing of the horror which was consuming him. The knowledge that Clare had almost certainly been kidnapped and was in mortal danger was so appalling that he could barely think. Only the habits of a lifetime kept him from sitting down and baying uselessly at the not-yet-risen moon, or at the God who had allowed this thing to happen.

Mostly he reproached himself.

Yet when he met the Brigadier in the drawing-room from which Gordon and Clare had disappeared the Brigadier was impressed most of all by his calmness. Dealing with three hysterical women had left him raw: to meet a fellow officer speaking in cool tones was a boon indeed.

Only Ralph could have told him how false was the image that he was displaying.

'Now, sir, Armstrong has told me something of what has happened but I would appreciate if you would tell me exactly how Clare came to be left alone with Stewart.'

The Brigadier was immediately as formal, precise and succinct as though he were reporting to a general in the field. Ralph heard him out.

'Thank you,' he said. 'And now I am going to trust you with information which is secret, and which must not go beyond this room. I haven't time to swear you in, to read the Official Secrets Act to you, but I am depending on your honour as an officer and a gentleman that you will do as I ask.'

And then he told the Brigadier as much of what had happened as he thought politic, as quickly and emotionlessly as he could, from the moment when Clare had come upon Boy Mallory with a man two days before her wedding, up to the moment when, under Armstrong's protection, she had visited South Farm Street. He was frank about his own role as a secret agent, the discovery of the spy ring, and Pryde and Gordon Stewart's treachery.

'So,' said the Brigadier heavily, suddenly looking older than his years, 'I have misjudged my daughter completely. She was brave and true. I hope that I have not lost her before I can apologise to her. You say that this man Stewart has almost certainly kidnapped her—for what purpose?'

'Either to use her as a hostage, or, and I pray God that I am wrong, to kill her because she knows too much.'

His face and voice betrayed the agony he was in. The Brigadier looked keenly at him. Whatever else, Ralph Schuyler loved his daughter.

'Now,' said Ralph. 'Gordon must have gone through the back way towards Berkeley Square. I don't believe that he has taken Clare to his own flat because he must know that sooner or later we would discover that they had disappeared and that the first place we would search is his. So my bet is that he has taken her to George Pryde. I fear that my ploy to frighten him into flight worked only too well, since not only is he about to fly the country with Gordon Stewart, but he is taking Clare with them as a hostage. He must know, however, that Clare's disappearance will set off a hue and cry so it's likely that he has a well-thought-out plan for escape. . .

'I'm only guessing, mind. I've nothing to go on, but I propose to go to Pryde's rooms. They're not far from here. I shall also send Armstrong to Stewart's flat, as well, and tell him to hold him in a citizen's arrest if he's there. He's a resourceful fellow, Armstrong.'

'As I have already discovered,' remarked the Brigadier a trifle ruefully. He was not used to being ordered about and harangued by a mere sergeant.

'If we find nothing at either place,' Ralph continued, 'then pray, Brigadier, for there is nothing else we can usefully do, other than set up a hue and cry at every port. . .which probably wouldn't be useful at all.'

On the way out Ralph met Clare's mother, her eyes

red, her face ashen. 'Oh, Major Schuyler,' she said in her gentle fashion, 'try to bring Clare back to us. I've only just found her again, and to lose her so soon. . .'

What could Ralph do but say numbly, 'I'll do my best,' and set off to do exactly that. But Stewart and Pryde had a good hour's start on him, and only Ralph knew how vital that might be. He wondered desperately where Clare was, and what she might be doing—or what might be being done to her.

Gordon had a key to George Pryde's flat. He opened the door and pushed Clare in, holding the pistol trained on her. By now Clare feared that Gordon was no longer the rather mild man who had been Boy's toady, but she had no idea how far he was prepared to go to protect himself. She only knew that she must be careful. Gordon plainly thought that Pryde was not in. He was wrong. He came into the dining-room, shirtless, towelling himself off. He looked Clare cruelly up and down, then said to Gordon in the manner of a man throwing a dog a bone, 'Bravo, old chap, you've actually managed to do something properly for once. If I had time, I'd run up a flag.'

He didn't wait for a reply, but simply added, 'Tie her hands behind her back, Gordon. You'll find some stout picture cord in a drawer over there,' indicating a tallboy. He spoke of Clare as if she were a parcel.

'Oh, I say,' began Gordon, 'a bit extreme, isn't it?'

Pryde laughed at him. Clare felt like doing the same. It really was rather rich that Gordon should object to tying her hands when he had just been proposing to take her life if she disobeyed him.

'Don't be a bigger damn fool than you already are, Gordon,' Pryde said pleasantly. 'I don't want her making a nuisance of herself, fighting about. If she makes a noise, or tries to shout, there's some sticking plaster in the drawer as well. Put that over her mouth if she does.'

'Fully prepared, are we?' Clare flung at him nastily.

'One more word out of you,' Pryde told her, 'and I'll put the plaster on myself. And you won't like the way I'll do it, I promise you.'

'Look here. . . .' began Gordon feebly. He had the cord in his hand and was looking at Clare with an agonised expression. She suddenly realised that, although Gordon was very brave in making threats, he was not so happy when he was actually having to carry them out. She cursed herself for not realising that he wouldn't actually have shot her if she had tried to escape. He was all talk and no performance,

'Shut up and get on with it.' Pryde said this with the greatest good humour, Gordon grumblingly complying the while by tying Clare's hands rather amateurishly. The cord was thin and bit into her wrists.

'And tie her ankles to the chair legs while you're at it,' Pryde ordered. He laughed at Gordon's agonised attempts to evade Clare's kicks, before he came over to hold her ankles down whilst Gordon finished his unwanted task.

After that Pryde dressed himself in anonymous-looking Oxford bags and a sports jacket, both rather worn-looking. He looked very different from the stylish man Clare had met at Mrs Norton-Norris's party, then at her own wedding.

'Did anyone see you coming here?' he asked Cordon abruptly.

Gordon shook his head. He was looking increasingly

nervous and appeared to be about to develop a nasty twitch.

'Did we really have to do this?' he asked at last.

'Do what?' Pryde's impatience with Gordon was growing more evident by the minute.

'Kidnap Clare. It's a damned dangerous thing to do.'

'So it is. But it's a damned dangerous business you've got into, Gordon. You should have known that from the start. Clare's going to make a useful hostage, if we're unfortunate enough to be tracked down.'

'I think we're making a mistake, Pryde. Why don't we just give ourselves up? Tell the authorities all we know — and get a pardon in exchange? Too many have died already, what with Jeremy's murder and Boy's suicide.'

Pryde, who had been shovelling up papers from a desk, now turned and stared at Gordon, who was fidgeting by the window.

'Boy's suicide? Come on, Gordon. Grow up. Of course Boy didn't commit suicide. He had to be liquidated. He was getting cold feet — like you — threatening to go to the authorities. Just as well that darling Clare here had jilted him — gave everyone a reason to think that he *had* committed suicide.

Clare listened to this disagreement, fascinated as well as horrified. So Boy hadn't committed suicide, after all! And seeing how reluctant Gordon had become when faced with real, rather than imagined or reported violence, they might come to blows, or do something that would enable her to get away. She decided to put her oar in.

'I'd go to the authorities if I were you, Gordon. After all, you weren't the one who murdered Jeremy and Boy — and you could always tell them who did.'

Pryde rounded on her. 'I thought I told you to shut up. One more word and I'll. . .'

'She's right,' announced Gordon defiantly. 'I've nothing to lose, everything to gain. Besides I don't want to spend the rest of my life in the Soviet Union. . .'

'You don't?' Pryde was snarling now, his face a mask of ferocity. 'Think you're going to inform on me, do you, Gordon? Well, I hadn't quite made my mind what to do with you when I finally cut loose, but now you've done it for me.'

He whirled on Gordon, pulling an automatic pistol from his pocket as he did so, and shot him, without warning, at point-blank range.

Gordon fell to the floor to the sound of Clare's scream of horror. Pryde now whirled on her. 'I told you to shut up,' he gritted, 'and shut up you will.' So saying he gave her a backhanded slap across the mouth with such force that her lips were left bruised and bleeding. But for all her fear of him—especially after his brutal murder of Gordon—she still offered him mute defiance.

'That's that,' announced Pryde, kicking Gordon's body away from him. 'Now, we have to fly the coop, and two of us can do that better than three.'

'I don't want to fly at all,' Clare announced. 'I think Gordon was right.'

'What do I have to do to shut you up, woman?' Pryde roared at her. 'I pity Schuyler having you for a wife. Nag, nag, nag all day, I suppose.'

Frightened though she was, Clare could not resist further defiance. Since he was probably going to kill her at some point anyway—if Ralph didn't miraculously arrive to rescue her—then she might as well speak her mind. Keeping quiet wasn't going to save her.

'I've no need to nag Ralph,' she told him loftily. 'He

doesn't go round betraying his country and killing his friends. He saves that for his enemies.'

Pryde, who had finished stuffing his papers in a brief case, turned on her with an oath. 'Saint Schuyler, is he? Whoring and drinking and looking down on his betters, the damned bastard that he is.'

He fastened the brief case, retreated into his kitchen before coming over to where she sat. He was carrying a tumbler with what looked like weak whisky in it.

'I want a suitably reticent woman with me, not a damned noisy shrew,' he told her, 'so drink this. It's got something nice for baby in it,' he ended in a grotesque parody of a mother feeding a child. 'Not too much, just enough to keep you quiet until we get to—wherever we're going.'

Clare's loathing of him was increasing with her fear. She had noticed that Gordon was moving feebly, and was willing Pryde not to look in his direction. A worm of blood was crawling away from his body, but it was plain to her that he was not quite dead—leaving her to hope that all might not yet be lost.

She dodged the tumbler that was being held to her lips until Pryde struck her again. Her eyes watered, but she valiantly turned her face away from him until he suddenly grasped her by the nose—and the unpleasant liquid went down her throat willy-nilly.

'There,' said Pryde tenderly. 'That should shut you up. Chloral hydrate. Very effective. I'm going to untie your legs and help you down the stairs, and then we'll take a nice little ride to the seaside.'

The room began to swim around Clare. She was vaguely aware of Pryde holding her up, guiding her on failing legs down the stairs and into the mews at the back where his car was parked—at which point she lost consciousness.

She knew nothing of Pryde bundling her on to the back seat, throwing a light blanket over her, starting the car, roaring out of the mews, on his way to freedom—if ending up in the Soviet Union could be regarded as any such thing.

Ralph acted with all the speed he could summon. The dilatoriness of the Windhams had given Gordon and Pryde—for he was sure that Pryde was involved—a head start. The quickest way to Pryde's flat was on foot, but more than an hour had passed since Clare had been snatched away even before he began the journey there.

He made little of smashing open Pryde's locked front door. Inside, he found Gordon lying, not where Pryde had left him, but almost against the door to which he had crawled, passing in and out of consciousness as he did so. Of Pryde and Clare there was no sign.

Regardless of the pool of blood in which Gordon lay, Ralph went down on his knees beside him, praying that he was conscious enough to talk. He cradled Gordon's head in his arms. Gordon looked at him through glazed eyes.

'He shot me,' he muttered hoarsely. 'Pryde. As though I were a dog.'

He fell silent, and Ralph asked urgently, 'Where's Clare, Gordon? What has he done with her?'

Gordon said nothing. He was gasping, not breathing. Finally, he murmured weakly, 'So sorry, Schuyler, so sorry. I shouldn't have done it... He's taken her with him...a hostage...'

'Where?' demanded Ralph frantically. Time was of the essence, and Pryde could not have been long gone.

He wanted to shake the answer out of Gordon, but dare not. He thought that Gordon was probably dying, but Ralph's only hope was that he would not do so before he had revealed Pryde's destination.

'Where, Gordon, where? Where's he taken Clare?'

'Broadstairs,' muttered the dying man. 'Got a cottage there, and a yacht. . .cottage called Swan's Nest, not far from the quay. The yacht's the *Flying Swan*. We were going to France. . .and then overland to Russia. He shot me, Schuyler, shot Peele and Boy Mallory. . .I think that he likes killing people.'

Some last strength ran through him. He half raised himself by lifting a hand to grasp the lapel of Ralph's jacket. 'Stop him, Schuyler. . .before he kills Clare. . .'

His head fell back on Ralph's arm. Ralph laid Gordon gently down on the carpet. He thought that the ambulance he was about to telephone for was unnecessary, but nothing to that. Gordon had turned up trumps in the end, and deserved a chance to live.

After that, he had work to do.

His half-brother, Lord Longthorne, when Ralph finally reached him on the telephone, was as practical as ever. After Ralph instructed him to do so, he read the letter sent to him that morning. Ralph rapidly briefed him on what had happened since.

'I want you to send the whole sheriff's posse to Broadstairs,' he ended. 'Malcolm and Johnson from the Yard. Armed police. Special Branch, and the police at Broadstairs alerted, the yacht impounded—if he's not already sailed. Which pray God he hasn't.

'Nothing is to be done by anyone without my say-so. He's not to be approached in any way until I'm ready to go in. Clare's my wife and the murdering swine has made off with her. My one hope is that he'll have to wait for the tide.'

Nothing of his anguish and despair over his loss of Clare showed in his voice. Over the phone he could hear Gerard, steady and dependable, one of the powers behind the government, who would throw the whole apparatus of state security at George Pryde.

'Colonel B is not to be told,' were Ralph's final words. 'I don't think that he's a party to this, but I dare not take any chances. I'm driving straight to Broadstairs police station with Armstrong. It should take me about two hours. No grandstand plays, you understand. Everything by the book to begin with—but I might have to play it by ear if things go wrong. You understand me?'

'By the book first,' Gerard agreed, 'and then use your judgement, if necessary. Trust me, Ralph. You shall have everything you want. Arming the police might take a little time, though. And I trust you—whatever you decide to do.'

CHAPTER SEVENTEEN

'WAKE up, damn you, Clare. I want you conscious.'

Someone was shaking her and shouting at her in an angry voice. Clare struggled to move—but found that she could not. Whatever could have made Ralph so cross?

And then agonising consciousness returned. It was not Ralph shouting at her, but George Pryde, his face malevolent. She was tied to a chair again, her hands behind her back, her ankles secured to its front legs.

Pryde was holding a tumbler to her mouth. Remembering what had happened the last time he had made her drink, Clare shuddered away from it. He grasped her by the hair and forced her face round. 'Don't be a fool,' he told her. 'It's only water. You'll feel better when you've drunk it. I want you fully conscious.'

Clare doubted that very much. Her head was thundering, she felt sick, her mouth and face ached, and her wrists and ankles were paining her where she was pinioned. But the liquid in the tumbler was odourless and colourless so she took a chance and drank it. It was life-giving, whatever might be in it, and she gulped it greedily down until Pryde took it away.

'That's enough,' he said as he walked away from her.

She looked around her. She was in a pleasantly shabby room in what appeared to be a cottage. Pryde was now wearing sailing togs, and was busily packing away yet more papers into a rucksack. The fruits of his spying, no doubt.

He became aware that she was watching him, and asked jovially, 'Interested, Clare? You should be. These are the plans for the other bastard's monoplane. He thought that we had failed to steal them, but we had. Ever hear of photography?' The laugh which followed was a self-satisfied one.

So Gis's plans for a revolutionary plane were due to be copied by Britain's enemies if Pryde managed to escape.

'You won't get away with it,' she croaked at him.

'Care to bet?' he flung at her. 'I sail at eleven tonight when the tide is right. By then you'll neither know nor care whether I escape or not. Your purpose will have been served.'

'Ralph will stop you.' Clare's voice was steadier as she began to recover from her drug-induced stupor.

'Oh, the ineffable hero, Schuyler,' Pryde sneered. 'MC and all. England's St George, like Gis Havilland. What a prize pair they make.'

'Better than you, at any rate,' retorted Clare spiritedly.

'What a wagging tongue you have, my dear. It will be a pleasure to silence it. Be quiet from now on, or I'll gag you.'

Clare knew that she had made her point, so said no more; being gagged didn't appeal to her. Instead she thought of Ralph and her eyes filled with tears. Just as they had learned to love one another this treacherous swine had snatched her away. She had to believe, she must believe, that somehow Ralph would track them down. He was so resourceful—and surely God could not be so cruel as to part them when all life was opening up before them.

She wondered where he was.

Ralph was at Broadstairs police station after a mad drive into Kent which had frightened even Armstrong. He had arrived there in the early evening to find that they were expecting him: Gerard had begun to do his stuff.

He had stopped in Park Lane long enough to fuel the Bentley and collect Armstrong, who had returned from Gordon Stewart's empty flat, and to arm himself with his Smith and Wesson revolver, now secure in a shoulder holster. He was ready for anything.

One relief was that the tide was not in Pryde's favour. He would not be able to sail until eleven o'clock. Not that that mattered since the Broadstairs police were guarding his yacht—except that they were not yet accompanied by armed officers, and Pryde would certainly not hesitate to use his own weapons in order to escape. They showed Ralph where the Swan's Nest was on their big map, and Armstrong was sent with a police constable to keep secret watch on the cottage from a safe distance.

'Trouble is,' said the local Inspector, 'it was once a smuggler's hideout, and it's likely that there are secret hideaways and paths down the cliffs. But since we've men watching his yacht, even if he reached there. . .' He left his sentence in the air.

Time dragged. Ralph had to stop himself from looking at his watch every five minutes. The thought of Clare in Pryde's power was intolerable, but he must be patient. To go off half-cock might doom them both. It would take time for Gerard's promised troops to reach Broadstairs.

Ironically, perhaps, Malcolm and Johnson were the first to arrive. They had been snatched away from their current case, without explanations and told to report as soon as possible to Broadstairs police station where they would be informed of their duties.

Malcolm had protested at this, to be told sternly by the Commissioner, 'I am informed that this is a matter of national security. Special Branch are involved and it is essential that you arrive there as soon as possible, without wasting time listening to lengthy explanations from me.' He didn't add that he had no idea, either, why his two men were wanted so urgently at Broadstairs!

Johnson poked Malcolm in the ribs as they entered the briefing room in the station. 'Look, Guv, it's him, Schuyler. The Major. What's he doing here?'

Malcolm's face lit up. 'You don't think that we've been sent here to arrest him,' and then, mournfully, since it appeared that Ralph was instructing the Chief Inspector, not the other way round, 'No such luck. But what the devil can be going on?'

'Ah, Inspector,' said Ralph easily, as though on their last meeting they had not parted at daggers drawn. 'I'm pleased to see that you've made such good time. I'm afraid you'll have to wait for explanations until Special Branch arrive—I want to brief everyone at the same time, so that there can be no confusion about exactly what orders have been given.'

His ease was spurious, but Malcolm was not to know that. In any case he had not long to wait to find out why he had been sent for. Special Branch arrived, in anonymous saloon cars and a black van, dressed in plain clothes and—to Malcolm's surprise—armed. They, too, reported to Ralph, as instructed. Their leader was a burly man, whom Ralph had already met on a previous operation.

They shook hands and then got down to business as Armstrong would have said. Ralph had commandeered a blackboard, and began to outline his plan to 'do it by the book' as he had said earlier to Gerard.

He had scarcely begun when a constable put his head round the door. 'There's a bloke here what says his name's Havilland, and he's to report to Mr Schuyler. That right, sir?' he appealed to Ralph.

Gis, it must be Gis. How the devil had he got here so soon? But, of course, he must have flown.

'Send him in, Constable.' There was his cousin, large as life and twice as natural, wearing flying kit, and immediately dominating the room with his presence.

'Sorry to burst in like this,' he offered, all his celebrated charm immediately in evidence, 'but Uncle Gerard, Lord Longthorne,' he explained in an aside to the assembled constabulary and old Uncle Tom Cobleigh and all, as he privately and irreverently dubbed them, 'thought that I might be able to help you. I gather that Pryde may have stolen my plans and may even have them with him. So I flew down and left the old Moth in a convenient field. I gather that the swine has kidnapped poor Clare.'

Ralph threw an arm around him. 'I've never been so pleased to see you,' he said soberly. 'I'm sure that we can find something for you to do.' He introduced Gis to his troops—as he had begun to think of them.

Malcolm and Johnson stared at his golden presence. Stared even harder when Gis pulled something from the pocket of his flying jacket. 'Before you begin your briefing, cousin, I've a present for you. Whilst Gerard was talking to me I had one of my flashes—you know what I mean.'

Yes, Ralph knew what Gis meant. On odd occasions, Gis had flashes in which he saw, or became aware, that someone he loved was in great danger and needed help. He called it intuition but Ralph knew that sometimes he had a brief and disturbing vision of a future event. And now he had experienced one concerning him.

'It might have been nothing but my over-active imagination,' Gis went on quietly, showing no emotion himself, and he handed Ralph a parcel. 'But I saw you holding what's in this, and I knew, don't ask me how, that without it you were in mortal danger. Stupid really, but I brought it along.'

Intrigued, Ralph opened the parcel. Inside was a tiny, almost a miniature, pistol, some ammunition for it, and an odd contraption of elastic and cord. He knew what it was, but had never seen one before. He looked at Gis.

'A Derringer,' Gis explained. 'The pistol with which Booth shot President Lincoln. Deadly at point-blank range. Its small size is its advantage. Gamblers in the old West used to keep them hidden inside their sleeve— they then appeared to be unarmed. It gave them an advantage if someone tried to kill them with their Colt because they were seen to be cheating. You could wear it if it became necessary—and like them, seem to be helpless.'

Malcolm, watching this interchange, could hardly forbear to snigger. He whispered under his breath to Johnson as they turned away to sit down for Ralph's briefing, 'What a pair, eh. The pretty one looks too much of a gent to do a hand's turn!'

Always ready to show his superior that he didn't

know what he was talking about Johnson whispered back, 'Don't know about a hand's turn, guv, but that's Havilland, the World War air ace. Designs planes and test flies them himself, they say. Surprised you haven't heard of him. Races at Brooklands, too, devil of a fellow.'

Malcolm's reply to this was a grunt, and a stern recommendation to his Sergeant to shut up and listen to what Schuyler had begun to tell them. The operation to net Pryde and free Clare had begun in earnest.

Clare, her eyes closed to banish Pryde and his cottage, was walking with Ralph in a beautiful garden. Before them was a view of distant hills, behind them was a house. They were in the country, far from London, and must have been married for some time for a pair of children ran before them. Murder and mayhem took place on a different planet. Only by retreating inwardly into this world of fantasy could she bear the hours of waiting before Pryde made his move and took her to his yacht.

Watching her, Pryde saw that she was on the verge of sleep, and smiled grimly. So much the better. He was being spared the edge of her tongue. He had finished packing the one case and the rucksack which he was taking with him, and the time for leaving his old life was almost on him. He had looked out of the window several times, but he had seen and heard nothing amiss. He was alone, undetected. Killing Gordon had killed any chance that he might be followed and found.

If luck was with him, and it seemed to be, then in a short time he would be safe. So quiet was it that he debated whether or not to take Clare with him to the yacht: it seemed pointless to drag her along if it wasn't really necessary. Oh, well, he would decide that when the time came.

Bored by the dreary hours of waiting, he lit a cigarette, opened a novel—a thriller by Edgar Wallace—and began to read. . .

Until, suddenly, someone knocked on the front door.

Ralph had said that they must wait until night fell. That way they could post themselves in place around Pryde's cottage without being seen. He drove Gis, the local Inspector, Lewis, and the Special Branch high-up—known anonymously as Smith—in his Bentley to the end of the lane which led to the Swan's Nest, their cohorts following behind.

He had had a brief private talk with Gis before they left when Gis had helped him to strap the Derringer to his forearm, and shown him how to use it. Ralph did not ask Gis where the little pistol had come from, nor how he had learned to be so expert in its use.

'I blame myself for involving Clare in this,' Ralph had said to Gis, his expression bitter. 'Right from the beginning she has been a target for them.'

'From what you say,' Gis remarked gently, 'she was a target even before you met her.'

'True, but I should have hidden her away, done anything to prevent what has happened. It's a dirty business I'm engaged in, if a necessary one to protect the State. There have been times when I wished that I *were* simply a poodlefaker, a lounge lizard. If Clare and I come safely through this, I'm going to have a stab at quite another career.'

'Retirement with honour,' nodded Gis. 'Like the old Roman general, Cincinnatus, returning to his villa in the country to raise chickens and a family when his term of service was over.'

'Exactly,' agreed Ralph, 'barring the chickens, of course. Rearing dogs and horses is more my line—and Clare's, I suspect.'

He said no more. His mind was on the business in hand, and nothing must interfere with it, not even thinking of Clare and himself enjoying a country idyll. . .

It had been decided that after the armed police and Special Branch men had surrounded the cottage, he, Lewis and Smith would try to speak to Pryde. Their aim would be to persuade him to surrender peacefully, seeing that they had him cornered. Ralph privately thought that he was such a tricky bastard that he might be harder to capture than his companions realised.

The iron knocker of the Swan's Nest's oak front door concealed a small slit, as Ralph found when he lifted it. He heard Pryde's steps as he approached the door, and called, 'Pryde, is that you?'

'You know it is, Schuyler. What the devil do you think you're doing here?'

Ralph looked at the Inspector. The Inspector nodded, and Ralph spoke again. 'I've come to tell you that you are surrounded. Your yacht has been impounded. The best course for you is to open the door, to release Clare and to surrender to us immediately. If you then tell us all that you know of Bolshevik covert operations in Britain, I can promise you that your sentence after trial will be heavily reduced.'

Silence.

Pryde broke it by laughing. 'Oh, that's rich, Schuyler. Really rich. Why should I believe a word you say? Besides, I think I'd prefer my own Götterdämmerung, taking Clare with me on to the funeral pyre, rather than surrender to you.'

The Special Branch man spoke. 'I have the word of the Home Secretary, Mr Pryde, that what Mr Schuyler offered you is true. It's more than you deserve, but there it is. Why not accept the offer, and then we can all go home and have a good night's rest? You can't really wish to end up in front of a firing squad—or in the Soviet Union.'

Silence again.

'Of course I don't—but needs must when the devil drives. What I am prepared to do is to ask you all to retire—except Schuyler. He may come in and try to persuade me to surrender. He must be unarmed, of course. And I won't open the door until those with him have retreated at least two hundred paces. He might like to say a last farewell to his talkative bitch of a wife.'

Silence again.

'Well, sir?' The Special Branch man and the two Inspectors spoke together. Malcolm thought that now was the time for that Fancy Dan, Ralph Schuyler, to show his true mettle. He was not to be disappointed.

'I have no choice, have I?' whispered Ralph, so that Pryde might not hear him. 'The time for going by the book has gone. We ought to sit it out—but that's my wife in there—and he's not reasonable any more. He might set fire to the place any minute. I'll go in. But you must promise me that you'll not try to enter unless you hear firing—as we agreed beforehand when considering that such a situation as this might arise.'

Agreement was nodded.

'Well, Schuyler? Dally any longer and I won't let you in.'

'Yes, I'm coming in.'

'Unarmed?'

'Yes, I'm unarmed,' lied Ralph.

'I shall check, mind. Tell your fellows to retreat. If I think you are tricking me in any way, I shall shoot Clare on the instant.'

Inside, whilst Ralph did as he was bid outside, Pryde rapidly untied Clare's ankles and wrists, made her stand up, and pushed her roughly towards the front door. He held his pistol in her back.

Clare made no effort to resist him, nor did she speak. The sound of Ralph's voice, as calm as ever, had filled her with hope—as it had filled Pryde with silent dismay. He had not expected his enemy to have tracked him down so quickly—was it possible that he had not quite finished Stewart off? No matter, he had a few tricks of his own up his sleeve. . .

'Open the door for me, Clare,' he commanded, prodding her cruelly in the back. 'As little as will allow your husband in. Make a mistake and I'll shoot you without a thought. Be a pleasure.'

Ralph was inside. Pryde stood before him, with Clare between them, his purpose obvious—he would shoot her if Ralph made a false move.

'Lift your arms, Schuyler, and open your jacket. Right. I see that you did as you were told. Took your shoulder holster off, did you?'

'As you see.' Ralph was affecting a coolness which he did not feel. Clare's eyes, huge and fearful, were fixed on his, trying to tell him something. She was a little pale, but he could see at once that there was something indomitable about her.

He was right.

'Don't do as he wishes, Ralph,' she begged him, 'if it means that he'll get away. I'd rather die than have him escape because he blackmailed you with me. He killed Boy and Jeremy as well as Gordon; he deserves to die.'

'I'll do what I ought to,' Ralph replied enigmatically.

Pryde laughed. 'Noble pair, aren't you?' And then he gave Ralph the one advantage he needed—seeing that it was Ralph who had something up his sleeve. 'Put your hands behind your back, Schuyler, so that I can tell that you're not doing anything tricky with them. That's right.'

He watched Ralph obey him, apparently slowly and reluctantly.

'Now, I'm going to use the pair of you to get away. There's a smugglers' secret passage out of the cellar, across the cliffs. Oh, I know that you've found the yacht, but I can slip through the cordon you've put around the cottage, and there are other bolt holes out of the British Isles of which you know nothing. You're going to come with me, Clare as hostage. One false move, and I'll shoot her, you understand me?'

'I understand you,' Ralph told him evenly. He had slipped the Derringer from his sleeve into his right hand as Gis had shown him. One false move from Pryde—if he made one—and he was done for.

'Good. Because I've changed my mind. You know, Schuyler, I've always hated you. You with your money and your rich and powerful relatives, and your War career, and your medal. Why, even your womanising was thought to be clever, whilst poor devils like me, virtually penniless, had to take our pleasure in secret because what we wanted to do was not quite nice.' He minced and grimaced over the last words.

'It was so easy to fool you all—particularly Colonel B. Saved me once because I came out of the right drawer. What drawer did you come out of, Schuyler, you damned illegitimate peasant, eh? It's going to be a pleasure to kill you. I don't think I want the trouble of dragging you round the cliffs with me, so now, I'll do for you.' Thrusting Clare brutally to one side, he pulled his automatic from behind her back to point it at Ralph.

Clare, who had screamed at his threat to kill Ralph, now flung herself sideways in front of Pryde to try to spoil his aim. She did more than that for him.

Confident that Ralph was unarmed, Pryde half turned to give her a backhanded blow of such force that she was thrown across the room catching her head a glancing blow on a table leg—to lie silent and stunned on the board flooring.

Her action gave Ralph the opportunity which he needed. He stepped forward, bringing his hand from behind his back, and aimed his little pistol at Pryde at point-blank range, killing him, as John Wilkes Booth had killed Lincoln, instantly.

Pryde had no time to be surprised, no time to fire, living, at Ralph. The two shots he did loose off were the reflex action of his finger on his automatic's trigger as he was hit. The first struck Ralph high in the left shoulder, the second buried itself into the wall above Ralph as Pryde fell backwards, dead.

Silence.

Cold and deadly.

Ralph was flung backward against the wall. Pryde had fallen at his feet. Clare, unmoving, lay where Pryde had thrown her. Danger over, Ralph had but one thought in his head, and that was Clare.

But first he had to make sure—as Pryde had not done with Gordon—that his enemy was dead, a task which he soon accomplished.

Rising to his feet, Ralph thought of the men whom

Pryde had sent to their deaths, and those he had killed himself, as he would have killed Ralph had not Ralph forestalled him. He muttered what would have to serve as Pryde's epitaph, using a variant of Booth's words after he had shot President Lincoln — 'So perish all traitors.'

His duty done, Ralph made his unsteady way to where Clare lay. . .so white and so still. . . .

CHAPTER EIGHTEEN

A MOMENT or two later, alerted by the shots, and as they had promised him, after a small delay, Inspectors Lewis, Malcolm and the Special Branch man, followed by their respective cohorts—and Gis Havilland—broke in.

To find Pryde lying dead before them and Ralph, wounded but not mortally, sitting on the floor, propped up against the wall, Clare, unconscious, cradled in his arms, his head bent over her. He looked up at them as they entered.

'I couldn't have done it without her,' he said, lovingly stroking the hair away from her bruised face. 'She saved us both.'

And when they would have taken her from him, so that they might care for their wounds, he would not let go of her, but held on to her the more tightly.

Finally when Gis, his face compassionate, knelt down beside him, and said gently, 'Let her go, little cousin. I don't think that she's badly hurt, but she needs our help and so do you,' Ralph finally gave way and fell into the friendly darkness, honour satisfied and his duty done.

'I'm not really ill,' Clare protested. 'Not like you, anyway,' and she waved from her bed at Ralph who sat beside her in an armchair, his left arm in a sling.

'But you know that the doctors are adamant that, having had your head hurt twice by that swine, and being made to drink chloral hydrate on top of it, you must rest under observation for several days.'

'I want to go home,' she told him defiantly. 'To *our* home. With you. I want to thank you properly for saving me.' And her eyes sparkled mischievously. 'If you're well enough to stand it, that is.'

'With a little help,' he told her, equally mischievously.

It was three days since Pryde's death. Three days full of excitement and action. They had been driven to hospital in Broadstairs and from there to London. The papers Pryde had been going to take with him had been impounded: the plans for Gis's monoplane had been found among them. State security had swung into action. Pryde's death had been blamed on an accident whilst playing with the Derringer, whose workings he had apparently not completely understood.

'And,' as Ralph had said, quoting the late Duke of Wellington, 'if you believe that, you'll believe anything,' but it had been duly swallowed by everyone. There had even been a short obituary notice of Pryde in *The Times*, lamenting the untimely death of a promising public servant.

Clare had already thanked Gis, when he had visited her the day after the shooting, for giving Ralph the Derringer, and both of them had congratulated Ralph for doing his bit with it.

'I really believed you when you told him that you were unarmed,' she told him, 'but, of course, as usual, you weren't telling the truth.'

'Of course,' he replied gravely, 'you know that I rarely do. A useful trait, do admit. But I don't think that it would have been quite so easy for me if you hadn't distracted him. The credit really goes to you.'

'To both of you,' Gis had said, acting as umpire,

amused to see that Ralph, the great lover, had now turned into Ralph, the great family man. They were a right pair of turncoats, he and Ralph, he thought. And he could go home to Thea knowing that his plans had been saved, and that Ralph was as fortunate a man in finding his woman as he had been.

And now both Clare and Ralph were saying to each other, 'I've got something to tell you.' They began laughing together, the laughter of release from danger and death.

'You go first, Clare.'

'Father came to see me this morning,' she told him. 'We were reconciled.' She did not say that the Brigadier, his face working, had said, 'I shouldn't have misjudged you so dreadfully, my dear. I should have known that you must have had good and sufficient reasons for refusing to marry Mallory—especially when the wedding was so near.

'And then, when Ralph told us how brave and true you were when Pryde kidnapped you, I felt worse than ever. You have a good man there, my dear. He will make you an excellent husband.'

Clare offered her father the best olive branch she could.

'Dear father, it was your teaching when I was young which helped me to endure hardship and obloquy. What you always said about honour and duty and keeping one's word. I'm sure that you understand now that I had to keep my word to Boy.'

'Indeed. I've sent them away,' he added. 'Angela and her mother. They are to live in the Lodge at Windham Hall until they can find a new home, away from us. Angela is saying dreadful things about you, and the worst of it is that I can't silence her by telling her the truth. Ralph has sworn me to silence. She and her mother were an unhappy influence on me. Your mother was right there, I was wrong not to listen to her. She is coming in to see you when I have done my duty and made things right between us again.'

'But how was Gordon's death explained away?' Clare asked. In all the excitement she had forgotten him. Ralph had told her that Gordon had saved her by telling him where Pryde had taken her, and it seemed ungrateful to let him go without a thought. She would never be able to thank him for he had died in hospital at about the same time that Ralph had shot Pryde.

'Oh, he was killed in a car accident,' her father told her. 'And we explained your disappearance by saying that you and Gordon had wandered off after our cat when it ran away. Unfortunately just as you caught up with it, you were both struck by a car. He was killed and you were slightly hurt—hence your being in hospital.'

Well, it all seemed rather thin to Clare—but what matter—it would have to do if the horrible truth was not to leak out. She had her family back, and if she had learned wisdom through being rejected, then she had gained, not lost—although she could hardly tell her father so.

'And you, Ralph? What's your news?'

'Three pieces. You remember the letter which you sent on to me the day you were kidnapped? It was from my mother. In it she named George Pryde as the spy. She gave me a little more evidence which clinched the fact that he was working for the Bolsheviks: another brick in the wall of evidence against him. The man you saw with Boy had been arrested and was being sent home for trial—he had been selling his country's secrets, too.

'She wrote to me because she and her husband are leaving Britain, and not intending to return. She says that he is giving up his diplomatic post, sickened by the treachery he has seen, so she felt that she could tell me exactly what she had discovered, but that she could not tell me how she had done so.

'What's more,' and he hesitated, his face working a little, 'she told me how much she loved me, how much it grieved her that she had been compelled to give me up—especially as she had no more children when she did marry. She bade me be happy with you.'

His face was sad, so sad that Clare took his right, undamaged hand, and said impulsively, 'Oh, I'm so glad for you, but sorry, too. It's as though you found her and then lost her.'

'True,' he said, and they sat silent for a moment.

'The second thing is that Malcolm spoke to me after we were debriefed. I had told them all exactly what had happened when I went in to the Swan's Nest, ending with the reason why I had to kill Pryde. . .that he was about to kill the pair of us. He said that he felt compelled to apologise to both of us in view of the brave way in which we had behaved when facing Pryde.

'He said that he understood why I had had to fool him and Johnson. I apologised, too, for having done so—but pointed out that it was my duty to deceive him. We shook hands on it, and he sent you his best wishes.'

Clare smiled. 'I'm glad. I always felt sorry we had to deceive him, to pretend we were simply a pair of bright young things having him on. And your third thing?'

'Oh, that is more serious. This morning I was offered Colonel B's post. To be head of his branch of the Secret Service.'

He did not tell her that it had come as a great shock.

He had been summoned to the Foreign Office, to Colonel B's room. Only, when he had gone in, the Colonel was absent. Instead his half-brother, Gerard, Lord Longthorne sat in his chair. Flanking him were two personages so grand and important that he had stared at them in wonder.

It seemed that the Colonel's hushing up of Pryde's arrest, as well as various other mistakes, had done for him. He had been dismissed although it had been given out that he had resigned. Now it was Ralph that they wanted. Especially as he had been so right over Pryde and had brought the whole thing off, successfully, without publicity.

Clare looked across at him when he told her of the offer. She kept her thoughts to herself, and asked quite simply, 'And what did you say to that, Ralph?'

He answered her question with another.

'What would you have me say, Clare?'

'That you must do what you wish, Ralph, what you see as your duty. What I think is immaterial. A soldier's wife is a soldier, too, you know.'

He rose and sat by her on the bed, putting his good arm about her. 'Oh, Clare, you are a treasure. My treasure. When that swine Pryde knocked you across the room that night I think that I went slightly mad. And when it was all over, and I saw you lying there as white and as still as death, I thought that all I wanted was to die with you. I never knew until then how much I loved you. I had never believed that I could love anyone, and there I was, suddenly understanding what the poets meant when they sang of lovers choosing to die together rather than live apart. . .'

He fell silent. When he looked up there were tears in

his eyes, something which Clare had never thought to see.

'It hurts me to think of it,' he said.

She kissed his warm cheek. 'Oh, Ralph. You must know that I feel — and felt, the same. If Pryde was going to kill you then all that I wanted was to go with you...' They sat there for a moment, silent, Ralph marvelling at himself.

Finally Clare stirred, and asked, 'So what was your answer to them, Ralph?'

'I told them that I was conscious of the honour that they were doing me. But, I said, I was now a married man, and I owed a duty to my wife and the family I hoped to have.'

He stopped and kissed her at this point, and Clare blushed rosily at the thought of the family he was imagining for them.

'Were I unmarried, I said, I would have accepted without a thought, but seeing that I *was* married and that I had done my duty by my country, not once, but twice, I wished to be like Cincinnatus and retire to my acres. If he could do it with honour, so could I. They argued with me, a little half-heartedly, but they saw that I was not to be moved. Gerard sent his love to you, and an invitation to dinner as soon as we are both fit again. And that was that.'

'And you don't regret what you have done, Ralph? You are sure that you don't?' Clare was as earnest as she could be.

Ralph rewarded her with a shower of little kisses, innocent kisses, not like the devilish ones they would exchange when they were home again.

'Clare, I told Gis of my intention to retire when we were waiting to rescue you, and he agreed with it. So we can go home to our dogs and horses. You do want dogs and horses, Clare?'

'Of course, and children.'

'And children, most of all,' he agreed.

Clare remembered her dream of them both in the country when she had been Pryde's captive, hoping to be rescued. Ralph, struck, told her that he had been thinking of the same thing at almost the same time when he had been talking to Gis.

'Soulmates, that's what we are,' Clare murmured, settling herself more comfortably into his good arm.

'We really must restrain ourselves, Ralph,' she admonished him severely as his caresses grew ever more ardent. 'We shall shock the nurses. Besides, I have another important question to ask you. Most important.'

'And what is that, Mrs Schuyler?'

'You will allow me to finish translating my torrid French novel, won't you?'

'Willingly,' he promised her, 'but only after we have spent a torrid night together.'

'Many of them, Mr Schuyler, many of them. As many as you like. I can't wait to begin.'

Historical Romance™

Coming next month

MAJOR'S MUSLIN
Marie-Louise Hall
REGENCY NOVEL, 1810

Lallie Ross had lost everything in her life—her parents,
her fortune, and her dignity. She thought life couldn't
possibly get any worse—until Major Alex Haldane
reappeared from the dead! Alex relentlessly pursued
Lallie, but she *refused* to love a liar! She knew she needed
protection from the world and her gloomy future, but that
would mean sacrificing again to Alex the only thing she
had left in the entire world—her heart...

STOLEN HEIRESS
Joanna Makepeace
LONDON/BRUGES 1461

All of Robert Devane's family had been brutally killed by
the evil Peter Hoyland, and he was determined to avenge
their deaths. He was going to put Clare Hoyland through
the most pain she had *ever* felt in her life—by marrying
her! Revenge felt *so* sweet, because he knew that Clare
was totally under his control—until he fell in love! That
wasn't part of Robert's plan—but neither was the end of
his marriage...

GET 4 BOOKS
AND A MYSTERY GIFT

Return the coupon below and we'll send you 4 Historical Romance™ novels and a mystery gift absolutely FREE! We'll even pay the postage and packing for you.

We're making you this offer to introduce you to the benefits of Reader Service: FREE home delivery of brand-new Historical Romance novels, at least a month before they are available in the shops, FREE gifts and a monthly Newsletter packed with information.

Accepting these FREE books and gift places you under no obligation to buy, you may cancel at any time, even after receiving just your free shipment. Simply complete the coupon below and send it to:

MILLS & BOON® READER SERVICE, FREEPOST, CROYDON, SURREY, CR9 3WZ.

No stamp needed

Yes, please send me 4 free Historical Romance novels and a mystery gift. I understand that unless you hear from me, I will receive 4 superb new titles every month for just £2.99* each, postage and packing free. I am under no obligation to purchase any books and I may cancel or suspend my subscription at any time, but the free books and gift will be mine to keep in any case.
(I am over 18 years of age)

H6LE

Ms/Mrs/Miss/Mr _____

Address _____

_____

_____ Postcode _____

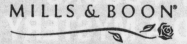